WHEN WE WERE WARM

A Futuristic Time Travel Romance

D1737020

A. B. Raphaelle

WHEN WE WERE WARM

Let not your heart

Hide like a coward

Instead, let it go forth

Armed with reason,

Standing in defense,

Of the one true thing—

Love

CONTENTS

A Note from the Author

1 ABBIE 1
2 AROYA 15
3 SKY PODS 35
4 GETTING TO KNOW YOU 40
5 GINA 54
6 THE ARCHANGEL 67
7 MARKUS 82
8 THE BEACH 90
9 THE REVERSION 103
10 THE LAKE 126
11 THE HEDGE-ROSE OPENS 132
12 THE WISH LIST 149
13 GOING HOME 155
14 THE MISSION 163
15 QUANTUM PHYSICS 173
16 CHANGING THE WORLD 180
17 BACK TO THE FUTURE 191
18 ELIJAH 2.0 201
19 ABIGAIL LITE 2.0 236
20 THE LAST FIGHT 278
21 THE CONVERGENCE 291
22 COMING OUT 298
23 TULIO'S BOX 313
24 EACH OTHER'S GAZE 319
25 LESSONS LEARNED 326
Afterword 330

A NOTE FROM THE AUTHOR

In 2012, I had an unusual experience. It was a vision; a kind of wide-awake dream that unfolded in real time–presenting me with a curious 'what if' question. It was more than just a random daydream, and several strange 'coincidences' eventually led me to wonder if there might be something more *real* about it than fantasy.

I was alone in my apartment in San Francisco. My 22-year-old daughter was living with me at the time–she was out somewhere, running around the city with her friends. I'm a person who easily enters altered states, and while sitting on my couch in the living room, I felt one of those states coming on. Since I was alone, with no pressing responsibilities–I allowed it to unfold.

I became aware of my surroundings in the vision; I was standing next to a tall building in the South of Market area of San Francisco–not too far from the Financial District. I came around a corner and suddenly found myself face-to-face with a strange-looking man. He was an attractive man with unusual silvery skin, and he began speaking to me. I felt as if he could read my mind because he addressed my thoughts even before I had said a word. He told me he was from another time–and he said that his unusual appearance was due to some sort of process that had been performed on him. Despite his appearance, I wondered what it might feel like to kiss a man like that; just a random thought, I guess. Although I said nothing, he spoke to my thought–warning me I would not enjoy the experience of kissing him because his skin was very cold. I asked him why he was here, and he showed me a shiny dark stone. He called it a 'key' and told me it was a crystal–

which confused me because it didn't look anything like a crystal. He said he came to warn us about an impending threat–a time when we might be faced with the possibility of losing our own humanity. When I asked him his name, he answered 'Aroya'.

This story is about Abbie–a woman who met a time traveler on the streets of San Francisco. It is based on my vision–a jumping-off point for the story–but everything else is fictitious. Although there are parts that do indeed relate to my own personal ideas and extraordinary experiences–overall, it is purely a work of fiction. Therefore, I hope the reader will forgive any inaccuracies or unsupported theories related to time travel or anything else, chalking them up solely to the author's creative interpretation.

Of course, this is also a romance; therefore, it is somewhat steamy at times–but mostly, it's a story about Abbie and Aroya's journey toward spiritual awareness, and their fight to save humanity.

I hope you enjoy my story.

A.B. Raphaelle (ABRaphaelle.com)

1– ABBIE

2019

San Francisco

Timeline 1.0

Beneath the shadow of a tall granite building, as the first rays of sunlight pierced the morning fog, Abbie met a man. He seemed familiar. There was a seriousness about his expression, but also a nervousness. In his hand, he held a dark, smooth stone that exploded into a kaleidoscope of color against the morning sky.

Abbie studied the stone. "What is it?" she asked.

"It's the crystal stone," he replied.

Confused, Abbie thought to herself, *but it doesn't look like a crystal*

The man focused his eyes on Abbie. "I need you," he said with sincere urgency.

Startled, Abbie opened her eyes. Her whole body was buzzing like a cell phone set on vibe. Wow, that was awesome! If it wasn't for work, she'd be riding this one all the way out.

Extinguishing the candle on her altar, she shook off the intoxicating vision–then, grabbing her coat and backpack, she rushed out the door to meet the bus.

Abbie was a nurse at the public hospital. Dressed in scrubs and booties, she hurried from room to room–hanging IV bags and entering data into the computer system. It was an old hospital–tired and rundown. A long train of recently expired patients rolled past in body bags–one after the other. The staff thought nothing of it. It was just another day.

Abbie checked the vitals of Tulio Guterres–a 37-year-old Latino man in room 29. He wore a nasal cannula for oxygen–and a big smile that lit up the room. Admitted through the ER, he came in with heart palpitations–but luckily, it was just anxiety. He felt much better now.

Abbie checked his oxygen saturation level and pulled up his chart on the computer. Everything looked fine.

"Mr. Guterres, we're still waiting on your labs. In the meantime, there's an order for an IV," she said.

When she moved his arm into position, he squeezed her hand gently. "Thank you, nurse. Please call me Tulio," he said.

Abbie wiped his arm with an alcohol pad. "Okay, Tulio. Just a little pinch," she said as she inserted the needle. She adjusted the IV flow, then comforted Tulio.

"If your labs look good, maybe you'll be going home soon."

Tulio let out a sigh of relief.

Abbie was at the nurse's station checking on his lab results when Dr. Eiffel–a short, dark-haired man with beady blue eyes–paraded down the hall with a resident in tow. He passed Abbie on his way to room 29. She hurried after him, entering Tulio's room.

Stone-cold, Dr. Eiffel examined Tulio's monitor and glanced at his IV bag. "Where's his meds?" he barked.

"I wasn't sure he still needed–"

Dr. Eiffel cut her off with a stern look.

Abbie said nothing more.

Retrieving the medications, she wheeled the bulky IV machine into Tulio's room. Tulio sat up–his eyes widening when he saw the machine; there were eight bags of medication hanging on that monster. Dr. Eiffel examined Tulio's oxygen saturation. "Mr. Guterres, you need help with your oxygen. I'm putting you on a ventilator."

Alarmed, Tulio turned to Abbie. "But you said everything looked fine."

Abbie's own shock was apparent. She didn't know what to say.

"Plug in his meds. I'll order the vent," Dr. Eiffel snapped.

Abbie re-examined the orders. "Excuse me, doctor– there's a problem with the Versed. The dose–"

"The dose is correct." Again, he cut her off.

Abbie started the medications for Tulio's IV line, but she refused to plug in the Versed.

"Where the hell are his labs?" whined Dr. Eiffel, glancing at the monitor.

"I'll go check," Abbie replied.

Abbie returned to Tulio's room, finding him sedated and woozy. "His O2 sats are between 90 and 92," Abbie said. "Can't we just use high flow?"

"Why use high flow when we've got a vent?" Dr. Eiffel replied. He studied Abbie's face while starting the Versed.

Tulio was now unconscious. Abbie's eyes locked on the Versed running through his vein. The dose was four times the recommendation.

Dr. Eiffel waved his hand across Abbie's face. "Snap out of it–fasten his restraints!"

Abbie was fuming with anger. She fastened Tulio's restraints–shooting Dr. Eiffel an angry look before leaving the room. Soon she returned with a crash cart and a syringe full of epinephrine.

Dr. Eiffel laughed. "What the hell is that for? Get rid of it–he's a DNR," he said.

Shaking her head, she double-checked the orders. "No. He's not a DNR. There're no orders and nobody's even notified his family."

"It's a new policy. We don't need the family's consent anymore," Dr. Eiffel smirked.

Abbie's jaw dropped in disbelief. "Whose new policy?"

"The higher-ups," Dr. Eiffel replied, resisting a smile.

Abbie couldn't believe what she was witnessing. Reluctantly, she wheeled the crash cart back out to the hallway. A young resident squeezed by, wheeling a ventilator into the room. The resident intubated Tulio.

"There's no DNR, so if this man codes–I'm jumping on his chest!" Abbie protested.

Dr. Eiffel smiled at her, smugly. "Go check his labs again," he said.

Reluctantly, Abbie followed orders.

While on the phone at the nurse's station, she heard the paging system announce *CODE BLUE, ROOM 29*. She dropped the phone, rushing back into Tulio's room. He was coding all right, and nobody was doing a damn thing to revive him.

"I'm calling it. Time of death 13:50," Dr. Eiffel announced. After removing the vent, the resident sheepishly left the room.

Dr. Eiffel stood defiantly next to Tulio's dead body like a gloating hunter posing with his trophy.

Infuriated, Abbie looked on silently.

"Abbie, you're a good nurse–but you're *way* too emotional. You really need to distance yourself," Dr. Eiffel said, with an air of satisfaction. He left Abbie alone with Tulio's dead body.

Abbie removed the IV line from Tulio's limp arm and shut off the monitor. Taking a moment, she addressed him. "Tulio, I'm sorry."

She wiped a tear from her eye, remembering his bright, smiling face just a few hours earlier–and felt the urge to squeeze his hand, just like he squeezed hers. She took his hand, but her warm memory soon transformed into the cold reality of death. She hated to admit it, but the sweet man with the cheerful smile felt more like a piece of meat right now–the difference between the living and the dead was disturbingly palpable. She tried to conceal her reaction, just in case the man's spirit was watching–but in truth, the sensation deeply repulsed her.

Abbie's shift ended. She rushed out the door to the bus stop—finally breaking down in tears. On this cool, foggy San Francisco afternoon in August, she waited for the MUNI train.

Still sniffling, she called her friend, Millie. "Hey, Mil'—it's Abbie. I had a really hard day today—" she said, fighting back tears, "but I'm keeping my appointment. Can you meet me after?"

"Sure, hon," Millie replied.

"I should be finished around 8:30. It's on the corner of Guerrero and 18th."

"Okay. I'll be there. No worries."

"Thanks, Mil'—I'll meet you at the curb."

Abbie arrived in front of an old Victorian-style apartment building. She entered the foyer, then climbed three flights of stairs. A Brazilian man named Carlos met her at the door, smiling. Carlos led her to a dark room, where a shaman smoking a carved wooden pipe sat cross-legged on a woven mat. He wore a feathered headdress with matching armbands and a jaguar tooth around his neck. His face and bare chest were decorated with red and black paint.

"We call him 'o Mestre da visão'…he is the Vision Maker," Carlos said.

Smiling, the Vision Maker stood to greet Abbie. "Hello," he said in his thick Brazilian accent, motioning for her to sit on the mat.

Walking slowly in circles, the Vision Maker began blowing tobacco smoke over Abbie's head.

"The smoke is for purification," Carlos explained.

Carlos and the Vision Maker now sat down on the mat, across from Abbie. The Vision Maker spoke softly, "Dor no coração."

"He says you have pain in the heart," Carlos said, translating.

Abbie thought of her patient, Tulio Guterres. She could still see his smiling face...then his lifeless body. Her heart felt like it was breaking into a million pieces. She fought to hold back the tears, but couldn't. She began sobbing.

"Yes," she sniffled. "My problem is...I feel too deeply about people I barely know. I don't want to feel that pain anymore."

Carlos handed her a tissue.

Abbie thought to herself: *I guess this happens all the time. He had those tissues handy, even before I started crying.*

"The people I work with are cruel. I can't stand being around such cold, unfeeling people," she said.

Carlos translated for the Vision Maker, but he was already nodding. Abbie assumed he understood.

The Vision Maker peered into Abbie's eyes and said, "O que você odeia, você se torna. Proteger o coração é bom. Fechar o coração não é bom."

"He says you are on your way to becoming the thing you hate. Protecting the heart is good–but closing the heart is not good," Carlos translated.

"But I don't know what to do. The pain is too much," she said, weeping.

The Vision Maker nodded again–he didn't need a translation. "Conflito no coração. Porque seu caminho não está correto."

"The conflict in your heart is because you are on the wrong path," Carlos said, translating.

The Vision Maker held a gourd rattle–swirling it around, creating a swishing sound. He moved the rattle to Abbie's right ear–then to her left.

"Olhos fechados. Escute," he said.

"Close your eyes and listen to the sound. Let it carry you," Carlos said.

Carlos puffed on his pipe. He held a large condor feather–using it to sweep more smoke over Abbie's head. The Vision Maker continued swirling the gourd rattle.

The swishing sound reminded her of wind blowing in her ears. Carlos began drumming softly while the Vision Maker sang in his tribal language. The sound of the swishing became louder, and soon Abbie saw the image of a condor in her mind; she felt like she was flying over an endless expanse of countryside far below. The feeling was exhilarating.

The Vision Maker put down his rattle. "Olha o jaguar. Seguir."

"See the jaguar. Follow it," Carlos translated.

In her mind, Abbie saw a jaguar; the big cat paced back and forth, waiting for her to engage. Then he turned, walking away. She followed him down a dirt path, entering a tropical forest. Pushing through the thick foliage, she searched for him. There was an opening in the trees, and she stepped through.

Now, she found herself standing on a sidewalk in the middle of downtown San Francisco. Surprised, she wondered how she got there. Remembering her instructions, she kept walking, looking for the jaguar.

She turned a corner–and came upon a man. He held up a dark stone–that sparkled in the sunlight. She thought she recognized him from somewhere. Could it be the man from her earlier vision?

The man took her in his arms and kissed her. The city faded away. Now, it was just her and the man, embracing and kissing passionately. Then she remembered she wasn't alone–and suddenly, she became self-conscious.

The man drifted away–but she could hear him calling out to her: "I need you."

Abbie's eyes popped open. The Vision Maker studied her face, smiling. Embarrassed, she suspected that he somehow saw her kissing the man.

Then he whispered something to Carlos, and both men chuckled. "Please, stand," Carlos said.

Abbie and the Vision Maker stood facing each other while Carlos poured hot water into a large bowl of herbs. The Vision Maker rubbed the mixture on Abbie's head–then on her face, arms, ankles, and feet.

"It's for protection," explained Carlos.

The Vision Maker stepped closer, placing his hand on Abbie's heart. Carlos translated, "You are protected–" then touching her right shoulder, he said, "by the condor–" and touching her left shoulder, he said, "and the jaguar." Abbie gasped–breathing in the powerful energy of the protectors. She trembled–a surge of energy coursed through her body.

The Vision Maker held her shoulders until the trembling stopped. In broken English, he said, "Now, close eyes."

Taking the pipe from Carlos, he blew smoke over her head–then he stood silent, facing her. She could hear Carlos in the background, singing softly.

Although her eyes remained closed, images emerged from a grey haze, one after another. She detected faint shadows in her periphery–then an image materialized in front of her. It was the face of Jesus; he was looking into her eyes. It surprised her–after all; she was with Indians–therefore, she expected to see condors and jaguars; she never expected to see Jesus! While looking into his eyes, Abbie experienced a sense of comfort and familiarity; as though she were in the presence of a loving brother. Then, slowly, the image changed. Now, it became the face of Mary. Abbie's relatives were Catholic, but she never learned to say the rosary–or even thought much about the holy mother. Now, however, she stood in silence–looking directly into the holy mother's eyes. Warm tears wet Abbie's cheeks– then suddenly, Mary's eyes transformed. The image was still Mary, but Abbie was now looking into her own eyes–and they were looking back at her. Overwhelmed by the sensation, a fountain of emotion rose from her heart, and she began to weep.

A hand gently squeezed her shoulder. It was the Vision Maker. "Mãe de Deus. Sim, ela vê a Mãe de Deus," he said.

"You see Mother of God," Carlos translated, with a hint of surprise in his voice.

Speechless, Abbie nodded.

"Good," the Vision Maker concluded.

Carlos set down the pipe and began arranging condor feathers, rattles, and dried herbs neatly on a table. The Vision Maker took up the pipe and moved closer to the opened window, looking at the sky while he smoked.

"Okay. All done," Carlos said. He motioned for Abbie to follow him, and they walked to the door. Carlos said goodbye–kissing her cheek in the customary Brazilian manner.

Abbie stepped out onto the street. Her whole body was still tingling; she could barely feel her feet touching the ground. She saw Millie waiting in the car and thought to herself; *I'm so glad I'm not taking the bus home tonight.* She got in on the passenger side, and Millie started driving.

Abbie was still feeling out of sorts. "Thanks, Millie," she said. Then she fell quiet.

"That's okay, hon'," Millie replied. "Tonight was light. No guests–just call-ins."

A drunken man stumbled off the curb–veering dangerously close to Millie's car.

"Besides, this neighborhood's kind of sketchy at night," Millie added. "I'm glad you called me."

Abbie's mind was still reeling from the day. In the morning, there was the strange vision–with the unusual man and the sparkling stone; then there was the drama at the hospital–with Dr. Eiffel, and the death of Tulio Guterres; and finally, there was a shamanic voyage, with an appearance by the same unusual man–and the vision of Jesus and Mary. Emotionally overwhelmed, she quietly wept–searching in her backpack for a tissue.

"Here, honey. Check the front pocket," Millie said, handing Abbie her purse. "Was the session intense?"

"Yes…very intense." Abbie found a tissue and blew her nose. "I'm not quite ready to talk about it."

"Okay. No worries. Whenever you're ready."

"But it's not just about the session," Abbie clarified. "It's about the hospital, too. In fact, it's mostly about the hospital." She straightened up, angry and frustrated–thinking about Dr. Eiffel.

"What's going on?" Millie asked, noticing Abbie's changed demeanor. "Are you mad about something?"

"It's that narcissist, Dr. Eiffel. He murdered another one of my patients today–and I just flipped! I swear, the chance of a patient leaving that hospital alive–is now slim to none!"

"Fuckin' narcissists," Millie responded. "The only thing worse than a narcissist boyfriend–is a narcissist doctor." A shiver ran up her spine. "God, just the thought of it!"

"It's worse than that…he's a murderer. And there's not a damn thing I can do about it." Abbie reflected on how hard she fought to save Tulio. "It's so weird 'cause nobody even seems to notice. It makes me feel like *I'm* the crazy one."

"You're not crazy, Abbie. It's that place! It's turning into some kind of insane asylum–or *worse!*"

"Yeah. It's starting to feel like the fuckin' *Twilight Zone!*" Abbie took a deep breath. "I just feel so empty inside…like I have nothing left to give."

"Job burn-out?"

"Maybe. It's all that death…bodies on top of bodies. Just roll 'em in, and roll 'em out."

"Abbie…if you think he's intentionally killing people, then you really need to say something."

"It's not just him. Hardly anyone leaves that hospital alive anymore." Abbie considered her options. "Who would I tell, anyway? According to Dr. Eiffel, the orders are coming from the 'higher-ups.'"

"Who are the 'higher-ups?'" Millie asked.

"I don't know. But whoever they are, apparently they tell the doctors what to do–and they just do it–even if it means murdering patients."

"People need to know what's going on. Why don't you come on my podcast, as a whistleblower?"

"Naw...that's not me. I'm ashamed to admit it, but I don't have the courage. Besides, it could destroy my career."

"Just think about it–okay?" Millie changed the subject. "You don't have to tell me anything...if you don't feel ready. But did the shaman thing go all right?"

"Yeah. First, I saw a condor–and I actually felt like I was flying. Then I saw a jaguar."

"Wow. Did you get any messages?"

"The shaman guy–he's called the Vision Maker–he told me I was on the wrong path. Maybe he's right. But there was lots more."

"More messages?"

"No. There were more visions. A jaguar led me to a place where I saw a man. I was in a tropical forest–then suddenly, I was in downtown San Fran–somewhere around the Financial District. That's where I met him. He was holding a shiny dark stone in his hand...and he *kissed* me."

"He *kissed* you? What did the shaman guy say?"

"Nothing. He just smiled, like he somehow saw it. But that's not the weirdest part. The weird part is–I saw the same man during my meditation this morning–

minus the kissing. It was almost like I was watching a rerun. Both times, there was this dark stone with swirling colors. And in my head, I heard the man call it a crystal, but it didn't look anything like a crystal."

"What do you think it means?"

"I don't know. Maybe it just means that I'm burnt out and need some kind of distraction. Anyway...both times, it ended in a disturbing way–with the man saying *I need you*...before fading away. It was really weird."

"Yeah, weird. Maybe he's stuck between dimensions or something. Did you see anything else?" Millie asked.

"Yeah, but I need more time to digest it."

Millie changed the subject. "How about grabbing something to eat? There was a street fair in the Haight today. Maybe there's still something going on."

"Sounds good," Abbie said.

Parking was a bitch in the Haight. Trekking four or five blocks, all of them thick with people, Abbie and Millie finally arrived at a funky little café. A group of street artists stood on the sidewalk performing–and a juggler tipped his hat at Abbie. A dark stone tumbled out from under his hat–hitting the pavement and cracking– revealing a dark crystalline structure inside.

The juggler handed the dark stone to Abbie. "This must be for you, my dear." He smiled, tipping his hat again–then he went on his way.

Abbie examined the stone. Then her eyes grew big. "Oh my God...you're not gonna believe this! Oh Jeez– I'm getting chills!"

"Why? It's just a rock."

Abbie turned the stone toward the light, revealing the iridescence–and the crystal inside.

"Is that the stone from your vision? Oh, shit–it is! I don't believe it!"

"Why not?" Abbie said. "It's an absolutely fitting finale to one of the weirdest days of my life!"

2– AROYA

2050

San Francisco

Timeline 1.0

The year was 2050. It had been 20 years since the catastrophe, and San Francisco was in a progressive state of decay.

It was a cold day in August–but then again, all summers were cold now–and the freezing winters took many in their sleep. Those who hid under sturdy structures, sheltering from icy winds, often met their fate when the temblors shook everything apart.

Surface dwellers were used to the shaking, but the elite got tired of it long ago. When they finally crawled out of their hidey-holes, they began utilizing hidden technology to build their own communities in the sky, high above the chemical particulates that drifted at the lower levels. These elite sky communities called themselves the Sky Council–and they assigned dwellings according to rank–from the Sky Council Elite all the way down to the common sky pod communities. The Sky Council dwellings were far removed from the surface dwellers, perched high in the sky, fastened magnetically to tall pedestals serving as docking stations. Shaped like deep dishes, the docking stations provided a magnetic current–levitating each saucer-shaped dwelling about 6 feet higher. The dwellings swayed atop their pedestals during earthquakes–but not being solidly attached to the dock or the ground–they risked little damage. On tall earthen hills, beneath the docking stations, enormous towers stood generating electricity. Tesla technology finally realized.

On the ground, in zone 9–there was no electricity at all. Not one woman walked alone on the streets–if you don't count the porcine chimera girls. (Human girls were a protected commodity–surface dwellers rarely saw them.) The pig people were a sad result of genetic experimentation. After the catastrophe, they had escaped from underground laboratories–and though presumed to be sterile and eventually destined to die out–they somehow found a way. Make-shift houses lined the streets, pasted together with mud and lightweight materials, periodically crumbling to the ground–especially when the earth shook. Humans inhabited most of these Hodge-Podge houses–while porcine dwellings were constructed from tree branches, few even having a formal roof. Most pig people had an IQ comparable to a chimpanzee–although a few possessed the intelligence of a 12-year-old human. They were definitely pig-like, but some had very human features–walking up-right and using their cloven forefeet similar to human hands. The ones with higher IQs suffered the most–and often found themselves outcast from all other groups.

Zone 9 was lawless, except for the overbearing rules enforced by the Sky Council Elite. Hideous predator chimeras roamed the streets at night, with their human faces and large cat-like bodies, looking for a meal. Their behavior was unpredictable, and their vocalizations were loud and creepy. Some of them enjoyed pork–but others thirsted for human blood. Because of this, every night before sundown, all human dwellings barricaded their doors and windows. The pig people huddled together on their straw beds, inside their haphazard dwellings. The little ones hid deep inside the center of the huddle–and the ones that didn't were easy pickings.

On the edge of zone 9–Aroya, a long-haired public worker–spent his afternoons secretly teaching teenage boys to read and write; a skill strictly prohibited by the Council–especially for zone 9 surface dwellers. In an old deserted warehouse, the boys practiced their writing, using scraps of tree bark or anything else they could find for paper, and crow's feathers filled with blackberry juice for pens. Dirty fingertips stained with purple juice offered proof of what they'd been up to–if anyone had an inkling about surface dwellers knowing how to write.

An orange and crimson sky announced the coming of nightfall. Aroya's students trickled out from the warehouse, making their way home over the desolate landscape. Soon, the doors would shut tight–and any man showing up between sunset and dawn would be highly scrutinized. Only a handful of regulars were welcomed beyond the bolted doors–all of them close friends, and all of them "dreamers." Although considered typical hard-working men; their ideals and intelligence were anything but typical. In another time, they would have been philosophers, professors, entrepreneurs, or scientists. These five men were old enough to remember life before the catastrophe; some of them even had a few years of schooling before it all came tumbling down. On this night, they read passages out loud from fragile old books kept hidden inside an underground vault. It all took place inside the huge empty warehouse, with high ceilings and spinning roof vents that turned noisily in the wind. The warehouse was windowless, of course, for privacy–and barricaded for safety.

Since the catastrophe, pleasant memories and fanciful dreams had become valuable commodities for the surface-dwellers. Most preferred to keep their dreams private–hidden away safely in their mind–but some traded them for useful items or simple pleasures. Nearly all pleasures were prohibited since the catastrophe–and 'eyes-in-the-sky' kept watch 24/7 to ensure that nobody enjoyed themselves too much.

Sitting around the fire of an old open furnace, the men took turns reciting passages from poetry, interwoven with drumming and fluting–all intended to induce sleep and encourage dreaming. Here, in this secret place–the men allowed themselves to imagine beauty in all forms: sight, sound, smell, and taste–all that was now sorely lacking in pleasantness. Some of these men hadn't slept in days–and many hadn't dreamt in months. On this night, they recited poetry around the fire–and for those who were lucky, they would dream.

The dream circle began with a large, 42-year-old bearded man named Elijah, bringing a stranger to the front. The other men scrutinized him, wondering if he was trustworthy. The stranger was tall and fair, with hair as white as snow and blue eyes, clear and cool as ice. He held up a dark stone, offering it as payment for a few lines of poetry. Most of the men turned away, uninterested in the trade.

Elijah shrugged his shoulders. "He's traveled a long way," he said. "It's all he's got."

Aroya accepted the challenge. "I'll trade a few lines from Walt Whitman," he offered.

The stranger smiled, handing Aroya the stone.

Aroya examined the dark stone against the fire's glow, noticing something unusual. There appeared to be light captured inside, creating an iridescence. The other men took a closer look. Some were sorry they didn't make the trade.

Aroya was quite pleased with his good fortune. "Let's begin," he said, standing before the men.

One man played a soft, airy tune on a rough, handmade flute–while others began drumming softly, drifting into a gently pulsing rhythm. Aroya prepared himself by rehearsing the poem in his mind–planning each rise and fall of pitch and every strategic pause. He began:

*"My tongue, every atom of my blood, form'd from
this soil, this air,
Born here of parents born here from parents the
same, and their parents the same,
I, now thirty-seven years old in perfect health
begin,
Hoping to cease not till death.*

*"Creeds and schools in abeyance,
Retiring back a while sufficed at what they are, but
never forgotten,
I harbor for good or bad, I permit to speak at every
hazard, Nature without check with original
energy."*

Finished, Aroya stepped away from the fire,
reclining on a lumpy hay bed. He waited for Elijah to
echo the poem, as was customary for each man in the
circle. Now the flute was quiet. Only the soft drumming
remained to accompany Elijah's husky voice. Although
a giant man, Elijah recited poetry softly–sometimes
verging on a melodic whisper. Echoing Aroya's poem,
he began:

*"My tongue, every atom of my blood, form'd from
this soil, this air,
Born here of parents born here from parents the
same, and their parents the same..."*

Elijah's voice, and the soft drumming, worked their
magic on Aroya–and he fell into a deep sleep. On this
night, he had a powerful dream–about his newly
acquired crystal stone.

In the dream, an unusual man with a painted face and feathers on his head spoke to him. It was the Vision Maker–the same man who had given Abbie her vision. The Vision Maker said to him: *hold the stone in your hand and close your eyes. See your desire–like a wave in the water...rippling–flowing–formless. Now, move the other hand beneath the stone–and see your goal. It is very still–no more rippling–it is solid. Drop the stone from one hand to the other, and let the moving waters of your desire...take you to your destination.*

Now, an attractive woman entered Aroya's dream. Consumed by desire, he caressed her and kissed her lips. The Vision Maker's voice instructed Aroya: *let her be your desire...and let your desire take you to your destination.* Aroya's worries dissolved–as he passionately made love to the woman in his dream.

When dawn approached, Aroya refused to let the dream go. He knew it was time to rise, but he stubbornly closed his eyes–surrendering to each lingering moment–replaying the dream over and over again in his mind.

Finally, Elijah shook him awake, hastening him to leave with the others before the sun broke through the morning fog. In 2050, being in the wrong place at the wrong time was a punishable transgression–and so far, Aroya's record was clean.

Aroya worked as an apprentice for the zone 9 surface maintenance crew. Today he dragged his butt into work–clocking in without a minute to spare. He was on assignment with his supervisor, John Cooper–who always did the driving. Slumped against the dusty passenger side window while catching a few z's–Aroya slept all the way to the job site while the hover truck jumped and jerked along.

Cooper teased Aroya. "What's wrong, Roy boy? Were you up late last night…with one of those pig girls? *Oink-oink!*" He let out a belly laugh. "You'd better watch out–I hear those oinkers got the cooties!"

Aroya reluctantly opened his eyes. "The only wild thing about my night, Coop…were my dreams," Aroya said–still groggy.

"You still dream? How d'ya manage that? Hell, I'm lucky if I even sleep," Cooper said.

"Well, not like I used to…but occasionally, I'm lucky," Aroya replied.

They arrived at their destination–a dirty old town on the outskirts, where only 'pig people' feel at home. The air was thick and gray from particulates that blocked the sun, and rubble littered the landscape. The soil and shrubs were either bone-dry or muddy–depending on the current weather program. On most days, the pig people dug mindlessly for roots and garbage–but today, the scene was chaotic.

Aroya dragged himself out of the hover truck and slipped into a metallic jumpsuit for protection against contamination. A giant hologram hovered in the air above an enormous black cube, situated against a rocky wall, near the mouth of a cave. The hologram flickered off and on, flashing fractured bits of digital numbers– accompanied by fuzzy images of government officials shouting confusing commands. A static sound crackled between the glitched words: *REPORT-REPORT-PENALTY-PENALTY!* An even larger holographic screen hovered higher, depicting horrific scenes of pig people melting under targeted death rays from the sky. All the pig people were in a frenzy–confused and panicked.

"It looks like another leak," Cooper said. Reaching into his truck, he pulled out two stun guns–handing one to Aroya.

Activating a communication device implanted inside his forearm–Cooper held his wrist to his mouth and reported to base.

"Connect! …John Cooper reporting. Inspecting a leak at porcine village, Bayside. Check back in five. Out."

Aroya hadn't seen Cooper's new device yet–a reward for reporting on another co-worker.

"When you finish your apprenticeship, and you're all certified–you'll be eligible for one of these too!" Cooper announced, gloating.

Nearby, a deranged pig-man was seriously flipping out. Covered in dark goo–his eyes were black as ink. He rushed forward, pleading with Aroya, "Shoot me! *Snort-snort*. Shoot me, shoot me!"

"Get back!" Aroya shouted.

The angry pig-man spat a dark oily wad that landed on Aroya's jumpsuit and oozed down the front. It absolutely wreaked!

Cooper hit the pig-man with a powerful jolt from his stun gun, knocking him out cold in the dirt. "Crazy oinker!" Cooper yelled. "Next time, I'll use a real gun!"

Aroya stepped out of his soiled jumpsuit, dropping it into a metallic refuge bag.

"Did he get any on ya?" Cooper asked.

"No, I'm clean," Aroya replied, glancing at the pig-man, motionless in the dirt. "You know, it's not their fault," he said, shaking his head.

It took courage to stick up for the pig people, especially when it came to idiots like Cooper–but it was the goo that made the pig-man crazy. They weren't typically aggressive–and most of them were actually more human than pig; intentionally engineered that way to supply organs for human transplants. After cloned humans began supplying 100% compatible organs, most of the chimera facilities shut down, but there were still a few old research facilities that used chimeras of all kinds. Following the catastrophe, porcine chimeras remained stranded out in zone 9–left to fend for themselves.

Cooper sneered with disgust at the pig-man in the dirt. "They should've exterminated them all," he said.

Aroya ignored Cooper's comment–knowing full well the kind of trouble he could cause him.

The two men crawled over large boulders to reach the 13-foot-high black cube. Aroya noticed a fracture at the top of the cube–a dark gooey substance bubbled out, oozing down the side. A glob of it landed squarely on Aroya's bare arm. Using a rag from his back pocket, he wiped it off without a second thought.

Cooper freaked out! *"Oh, man!* I never should've let you go in without a suit!"

"Don't worry," Aroya said. "It doesn't affect me. I used to play with it as a kid."

"You used to play with it?"

"Yeah. After the catastrophe–when we were bored. Me and my friend–we used to mess around with it."

"Your friend didn't get sick, either?"

"Nope. We never had any problem with it."

"You wouldn't be one of those *mutants*, would you?"

Aroya laughed. "No, Coop. I'm just an ordinary guy."

Cooper turned away, suspicious. "Go ahead and inspect the leak. I'll call in the report." Cooper returned to the truck.

Aroya examined the cracked cube, climbing high on jagged rocks to get a better look. A noisy commotion came from outside. He dropped down, peering over the boulders. A Surface Squad commander, fully outfitted in ultra-secure body armor, joined Cooper near the truck. Extremely animated, Cooper pointed to his arm, then gestured toward the black cube.

The Squad commander looked in Aroya's direction. *"MR. WALLACE! THROW OUT YOUR WEAPON AND COME FORWARD!"* he shouted.

Bewildered, Aroya tossed his stun gun out–and stumbled into the open. He approached the commander while a swarm of drone-nets hovered in the sky–ready for capture if he dared run. Terrified–he imagined it must be some sort of mistake. A pack of jackal-bots came out of nowhere. They encircled him, threatening him from behind–pushing him forward toward the Squad.

The Squad commander aimed his weapon at Aroya. *"STAY WHERE YOU ARE! DO NOT MOVE!"* he yelled.

While the Squad steadied their guns on Aroya–the commander approached, grabbing his arm. "Come with me–and don't make any sudden moves!" The jackal-bots were right on their heels–growling and bearing their razor-like teeth.

The armored transport doors opened, and the commander shoved Aroya inside. *"Sit!"* he hollered. *"With your hands in your lap–and your back against the wall!"*

Aroya leaned back, and two large clamps moved in from either side–securing his upper body.

In the distance, Cooper watched. "I hope you rot in hell–you *mutant freak!*" Cooper yelled, crossing his arms over his chest.

Aroya shot back an angry look. The doors closed.

At a deep underground facility, known as the *Center for Trans-Human Processing*, armed guards marched Aroya inside, wearing a new metallic jumpsuit over his clothes. Administrator Burk followed behind.

Dr. Biegel, nearly 60 years old–stood in his lab, facing an animated holographic model of a human body–hovering atop a 3-foot-high black cube. His medical assistant, Betty, announced Administrator Burk's arrival as the guards escorted Aroya into the laboratory.

Burk handed a tiny black cube to Dr. Biegel. "We've got another *mutant* for you, doc. We're consulting with Sky Council about VIM transformation–once he's fully trained…depending on how the *processing* goes, of course. Keep us informed."

"I most certainly will, Administrator," replied Dr. Biegel.

The glass doors opened for the Administrator's departure, and Aroya caught a glimpse of the guards still standing outside. Dr. Biegel activated the small data cube–and a hologram popped up, displaying Aroya's data:

AROYA WALLACE:
BIRTH DATA–DESTROYED, PARENTS–
UNKNOWN. COLLECTED IN 2030 SWEEP.
SUBJECT REPORTS TO BE 37 YEARS OLD.
CURRENTLY IN TRANSIT BETWEEN ZONE 9
SURFACE DWELLINGS. LABOR ASSIGNMENT–
SURFACE MAINTENANCE, SUPERVISOR–JOHN
COOPER. PRIMARY SOCIAL RELATIONSHIPS–
NONE. TRANSGRESSIONS–NONE. SUBJECT
FREQUENTLY OBSERVED IN ZONE 9 PORCINE
VILLAGE, BAYSIDE. PERIODICALLY OBSERVED
IN THE COMPANY OF ELIJAH STEWART. HEALTH
STATUS–FUNCTIONAL.

REPORT:
COLLECTED BY ZONE 9 SURFACE SQUAD ON
AUGUST 7, 2050. TAGGED BY MAINTENANCE
CREW SUPERVISOR JOHN COOPER, WHO
BELIEVES WALLACE TO BE A MUTANT. COOPER
STATES THAT WALLACE INTERACTED WITH
THE VIM, SUFFERING NO ILL EFFECTS.
ACCORDING TO COOPER, WALLACE ADMITS TO
PLAYING WITH VIM AS A CHILD. IN
COMPLIANCE WITH ADMINISTRATOR BURK'S
ORDERS, AROYA WALLACE IS TO BE
PROCESSED IMMEDIATELY IN PREPARATION
FOR ELITE GUARD TRAINING. BY DIRECTION OF
THE SKY COUNCIL, DR. BIEGEL IS ORDERED TO
MOVE FORWARD WITH FULL VIM
TRANSFORMATION ONCE WALLACE IS
SUCCESSFULLY PROCESSED AND TRAINED.

Aroya stood behind Dr. Biegel, reading his data hologram. "What is VIM transformation?" Aroya asked, curious.

"VIM is an acronym for Viscous Intelligent Matter…known commonly as 'the goo.' That's why you're here. Your record indicates that you've recently had contact with the VIM–but suffered no negative consequences, which is highly unusual."

Aroya shrugged. "It fell on my arm, and I wiped it off. What's the big deal?"

Dr. Biegel closed the data cube and dropped it into his pocket. "Mr. Wallace, please follow me to the next room. I need you to remove your clothing, so I may examine you."

Aroya followed Dr. Biegel–still very confused. "I don't understand why you need to examine me."

"We need to determine if the VIM has invaded you internally."

"Invaded me? I don't think so," Aroya said. He removed his clothing and stood naked in front of the doctor.

Dr. Biegel scanned his entire body with a hand-held device. He projected a semi-transparent holographic diagram in the middle of the room. "I don't see any spots or flares," he said, "and the projection is exceptionally bright and clear. Everything looks completely normal."

"I told you."

"But you said you played with the VIM as a child? What did you mean by that?"

"I didn't mean anything. Kids play with stuff. And I was 17–so technically, I was a teenager…just a bored teenager."

"Mr. Wallace, please have a seat."

Aroya grabbed his clothes from the table (minus the metallic jumpsuit) and began dressing.

Dr. Biegel didn't intend for Aroya to get dressed–but he was attempting to win his cooperation–so he thought it best to allow it.

"You must realize that ordinary humans cannot withstand physical contact with the *VIM,*" Dr. Biegel said.

"I don't know what you're talking about," Aroya said while dressing.

"Do you know what this place is?"

"The guards called it, *The Center.* That's all I know."

"Its full name is the *Center for Trans-Human Processing.* We process people here. We physically process them–in order to make them more useful to the Sky Council."

"Okay. I've been processed. Can I go now?"

"I'm afraid the *Council* won't allow it. They have special plans for you."

"What kind of plans?"

"The Council plans to train you for the *Elite Guard.* That's why you've been brought here–"

"Brought here? More like *dragged* here."

"Yes, well...you were brought here for processing. It's mandatory for all surface dwellers before they leave the surface–especially when they've been recruited for the Elite Guard."

"But I don't wanna leave the surface–and I don't wanna join the Elite Guard."

Dr. Biegel took the data cube from his pocket, setting it down on the table. He reactivated it–pointing to the hologram floating above the cube. "See here, Mr. Wallace–they're preparing you for the Elite Guard. It's a direct order from the higher-ups." The data cube displayed Aroya's history again.

"Why me? I'm just a maintenance apprentice–not exactly *Elite* material."

"I suppose they want to use your special abilities. And also...there's the control issue."

"What special abilities? I don't have any special abilities."

"Do you still dream, Mr. Wallace?"

Aroya turned away, silent.

"Do you sometimes know things about people–before you've been told?" Dr. Biegel asked. "Maybe you even know what others are thinking?"

Still looking away, Aroya remained silent.

Dr. Biegel spelled things out for Aroya. "I'm afraid you have no choice. Even if you weren't being recruited–it would still be mandatory. All *mutants* are processed."

"I'm not a *mutant,"* Aroya protested.

"Please, Mr. Wallace–"

"My name is *Aroya."*

"Okay then, *Aroya...*ordinary men do not handle Viscous Intelligent Matter without effect–and that is why you are so valuable to the Elite Guard. When your training is complete, you will be considered for *full transformation."*

"Transformation into what?"

"Full transformation is what we call it when a mutant fully merges with the *VIM.* Unlike the process, which needs to be updated periodically–once you are fully transformed, you will be more than just a mutant–

and more than just a man. You will be *immortal*. And your abilities will be enhanced–beyond what the process could ever do. In a sense, you will become something like a *god.*"

"A god?" Aroya shook his head. "No, not me. I'm an ordinary man–and I prefer it that way."

"But there are some who think you might be more than an ordinary man. They think you're special...one of the *chosen.*"

"Chosen by who?"

"They think the *VIM* chose you, *specifically*. I suppose it's because–there's no other way to explain why the VIM doesn't harm you."

"How can the goo choose anything? It's just *goo!*"

"Have you ever wondered what the goo is? And why they distribute it throughout the entire surface?" Dr. Biegel asked.

"No. I never wondered. It's been there since the catastrophe–just like all the other weird stuff."

"Aroya, the VIM controls everything on the surface. Absolutely everything. And soon–"

"I can touch it–*so what!* Why is that such a big deal?"

"It's a *very* big deal–because it means we can transfuse it into your body without rejection."

"No freakin' way! You're not putting that creepy shit into my body!"

"If you don't consent to full transformation, there's really nothing we can do. You see, unlike processing– full transformation is not mandatory. You must be willing to surrender to it–freely and completely. Otherwise, it may not merge with you."

"*Good!* I don't *want* to merge with it. So, I don't *consent!*"

"Very well. But you still must undergo processing."

Aroya had enough of this nonsense. He bolted for the door.

"*GUARDS!*" Dr. Biegel shouted.

Three guards rushed in, taking hold of Aroya.

"*Get your hands off me!*" Aroya protested.

"Aroya, please listen," Dr. Biegel pleaded. "The process will give your mind and body new abilities–that you could never have imagined! Everything will function optimally, and your abilities will be enhanced. It's for your own good!"

"*NO! LET ME GO!*" Aroya shouted.

Dr. Biegel addressed the guards. "Strip him–then strap him down." Turning to Aroya, he said, "Fighting will only make it harder on yourself!" Exasperated, Dr. Biegel left the laboratory.

Aroya struggled against the guards. Dr. Biegel's assistant, Betty, looked on sympathetically.

Once securely strapped down to the procedure table, Betty wheeled him into a glass cubicle. She rolled the table over a large machine with switches and hoses, with even more hoses suspended from the ceiling.

Spotting all the hoses–Aroya's imagination went wild!

Betty walked around the procedure table, fastening devices onto his arms and legs. "I'm sorry, Mr. Wallace," she said, sliding something under his neck. "Please try to relax."

She fastened a device over his head–then reached for a lever.

"*Wait, wait!*" he pleaded, terrified.

Betty stopped. "Don't worry, Mr. Wallace. You won't feel a thing–and when it's all over, you won't remember anything."

Aroya focused on the words; *you won't remember anything.* He recalled his dream and wondered if he might lose his ability to remember it–or lose his ability to dream altogether. Panic flooded his every nerve and muscle with adrenalin. His heart pounded so thunderously that the monitor beeped a loud warning.

Betty leaned closer, fastening a sensor onto his chest.

"Will I still dream?" Aroya asked nervously.

Betty's eyes revealed her pity. "Your memory will be sanitized, and you won't have access to any information that might threaten the system." Sadly, she continued, "And I'm afraid…you will no longer dream." She shook her head, clearly disgusted.

*"Please…*is there any way to save my dreams?" he pleaded.

Nervous, Betty surveyed the room, glancing up at the camera. Again, she leaned forward–pressing the sensor more firmly onto Aroya's chest. With her back to the camera, she discretely whispered into his ear, "The cerebral processing will not initiate unless all circuits are closed. If I leave this connection near your ear loose," she loosened the connection, "then you might be able to shake it off. I'll silence the alarm. But please wait until I've left the room." She smiled at Aroya. "Good luck, Mr. Wallace."

Betty stood on a stool to reach the camera–smearing the lens with greasy ointment. Then she pulled the lever and left Aroya alone in the room.

Multi-colored lights hovered in mid-air, above and around Aroya's body. He flinched, feeling a painful pinch on both arms and legs. The process was activating.

Betty rushed back into the room. "Mr. Wallace? Can you hear me?" she asked.

Aroya opened his eyes.

"I found this in your clothing," she whispered, showing him the crystal stone. "It must be special to you. When you receive your assigned attire, check the lining beneath the pocket."

Unable to speak, Aroya simply blinked his eyes.

Betty nodded–then hurried away.

Aroya's vision blurred. Sedated and groggy–he tossed his head back and forth, struggling to dislodge the wire from his headgear. Aroya lost consciousness...then, as if by magic, the wire popped out, falling to the floor.

3– SKY PODS

2050

San Francisco

Timeline 1.0

Hundreds of sky pods glowed at different altitudes, as far as the eye could see in the night sky. Aroya stood inside a sky pod, looking out through a glass wall–with his hair cut short, in a form-fitting jacket with an asymmetrical lapel. From all appearances, he was now a member of the Sky Community. His skin was pale and glistened like the silver moon. Distant and emotionless, his piercing eyes stared out across the expansive sky. He winced and rubbed his temples.

Klaus, his pod mate and trainer, entered the room–noticing his discomfort. "What's wrong, little goo-bot? Does your head hurt?" Klaus mocked. "It's just the processing. It'll be gone by tomorrow," he snapped.

"Do you know how to use it?" he asked, pointing to a large black cube in the center of the minimally furnished communal room.

"No," Aroya said as he turned away, disinterested.

"*Damn the Guard!* What were they thinking? Sending an idiot goo-bot for Guard training," Klaus said, clearly annoyed.

Aroya ignored him–and without a word, he retired to his bedroom.

That night, while he slept…he had a dream. It was the same dream–with the feathered man, the crystal stone, and the attractive woman. He now desired the woman more than ever. He awoke with an enormous erection–that would not quit!

In the communal room, Klaus was surfing–on a holographic veil–projected from the black cube.

Aroya shuffled in, half asleep, carrying his jacket to conceal his erection. He stared out at the docking station, studying the hovercraft parked there. He'd never driven a hovercraft before, but he suddenly saw the operating system flash in his mind. Thanks to Betty, the tech hadn't completely taken over his mind, but it still endowed him with extraordinary abilities–most of which he was still unaware.

"You won't be needing breakfast," Klaus shouted. "A processed body can go for days without fuel." Klaus stepped off the surfing veil. "Hey Wallace, catch!" Klaus yelled, tossing him a black data cube.

Aroya reached out, catching the cube and dropping his jacket.

"It's your itinerary!" Klaus added. Then, noticing Aroya's erection, he pointed, laughing. "It looks like the processing worked somewhere," he teased, "or maybe, you're just happy to see Klaus?" he said, winking. His smile faded. "I heard you talking in your sleep last night! Were you perhaps, dreaming?!"

"No. I was sleeping," Aroya replied, picking up his jacket.

Aroya walked away, but Klaus blocked him.

"Wallace? Did your processing fail? *Answer me! Are you still dreaming?!*" Klaus yelled.

Aroya pushed past Klaus, retreating to his bedroom to contemplate his situation. He suspected Klaus was ready to file a report, so he began preparing for a quick departure.

Klaus stood outside Aroya's door, shouting relentlessly. *"You don't get it, do you?! They don't just allow any surface dweller up here! You're only here because you're a freakin' goo-bot! They're preparing to fully transform your gooey ass–but apparently, your processing failed–so now that's impossible!"*

Aroya heard Klaus making a call.

"Call Administrator Burk," Klaus ordered the cube. "Connect!" Burk's hologram materialized above the cube. "This is Klaus Wolf reporting on Recruit Wallace."

Aroya was sure the Elite Guard would be arriving soon. He grabbed his jacket, checking his pocket for the stone. It was there, inside the lining–just like Betty had told him.

"Sir, I believe Recruit Wallace's processing failed," Klaus told Burk. "I'm certain he was dreaming last night."

"I'll dispatch a team for examination," Burk replied.

Aroya darted from his bedroom, alarmed. He ran to the docking station–boarding a hovercraft.

"Where do you think you're going?!" Klaus screamed. *"You can't hide, you mutant freak! You'll be tracked within the hour!"*

Aroya sailed off, gliding down to the surface–in the direction of zone 9.

Unsure of where to hide, he landed near the bay–at the edge of the porcine village. Pig people gathered around the hovercraft, easily impressed by anything out of the ordinary for this wretched part of zone 9. Some of them were still behaving strangely. The holographic screen continued glitching–and a black puddle oozed over the ground. Most humans avoid the VIM–so Aroya thought it best to hide in the cave behind the leaking cube.

Walter, a teenage pig-man, joined the crowd. "Aroya! Aroya! *Snort-snort...*" he called out.

Spotting Walter near the back, Aroya beckoned to him. "They'll be coming for me soon," Aroya informed Walter. "Take the hovercraft and hide it–but don't let anyone catch you with it." he warned.

"They're coming for our friend! *Snort-snort...*" Walter announced to the crowd. *"DANCE! Snort-snort. DANCE! Snort...*" he cried out.

All at once, the pig people squealed and danced in their own chaotic style–a tactic they commonly employed to confuse outsiders...especially authorities.

Walter and his pig friends pushed the hovercraft over the rubbish–hiding it beneath a pile of debris.

Aroya headed for the black cube. Crawling over boulders and stepping over puddles of goo–he lowered himself into the cave.

The rumbling of Surface Squad vehicles now accompanied the piercing sound of pig squeals–

ramping up the chaos. Aroya had witnessed pig people creating chaotic distractions on multiple occasions–as cover for an escape. He could easily imagine the riotous scene outside. The squealing was unnerving. He figured the Squad would eventually shut down their antics…and then they'd be coming for him.

Sitting on a rock, he thought hard–trying to devise a plan–but he knew it was only a matter of time…and there was no way out. Suddenly, a voice spoke in his head. It was the feathered man. Again, he said the words: *let her be your desire…and let your desire take you to your destination.*

Aroya took the crystal stone from his pocket. Closing his eyes, he remembered the Vision Maker's instructions. He placed the stone firmly in his right hand and envisioned Abbie.

"I need you," he said aloud while holding Abbie's image in his mind.

He placed his left hand below his right–imagining himself beside her. Dropping the stone from one hand to the other–the raucous noise of squealing pigs faded away. Everything rippled like water–the *wave* grew stronger, finally knocking him to the ground. Then suddenly…everything was still.

4— GETTING TO KNOW YOU

2019

San Francisco

Timeline 1.0

When Aroya looked up, he found himself in an unfamiliar world. He had fallen onto a stretch of pavement in a dirty San Francisco alleyway—surrounded by tall buildings and meandering street people. It was still morning—and the air was windy and wet. He watched a drug deal go down, assuming it was normal. Then casually, he wandered out onto the street until he found a newspaper stand. He read the date beneath the headlines: *August 9, 2019.*

A car stopped in the street, blasting music—waiting for the light to change. Aroya moved closer, listening to the music—catching the eye of the driver.

"Damn bro! You in a band or something?!" the driver hollered, referring to Aroya's silvery skin.

Aroya just stared at him, confused.

The traffic light changed. *"Fierce look!"* the driver added, speeding away.

Aroya recalled this time period from when he was a child. It had been 31 years–but he still held on to those memories, like a drowning man grips a rope. He kept on walking.

Abbie stepped onto the windy street–moving briskly, with her head tucked down, and her collar pushed up. She turned down a side street, entering a nondescript shop with a sign that read, *We Rock!* It was a funky little place, filled with all sorts of minerals and polished stones.

She showed her crystal stone to the rock hound behind the counter. "Can you tell me what this is?" she asked.

The rock hound glanced at the stone. "I believe that's labradorite," he said. He switched on his desk lamp and held the stone under the light for Abbie. "You see those shimmering colors? That's called 'labradorescence.' The light bounces around–striking the surfaces of the crystal inside."

"It's a crystal?" Abbie asked for confirmation.

"Oh, yeah–it's a crystal. A somewhat unique crystal, for sure."

"Okay. Thanks for your help!" Abbie said.

"My pleasure."

Abbie tucked the stone into her pocket and ventured on down the street. To avoid being slapped by the chilly wind as she made her way, she stuck close to the sides of the tall buildings.

Nearing her favorite café, she turned the corner. Suddenly, she stopped dead in her tracks–coming face-to-face with an unusual-looking man. The man didn't move or speak–he just stared at her nervously–hoping she would recognize him. Abbie thought she'd seen him before, but she just couldn't place him.

Aroya heard her thoughts in his head, and he finally spoke. "You're right," he said. "We've met before. I'm here…*because* of you."

His words made her uncomfortable, and yet there was an odd familiarity about this man. His face was extremely pale, and his skin odd-looking–but she still found him somehow attractive. His lips were nearly blue against his silvery skin–and she couldn't help but wonder what it might feel like to kiss a man like that. Again, he heard her thoughts.

"You probably wouldn't enjoy it," he said.

"What did you say?" asked Abbie.

"You were thinking about kissing me. But my mouth is cold–and probably not very pleasant."

Taken aback, Abbie noted he was dressed warm enough. "Are you sick?" she inquired.

"No. I'm not sick."

Abbie was losing her patience. She attempted to walk around him, but he blocked her way.

"I'm not sick," he said. "I've been *processed.*"

She studied his face, wondering what he meant.

"Inside of me is a web of metals and plastics," he continued, "and technology that controls it all."

Abbie suspected he might actually be crazy–but his serious manner and vulnerable disposition kept her attention. Instead of running away, she chose to show some compassion. There were people on these streets with spiky hair, lizard scale tattoos, and more piercings than skin. Considering this, she assumed the shimmering silver patina of his skin might be due to make-up.

"You said you have wires inside of you? Do you think you're a robot?" Abbie asked.

"No. I'm not a robot. I'm a man."

Abbie still wondered if he might be crazy.

"I've been *processed...*" he continued, "filled with technology. But the processing wasn't complete. I'm still very much a man."

"What do you mean, 'the processing wasn't complete?'" Abbie asked.

"It didn't affect my mind," Aroya replied. "I can still remember my life before...and I can still dream. That's why I'm here."

Abbie considered his strange story. She wondered what any of it had to do with her. There were lots of crazy people roaming the streets of San Francisco–digging through trash, talking to imaginary people–but this man clearly wasn't one of them.

"You say we've met before?" she asked.

"Yes. In a dream," Aroya replied, patiently waiting for her to remember.

Abbie's mood suddenly changed. She wondered if this might be a pickup line. Even so, there was something about his eyes that pulled her in.

He ran his fingers through his hair, trying to make it look longer. "When we met in the dream, my hair was longer, and my skin was…more normal."

Suddenly, Abbie remembered the vision!

"Yes. That was me," Aroya said. "I was with you in that dream…with *this.*" He reached in his pocket, pulling out the crystal stone–holding it up for her to see.

Abbie's jaw dropped–she felt her heart racing. Nervously, she reached into her coat pocket–retrieving her own crystal stone. She held it up next to his.

Aroya never expected she would have one too! "Where did you get it?" he asked, surprised.

Feeling light-headed, Abbie searched for a place to sit.

Aroya pointed to the café. "Come. Let's go sit down," he said.

They found a small table near the window. "Should we get some tea…or coffee?" Abbie asked.

"I'm sorry–but I have no money. We haven't used money since the catastrophe," he said.

"The catastrophe? Where are you from?"

"I'm from here, but it's been 20 years…and it's been 31 since I've seen 2019."

"Where have you been for the last 20 years…or 31 years?"

"I've been here, but in the future."

Abbie raised an eyebrow. If he was referring to time travel, maybe she didn't want to press him–because he might actually be delusional. But then again, there was the vision…and the crystal stone. She placed her own stone on the table, just to remind herself that this unusual man might actually be telling the truth.

"When we met on the street–you said you were here because of me?" she asked.

"That's right. The feathered man with the painted face introduced us."

"The *Vision Maker*. I went to him for help." Abbie said.

Aroya nodded. "I saw you in a dream. The feathered man brought you to me. He told me how to get here by holding your image in my mind while dropping the stone."

Abbie remembered the call for help at the end of her vision. "Why did you come?" she asked. "Did you need help?"

"Yes. I needed help. I was about to be captured. But the stone, and my memory of you, helped me escape."

"Who was trying to capture you? Are you in trouble? Did you do something?"

"No. It's not like that. They wanted to use me for something. They wanted to do something to my body."

"Didn't they already do something? Because your skin it's…kind of unusual."

"Yes, I told you. I've been *processed*. That's what they call it when they put technology into your body. I resisted–and the process wasn't complete. I escaped, but they were tracking me. Time travel was my only way out."

"Why would someone want to do that to you?"

"They think I have a genetic mutation. They use people like me for special purposes. They *process* us…for the Elite Guard."

"Who are the Elite Guard?" Abbie asked.

"They are the enforcers–in my time. They do the bidding of the controllers."

"They *forced* this on you?"

"Yes. They tied me to a table–I couldn't stop them. I lost consciousness, and when I awoke, it was done."

"Oh, my *God*. That's *terrible!* Is it reversible?"

"I don't know," he replied. "I know what I look like–but what's worse is what's inside me…that's what turned my skin cold. But my memory was spared. I still remember when I was warm."

"That's quite a story," Abbie said. "If it wasn't for my own stone–and the vision, I might think you were crazy. But I don't…because of this," she said, picking up the stone.

"Thank you," Aroya said.

"But I'm not sure what I can do for you. You say they put technology inside you?"

"Yes. Tiny particles, like miniature machines. They're inside me–controlling certain functions. I can see some of it in my mind–but not all of it. The purpose is to enhance my abilities–but I resisted training, so I don't know what those abilities are."

"What were they trying to do? Make you into some kind of Superman?"

"Whatever it was supposed to do–I don't want it. I just want to be an ordinary man."

"I wonder if there's a way to remove it," Abbie said. "You say it's made of microscopic particles of metal?"

"Something like that. There's more to it–but I can't access the system fully."

Abbie recalled a method used for removing metals from the body. "Have you ever heard of chelation?" she asked.

She took her cell phone from her bag and began entering search terms.

"What are you doing?" Aroya asked, alarmed that she might be alerting the authorities.

"I'm searching for information about chelation," she replied. "To help you."

"Oh," he said, relieved. "I remember now."

"Remember what?"

"Your cellular phone. It's been a long time."

Just then, Millie stopped on the sidewalk in front of the café–rebalancing an armful of groceries. Noticing Abbie through the window, she waved–then entered the café, lugging her groceries over to Abbie's table.

"Hi, I'm Millie–Abbie's crazy neighbor," she said to Aroya. Millie was pleased to see Abbie with a man, but his strange appearance confused her.

Abbie began introducing Aroya–then realized she didn't know his name. "This is my new friend," she said awkwardly.

"Well, hello…new friend," Millie said, amused. "Do you have a name?"

"My name is Aroya."

"What a unique name. Is that Spanish?"

"No. It's a family name–from up north, somewhere."

Abbie held up her phone, showing Millie her Google search. "We've just been talking about chelation. I'm wondering if it can be done at home."

"What about Markus? Doesn't he do chelation?" Millie asked.

"Yeah–but it's for an unusual condition. I'm not sure Markus is familiar with it."

Millie noted Aroya's skin. "Oh, I see." She didn't dare ask about it. "You know…" she said, "I interviewed a guy last week who nearly died from mercury poisoning. He wrote a book all about chelation–and how it saved his life. I need to get ready for my show now, but I can drop the book by your place in the morning."

"That would be great. Thanks, Millie," Abbie said.

Abbie treated Aroya to tea. Afterward, she brought him to her apartment.

Abbie's place was cozy–a harmonious blend of Bohemian and Modern. A Persian rug and some floor cushions adorned the hardwood floor, and a small mahogany altar leaned against one wall–crowded with pictures and other various items. On another wall was a fireplace–and a sliding glass door leading out to a small patio. All were rare amenities for an apartment in San Francisco–luxuries she accepted in trade for living in a rather sketchy neighborhood.

Abbie prepared sandwiches for lunch. They discussed their dreams and visions, the crystal stone, and the Vision Maker. The day passed quickly, and the sun was now setting.

"Where will you stay tonight?" Abbie asked.

"I have no plans."

Abbie already assumed he had no arrangements, considering how he arrived. Again, she reached into her pocket for the stone. She needed it now, to remind her once again that Aroya was more than just a stranger off the street.

"Would you like to stay here on my couch tonight?" she offered.

"Thank you. That would be nice," Aroya said, smiling.

In the morning, there was a knock at the door. Abbie opened it, and Millie peeked inside, noticing Aroya asleep on the couch. Raising an eyebrow, she handed Abbie the chelation book. She whispered so as not to wake Aroya. "Please reconsider the interview. There are more rumors about mysterious deaths at the hospital. If you know something, you could save lives."

"I'll think about it and let you know," Abbie replied.

She took the book from Millie, closing the door quietly. Setting the book on the counter, she put a teakettle on the stove–then went to her bedroom to dress. From her bedroom, she heard the teakettle whistling. She hurried into the kitchen and found Aroya removing the kettle from the burner.

"I remember these," Aroya said, amused. "My grandmother had one. It had a little bird on the spout– just like this one."

Abbie opened the cupboard and grabbed two cups. "Would you like some tea? I'm sorry, but I don't have any coffee."

"Tea is fine. You have no idea what a luxury something as simple as tea is for someone like me."

Abbie poured two cups of tea.

"Would you like bacon and eggs for breakfast?" Abbie asked.

"Eggs would be wonderful. But no bacon, thank you."

"You don't eat pork?"

"No. I can't eat pork." He wrinkled his nose. "I can't even imagine it."

"Is it a religious thing?" Abbie inquired.

"No. It just doesn't feel right...eating my neighbors."

Abbie never expected that response. "Your neighbors were pigs?" she asked.

"It's hard to explain. Things are different in the future."

Abbie thought maybe it was too soon to press him for more information. "Okay, just eggs and toast, then. Maybe an omelet." Then it occurred to her that fresh herbs might be good in the omelet. "Hey, come with me...let's go get some herbs from my garden."

Abbie led Aroya to the rooftop of her building. There, she showed him her secret garden–filled with fresh flowers and herbs. The view from the rooftop was gorgeous–even on a foggy day.

They stood on the roof, surveying the city. "I love it up here. It's just like living in the sky!" Abbie said.

Aroya thought of the sky pods. "I prefer the ground, myself. But I love your garden!"

"Yeah, I love it too," she said, snipping a few fresh leaves of basil. "Sometimes, it's hard to feel like I'm living in a real home–with all this glass and concrete around me. The garden makes me feel more comfortable here."

Aroya found some delicate pink roses growing in a wooden planter. "Oh, these are beautiful. I haven't seen a real rose...in so many years."

Abbie lovingly stroked a rosebud. "I love roses," she said.

Aroya focused on her hand, caressing the rose. He imagined her stroking his skin the same way–with those tender hands that had undoubtedly soothed and tickled at least one lucky man. He closed his eyes to savor the image in his mind. When he opened them, he saw Abbie's hands cradling another rose in full bloom.

She parted the petals with care, sniffing at its fragrance. "Mmm…it smells heavenly. Come smell it!"

Aroya moved closer. The rose's perfume was intoxicating. Coupled with Abbie's exquisite hands and his over-active imagination, he could barely conceal the waves of emotion sweeping over him.

"Such beauty…for so many of the senses," he said. "The eyes, the nose, the touch…"

Returning to the apartment–Abbie served up two perfect omelets stuffed with fresh herbs and vegetables.

Aroya ate very little.

"You didn't like your omelet?" Abbie asked.

"Oh, no–I enjoyed it! It's just that…since the process, I can't seem to eat very much."

Abbie wondered about the reason, but it felt invasive to prod him about it. "This morning, while you were sleeping, Millie brought us the book about chelation," she said, changing the subject.

"I like the name, Millie. I had a dog named Millie once," Aroya said.

"Millie's a good friend. She has a podcast, and she wants me to do an interview on her show."

"You don't want to do it?" Aroya asked.

"I don't know. It might be dangerous. I'm not a very courageous person."

Abbie's hesitancy piqued Aroya's curiosity. "Dangerous? But why?" he asked.

"When I went to see the Vision Maker–the 'feathered man'–I was having a really bad day. But honestly, it was just another of many bad days, stretching on for months. I'm a nurse at the public hospital, and a couple of days ago, I witnessed something horrible."

Aroya closed his eyes to envision the scene in his mind. "Yes–I can see it. And I can feel it. Oh, how terrible."

"Yes, it was terrible. And Millie thinks I should tell people about it."

Aroya sensed the emotions moving through Abbie's heart. There was so much pain and so much beauty–all at the same time.

Again, Abbie changed the subject. "C'mon. Let's look at Millie's book."

She brought the book into the living room and sat in a chair, placing the book in her lap. Aroya sat on the couch, watching her scan through the index.

She found what she was looking for. *"Chelation! Here it is!"* She read the definition: *"Chelation is a type of bonding of ions and molecules to metal ions."*

The shiny new book drew Aroya's attention. He was used to reading old dusty books, with stained covers and dog-eared pages. He hadn't seen a shiny new book for many years. Leaning forward, he examined the book more closely.

"Would you like to read it with me?" Abbie asked.

"Yes, I would."

Abbie moved closer with the book in her lap. Aroya touched the book's smooth pages, admiring the colorful illustrations.

"Don't they have books in your time?" Abbie asked.

"Well, yes and no," Aroya replied. "They're not allowed anymore, and most were destroyed...but we found some, hidden away. But ours are all very old."

Abbie prepared to move the book to Aroya's lap–but when she moved his hand to make space, the feeling of his cold, plastic-like skin startled her. The sensation reminded her of a cold piece of meat, wrapped in cellophane–and then the vivid memory of Tulio Guterres' dead hand came flooding back to her mind. Her repulsion was obvious.

"It must feel strange," Aroya said. "I'm still not used to it myself."

Abbie pretended that it didn't happen. She turned the pages of the book in Aroya's lap–then the book began to tilt. Confused, she lifted the book–discovering Aroya's enormous erection.

"Whoops!" she said, smiling nervously–scooting back into her chair.

Confused by his own body, Aroya apologized. "I'm sorry. It's a side effect from the process." He handed the book back to Abbie.

"No worries," she said. "I'm a nurse. That stuff happens all the time." She turned her attention back to the book's index. "Here it is, *chelation for heavy metals.*" While reading, she suddenly grew concerned. "I've never done anything like this before. I'm not sure how it will go with someone...like you."

"I know the process changed me–but I assure you, I am still a man."

Playfully, Abbie replied, "Yes, I can see that."

5– GINA

2019

San Francisco

Timeline 1.0

Abbie and Aroya returned to the neighborhood café. While enjoying their tea, Gina, a woman from the AR department at Abbie's hospital, entered the café. She was young, cute, and eight months pregnant.

"Gina! What are you doing here?!" Abbie said, surprised.

"I'm looking for you! I went to your apartment and ran into your neighbor, Millie. She told me you might be down here."

"You were looking for me? Why–what's going on?"

Gina acknowledged Aroya at the table. "I'm sorry. I can come back later…."

"Oh no, it's okay…" Abbie said, "this is my friend, Aroya." Then turning to Aroya, she explained, "Gina works with me at the hospital."

Aroya could sense Gina's urgency–and thought it best to allow them some privacy. "You know…I noticed that bookshop, across the street. Do you mind if I go check it out–while you ladies chat?" he asked Abbie.

"No, I don't mind," Abbie replied, a little surprised.

Aroya stood, glancing at Gina's pregnant belly. "It's nice to meet you, Gina," he said, with his hands tucked into his pockets; a tactic he employed to avoid shaking hands.

Abbie wondered how he might fair, on the streets of this unfamiliar time. "Are you sure you're okay?" she asked Aroya.

"Of course. I'm fine," Aroya replied with a smile.

Gina watched Aroya leave. Then she leaned forward, whispering, "He's *fine.* Wow, that's an understatement," she said with a giggle. "But what's with his skin?" she asked.

"It's some sort of medical condition," Abbie replied.

Gina cringed, wondering what it could be.

"Don't worry, it's not contagious," Abbie reassured her.

"Well, that's good…I guess." Now, Gina changed her tone. "I'm sorry for dropping by like this–but I'm kind of nervous about using my phone."

"Why? What's up?" Abbie asked.

"There's something weird happening at the hospital. For months now, our revenue's been skyrocketing! Not only are we billing for record amounts–we're collecting in record time! I looked into it, and it's all coming from government programs…no private insurance. And every patient connected to those accounts *expired*…none of them were discharged home!"

"I know what you're talking about," Abbie said. "That's why I needed some time off. I saw the same thing on my end, and it freaked me out!"

"Really?" Gina replied. She leaned forward, whispering, "And you know what else? Some of the doctors are suddenly driving flashy new cars. It's weird. And they're like, making sure everyone sees them too!"

"I bet that includes Dr. Eiffel," Abbie said.

"You bet! He's driving a Tesla now!"

"I would've pegged him for something more traditional…but yeah, it figures."

"What do you think is going on?" Gina asked, puzzled.

"I don't know–but you're not the only one noticing things," Abbie replied.

"I know. Even your neighbor Millie knew about it. I told her what was on my mind…I hope that's okay. She said she's like your bestie–so I thought it was cool."

"Yeah, Millie's cool. No worries."

"She wants me to come on her podcast…but I'm too scared. I'm even scared to use my phone," she whispered. "I've got a real bad feeling about this, Abbie. I think something huge is going on!"

"I know. I'm nervous too," Abbie said. "Have you told anyone else?"

"I mentioned it to a few people at lunch. After that, my phone started acting really weird…like there was a clicking sound, and I could hear people whispering in the background." She took a deep breath. "I thought maybe I should file a report of some kind, so I documented everything–then I sent it over to the Big Chief."

"Wow. I hope he's not in on it too–'cause Dr. Eiffel said the orders were coming from the *higher-ups!"*

"Oh no! I thought it was just a few bad doctors! Maybe I should have contacted a government agency, or something!"

"Yeah, maybe. But which one? I thought about it too–but I don't know where to go," Abbie said.

Gina rubbed her temples. "God, I've been losing sleep over this–and I know it's not good for the baby." She caressed her pregnant belly. "But I do have some good news!" she said, smiling. "Dave's company just went public! That means I can quit! I'm giving them notice tomorrow!" She leaned back in her chair. "I just wanna stay home now–and focus on the baby," she said, with a sweet smile on her face. "I'm still not finished decorating the nursery–but oh, you should see it, Abbie–it's so cute!"

Abbie thought to herself, *it's so nice to see Gina happy. If she wanted advice–then she was gonna give it.* "I know it's hard to ignore what's going on–," Abbie said, "but you need to forget about it. Just go home and enjoy your life…and take care of that baby. Eventually, it will all come out anyway. It always does."

"Yeah, I know," Gina replied. "But isn't that kind of selfish? What if *me* coming forward can somehow stop what's going on?"

"I know what you mean. But with the baby coming, nobody would blame you for wanting to steer clear of this mess. Maybe you should talk it over with Dave…and pray on it."

"I'll do that," Gina said, preparing to leave. "You know…I'm gonna miss our talks in the cafeteria. You were my only real friend at the hospital."

"Don't worry, we can still get together…and you can call me."

"Thanks, Abbie–I will."

"Just go home now, and take care of yourself."

They hugged, and Gina left the café.

Aroya returned with a book. It was used and a bit worn, but he seemed pleased with it. He set it on the table. "It's Alfred Noyes," he said. "Love poems."

"I thought you didn't have any money," Abbie responded.

"I don't. I was talking about the book with the owner–and then when I was leaving, he just told me to keep it! I've never even seen book *three* before," Aroya said, holding up the book. "Ray, the owner, told me it's a rare copy…but he has no idea how rare it is in *my* time!" Aroya said, smiling.

"You really love poetry, don't you?" Abbie said, impressed by Aroya's passion.

"Yes, I really do," Aroya replied. Leaning back in his chair, he thought about the misery of zone 9. "In the year 2050," he explained, "there is very little beauty left in the world…it's simply not allowed. No more art or music of any kind–and the laws are very strict about books. But in secret, some of us still read old books. We recite poetry to help us remember beauty. It's impossible to hide something like a painting, but if we memorize a few lines of poetry, we can carry that beauty in our minds completely undetected. And we can trade with it, just like money."

Abbie finds Aroya's description of the future horrific. "I never imagined there'd come a time when beauty itself would be outlawed," she said.

"Unfortunately, that time *did* come. But now, here I am in 2019–and there's so much beauty here, just in everyday things that no longer exist in my time–for instance, the beauty of a pregnant woman. We don't see that anymore in my time. Your friend, Gina...she was absolutely radiant."

Abbie smiled, remembering Gina's comment about Aroya. "Gina thinks you're *fine,*" Abbie joked.

"Well, she's right! I *am* fine," Aroya said, flipping through the book. Then closing it, his mood changed. "Abbie...your friend...."

"Gina came to me for advice," Abbie said, interrupting. "She's scared."

"Yes. She *should* be scared,*" he said, pushing his book aside. "Please listen...there's nothing you can do. I'm only telling you this to prepare you–"

Just then, Millie entered the café, making a beeline for Abbie's table. "I *thought* you guys were down here," Millie said. "Did Gina find you?" she asked, sitting down.

"Yeah, she did. The poor girl is so stressed out about the hospital."

"I know she is. She told me all about it. Do you think she'll do an interview?"

"No. She's too scared."

"I know–" Millie said, "and I totally understand. But it's a shame you guys can't tell the world what's going on. It might actually save lives!"

"Millie's right," Aroya agreed. "More people will die if something's not done." Then he turned to Millie and asked, "What if you revealed the information yourself? Without mentioning names?"

"I'm not sure that would fly," Millie replied. "I mean…why should anyone believe *me? I'm* not a witness to anything."

Abbie stared off into space, thinking about that day at the hospital–fighting for Tulio Guterres.

Aroya felt her pain. "Abbie, it wasn't your fault," he said, reassuring her.

Abbie was about to say, *how did you know what I was thinking?* But after considering Aroya's extraordinary abilities, she simply replied, "I guess I'm just tired."

Millie picked up on the conversation. "Is this about that patient…and Dr. Eiffel?" she asked.

Aroya's face turned sour. "Dr. Eiffel is a very bad man," he said, shaking his head.

"That's for sure," Abbie replied under her breath.

Millie suddenly had an idea. "Hey, Abbs'…what if we disguise your voice. You could be my super-secret whistleblower–who, of course, *must* remain anonymous."

Abbie looked to Aroya for his reaction.

Although he agreed that someone must come forward, selfishly, he didn't want it to be Abbie. "It's a complicated situation," he said.

Finally, Abbie shook her head. "No. I don't think so."

Millie gave up. She knew Abbie had a lot on her mind, and she didn't want to burden her with more. "Okay. But if you change your mind–let me know."

She tapped on the table, smiling. "I better get goin'…I'm on the air in 30 minutes. See you guys later."

Back at the apartment, Abbie and Aroya enjoyed a large cheese pizza (no pork). It was Aroya's first pizza in more than 20 years. Later, they curled up in different chairs, reading books.

In the morning, way too early–Abbie's phone rang. She answered it, with her head still on the pillow.

Aroya suddenly appeared at her bedroom door–studying her face while she spoke on the phone.

"Who's calling?" Abbie asked sleepily. "Yes, this is Abigail Lite. ...Yes, I know Gina Henderson. ...*What?! ...No!!!"* Abbie sat straight up. *"But how?! ...No way–she never would have done such a thing! I just saw her yesterday–and everything was fine! She was so excited about the..."* Abbie broke down, sobbing. Between tearful gasps, she replied, "Yes. ...Okay. Thank you. Goodbye." Ending the call, she dropped her phone on the bed. Then she noticed Aroya standing in the doorway. With one look at his face...*she* knew that *he* knew.

Aroya swallowed hard, nervous. "Can I do anything?" he asked.

"You *knew*...didn't you? Yesterday–you *knew.* That's what you were gonna tell me at the café."

"Yes, I knew. But there was nothing we could do."

"They said she committed suicide! Did she?"

"No, of course not. She was murdered."

"My *God*. She was eight months *pregnant!* What kind of *monster* would do that?!"

"I think you know what kind. You work with them every day," Aroya replied.

Abbie rubbed her eyes. She walked into the bathroom. Grabbing a wad of toilet paper, she blew her nose.

"Why couldn't we *stop* it?" she asked, sniffling.

"There wasn't enough time," Aroya replied. "Sometimes you can…but for big things–mostly you can't. It depends on the event…and the time."

"Do you know *everything* before it happens?" Abbie asked.

"No. Just sometimes, with certain people."

Abbie shuffled over to the kitchen table–slumping over, depressed.

"Shall I make some tea?" Aroya asked.

"Sure," Abbie replied, despondent.

Aroya put the kettle on the stove, then sat with Abbie at the table.

Abbie propped her head up with her elbow, contemplating the situation. "This is *so fucked-up…God, everything is so fucked up!"* she exclaimed.

"Gina–and the hospital…I know, it's all horrible." Aroya sighed, leaning back in his chair. "You might find this hard to believe, Abbie…but these are actually the *good* times."

"The *good* times? As compared to *what*?"

"As compared to what's still to come."

"God–I can't even imagine…."

"Trust me, you're fortunate to be living in 2019," Aroya said.

Millie knocked at the door, and Abbie let her in. Her eyes were red and swollen. It was clear she'd been crying.

"Gina called me last night," Millie said, between sniffles. "She left a voicemail saying she wanted to do the interview. I returned her call this morning, and a *detective* answered the phone." She wiped her eyes. "From the look on your faces, I assume you already know."

"Yeah," Abbie replied. "They say it was suicide–but it wasn't."

Millie took a chance, asking one more time, "Are you ready now…to tell the world what you know?"

"Fuck yeah–sign me up!" Abbie replied, with a new fire in her voice. *"Someone's gotta stop this!"*

"Abbie, you know you're my dearest friend," Millie said. "And you know I'll do everything to protect you."

Time was of the essence. They planned a live interview for that evening.

At 6:55 pm, Abbie arrived at Millie's home studio. She wore an oversized hoody that fell over her eyebrows– and a pair of cheesy dark glasses. With every strand of hair tucked neatly away, she zipped up her sweatshirt– leaving only her nose and chin exposed. She sat waiting nervously, while Millie outfitted her with headphones and a voice-changing microphone.

Aroya sat in the living room–on the other side of a glass partition. He kept his eyes on Abbie as she took deep breaths, preparing for the interview.

Millie signaled the show was about to go live. She held her hand up–then dropped it, as a sign flashed: ON

AIR. She began the show: "Well, hello out there! This is the *Millie Grace Show*–and I am Millie Grace. Tonight, we have a surprise guest. A whistleblower! Of course, our guest will be disguised to protect their identity…and their voice will also be disguised. They're about to share with us–some very shocking information about nefarious deeds going on right here in San Francisco, at our own public hospital. My regular listeners know that I typically like to keep this show light and playful–but I'm afraid tonight, things are gonna get really heavy…that's just a warning. Okay, let's begin."

Turning the camera on Abbie, Millie began the interview: "Hello, dear whistleblower. Please tell our audience what you witnessed at the hospital recently. And then, tell us what you know about the death of Gina Henderson. Take your time."

Abbie began: "Hello. I have been an employee at the public hospital for more than ten years–"

Millie interrupted, "And the population served by this hospital is mostly low-income. Correct?"

"Yes. And also trauma patients–gunshot wounds, automobile accidents–that sort of thing. But you're right; the hospital mostly serves low-income patients–covered by government healthcare plans."

"What did you witness while working there recently…that made you want to come forward?"

Abbie took another deep breath. "I witnessed many unnecessary deaths…daily…of patients who didn't even fit the criteria of being seriously ill. In recent months, very few patients were discharged home. Most of them left in body bags."

"You say when these patients were admitted–some of them were not even seriously ill? Then what happened to them...once they were in the hospital?"

"Their care was severely mismanaged–and some appeared to have been...intentionally murdered."

"Whoa! They're *murdering* people at the hospital?"

"Yes. I believe so."

"But why would they do such a thing?"

"I'm not sure–but it might have to do with money. A hospital employee was just found dead this morning– after she filed a complaint about unusually large sums of money being collected from government programs."

"And this hospital employee would be Gina Henderson. Correct?"

"Correct. Gina was telling people about what she had discovered, only a few days before her death."

"And Gina was only 26-years old...and eight months pregnant."

"Yes, that's right. Anyone who knew her–knows she was very happy, and she would never kill herself."

"They did report it was a suicide. I read that. Unbelievable! And eight months pregnant–eagerly awaiting her first child."

Abbie broke down, sobbing.

Millie turned the camera away from Abbie–then continued, "Okay, my heroic whistleblower. I think we've imposed on you quite enough. We currently have nearly thirty thousand people listening out there. I assume that some of you are San Franciscans...so let's hope that one of you has the courage to demand an investigation! We'll be right back after this quick break."

Millie removed Abbie's headphones–ushering her to the door. "Take care of our girl," she whispered to Aroya.

Abbie left Millie's apartment, still wearing her disguise. More than ever, Aroya had an overwhelming urge to hold her–but he resisted, knowing he couldn't offer her the warm embrace she so desperately needed.

Once inside the apartment, Abbie broke down. She threw off her sweatshirt and fell to her knees, bawling like a baby. Confused, Aroya didn't know what to do. He didn't dare touch her bare arms with his cold, cellophane hands–so he took a throw blanket from the couch and wrapped it around her, lifting her to her feet. He wanted so much to hold her against his chest–but instead, he awkwardly held her at arms' length, guiding her into a chair.

"Just rest," Aroya said. "I'll make you some tea."

When Aroya returned with the tea, Abbie was fast asleep in the chair. He set her tea on the table–then curled up on the couch, watching her sleep–imagining how good it would feel just to hold her. Ever since that amazing dream, Aroya wanted Abbie more than anything–but now his desire was growing into something more. He was falling in love.

6– THE ARCHANGEL

2019

San Francisco

Timeline 1.0

Abbie and Aroya were still asleep in the living room at daybreak–her in the chair and him on the couch. She opened her sleepy eyes and stretched her limbs.

Aroya sensed her movement and sat up. "How do you feel?" he asked.

Abbie rubbed the sleep from her eyes. "Actually, I feel kind of claustrophobic," she replied. "Let's go out and get some breakfast."

"Okay," Aroya said.

Abbie quickly showered and dressed. She walked into the kitchen, discovering Aroya standing over the sink–using a shiny pot lid as a mirror, arranging his hair.

"Oh, my God. I'm so sorry! Please use the bathroom!" she said. "You can even shower if you like. I've got some clean sweats that my brother left here. They might just fit you–"

"I'm fine. Really, I am," Aroya said.

Abbie thought about it, then realized she hadn't seen Aroya use the bathroom once since he arrived. "Why don't you ever use the bathroom?" she asked. "Is there something wrong?"

"I think it's the process. Apparently, my body is ultra-efficient now. There's very little waste."

"Is that why you eat so little?"

"I suppose so. But I assure you, I thoroughly enjoy every little bit."

"Okay then. Let's go get some breakfast–even if it's just a little bit."

Not more than an hour had passed at the café before they returned to Abbie's apartment. She took out her key, then noticed the door was slightly ajar. Giving it a little push, it swung wide open. Abbie stood there, staring into her apartment–bewildered at the sight of her upside-down furniture and pictures smashed and strewn across the floor. Even her pots and pans lay scattered about, and her plates and cups were now just a pile of ceramic rubble. Frozen in shock–she surveyed the chaotic scene that was once her comfy little home.

"Don't go inside," Aroya warned. "It might not be safe. C'mon, let's go to Millie's place."

Millie answered the door, still half-asleep, wearing a pink fluffy bathrobe and slippers.

"I can't believe it," Abbie said. "Somebody just tossed my apartment."

"Oh, my God. Are you alright?" Millie said, worried.

"She's fine," Aroya replied. "We were at the café when it happened."

"I'm afraid to go inside," Abbie said. "I don't know what to do."

"Stay here with Millie. I'll go check it out," Aroya said.

"Please be careful," Abbie said.

Several minutes later, Aroya returned. "It's a terrible mess...and they left a message. I'm not sure you want to see it."

Millie was now in her sweats. "Let me help. I'll bring my Angels for protection."

The three of them cautiously entered Abbie's apartment. It was truly a sad scene. Abbie lifted a few of her cherished photos from the rubble of broken glass and mangled frames. She walked into her bedroom, where Aroya and Millie stood waiting. Above her bed, she saw the words YOU WILL BE NEXT written in blood-red paint.

Abbie's heart sank. Then her phone rang. Still in a daze, she answered, "Hello? ...What? But why?" The caller hung up. Abbie appeared confused, tossing her phone on the bed. "That was the hospital," she said. "They fired me."

Millie put her arm around Abbie, comforting her. "But honey, you were planning to quit, anyway. They just did it *for* you, that's all."

Walking into the kitchen, Abbie spotted something odd. It was a little doll's chair, just 6 inches high.

Someone had placed it atop her kitchen table. A ceramic duck sat on the cushion with the name ABBIE written across its back in black marker.

"What the hell...? This isn't mine!" Abbie exclaimed.

Aroya and Millie examined the duck on the chair.

"Oh, Honey...it's a message." Millie shook her head, disgusted. "Those sick bastards!"

"What does it mean? I'm a duck?" Abbie asked.

"A duck–sitting in a chair. In other words, a sitting–"

"Oh, I get it. A sitting duck. Great."

"Should we call the police?" Millie asked.

"No. It would probably just make things worse," Abbie said. "Besides, what're they gonna do? Nobody's hurt...and I had nothing of value to steal. They won't investigate, and they sure as hell aren't gonna protect me."

"Why don't you take Abbie back over to your place," Aroya suggested. "And I'll clean up."

"No way!" Abbie responded. "I'm staying right here in my home! Besides...I've gotta take inventory." It suddenly occurred to her that anything of value might be in her bedroom. She rushed back in, surveying the scene. *They took my fuckin' laptop! Son-of-a-bitch!*"

Millie surveyed the room. "Well, of course, they did. That's probably what they came for in the first place. The rest of this mess...it's just to fuck with your head. Don't let it get to you, Abbie."

They loaded boxes and filled garbage bags with broken glass, ripped papers, and various other crushed items for the remainder of the day. Miraculously, although visibly roughed up, most of Abbie's books survived–even after the bastards tore her bookcase off the wall. Aroya brushed off the books, organizing them into neat stacks–then he piled pieces of broken wood from the mangled bookcase in the rear of Abbie's kitchen.

Abbie walked to where her altar once stood, sliding a narrow panel sideways near the baseboard. "They didn't find it," she said.

"Find what?" Aroya asked.

"My secret hiding place. There's nothing of real value in here–just sentimental things." She smiled, happy that this little nook somehow escaped molestation.

When they finished cleaning up, Abbie and Aroya walked downtown to shop for a new computer.

The devices in the store fascinated Aroya.

"Don't they have computers in 2050?" Abbie asked.

"Not like *these!*" Aroya answered. "I thought your computer was kind of old-looking, but I haven't seen stuff like this since I was a kid!"

"What do they use in 2050?"

"Everything's projected as holograms, from cubes."

"You have a holographic computer?" Abbie asked, impressed.

"No. Not me. Surface dwellers aren't allowed stuff like that. But we see them around–displaying messages and such."

Abbie finally found a laptop she liked. "It's not holographic, but I guess it'll do."

When they returned home, Abbie sat at the kitchen table, downloading software onto her new computer. Aroya reclined on the couch, reading *Walt Whitman.* Although ripped, the couch was still fully functional.

Tired of scrolling for new kitchenware, Abbie got up and stretched. "It's time for a break," she said.

Leaving the laptop open on the table, she sat in her favorite chair, cross-legged. The chair was also a bit sliced up, but she didn't seem to mind.

Earlier, Aroya had set two cups of tea on the coffee table, and one was still full. It was cold now, but Abbie didn't notice. She sipped her tea while studying Aroya's face–as he dozed on the couch. It was an attractive face, masculine but beautiful–adorned with deeply intense eyes. But it was his skin that was the problem; it reminded her of a fish–all shiny and cold. She wondered if she could ever get used to it. Again, she let herself fantasize about kissing his lips and recalled the experience with him in her vision. It all seemed so long ago, but in reality, it had only been about a week. Abbie's mind drifted to the image of the ceramic duck sitting in the doll's chair. She tossed it out with the rest of the garbage, but the image was still burning in her mind. She glanced toward the kitchen table, where she first discovered it. Her eyes were tired, but she thought she saw something move on her computer screen. She jumped up to get a better look. The curser was skipping around on its own, and while she puzzled about it, a document popped open. It said, SITTING DUCK–repeatedly, maybe a hundred times. Abbie stared at the computer screen, dumbfounded. It was a brand-new computer, right out of the box. How could anybody hack it so quickly?! She felt her heart pounding and her face flushing. Finally, she screamed, *"NOOO!!!"*

In less than a blink, Aroya was standing at her side, bewildered.

"How did you do that?" Abbie asked, startled.

"I don't know. I just heard you scream. And then I was here." He studied Abbie's face, concerned. "Abbie, why did you scream?" he asked.

"My new computer. It's been hacked already. They're inside my fucking computer, and they're mocking me!"

Aroya glanced at the message. "Abbie...it's really not safe here."

Abbie slammed her laptop shut. "Where should I go? Should I run away and hide for the rest of my life?"

"I don't know," Aroya said. "I only know that you're not safe here."

Abbie sat down at the table, angry and exhausted. Taking a deep breath, she closed her eyes. "I think it's time to pray," she said. She turned toward the wall where her altar once stood. "My God," she said, rubbing her forehead, "they even crushed my altar."

Aroya walked over to the garbage, piled high in the kitchen. He pulled out a few pieces of wood. "Maybe we can use this to make a new one. I mean...temporarily."

Abbie examined the broken wood. "Maybe."

The sun was setting, and they'd been so busy that they hadn't bothered to eat since morning.

"Do you like Japanese food?" asked Abbie.

"I don't know. Does it have pork?"

"Not so much, but it has lots of fish."

"Then, yes–I think I like Japanese food."

"What do you normally eat…in your time?"

"We're only allowed surface rations, once a day. And nobody knows what it's made of."

"You don't have any kind of meat?"

"When I was a child, we ate all kinds of meat. Hamburgers, steak, chicken…but later, right before the catastrophe, laboratories were destroyed, and a sickness was released. Lots of people died, and the crops were all poisoned. It killed a lot of livestock…and there was a huge food shortage. People eventually began eating their pets. It was terrible."

"Oh, my God. Someday, you'll have to tell me about the catastrophe. But not now. I've already had enough catastrophe for one day."

Abbie used her phone to order sushi. "The fish will be here in about an hour," she announced.

"Okay," Aroya said. "While we wait, why don't we see if there's a potential altar hiding in that garbage bag?" He pulled some wood from the bag and leaned it against the living room wall.

"Hey! That might actually work!" Abbie said. She grabbed her phone. "I'll text Millie to see if she has a few items to donate."

Finishing their sushi, they patched together a modest little altar. Abbie covered the rough wood with an old pillowcase, and she used a broken teacup for a candleholder. There was a knock at the door, and of course, it was Millie. She carried an armful of goodies over to the kitchen table.

"Sorry. I know it's not much," Millie said. "But look," she held up a picture, "here's a nice picture of Archangel Michael. I figured you could use his kind of protection right now. You want any incense or candles?"

"Thanks, Mil'…no incense, and I have a little candle. But do you have a lighter?"

"No. But I brought some matchsticks."

"Great!" Abbie took the picture of Archangel Michael, and the matchsticks, over to the altar.

Aroya looked on with great curiosity. He knew what an 'altar' was, but he'd never actually seen one in a person's home.

"And here's a little vase," Millie said. "It's a fake flower, but it's kind of nice."

"Oh, it's just perfect! Thanks!" Abbie set the vase on the kitchen table.

"Okay. Stay safe, you two," Millie said. "I'll be praying for you tonight." She hugged Abbie.

Once Millie had gone, Abbie removed the fake flower and examined it. Wrinkling her nose, she placed it on the table, dissatisfied. The altar was already sliding a bit, and Aroya worked to stabilize it.

"A rose! That's what it needs!" Abbie said, excited. "I'll go get one from the garden."

"But it's getting dark. You shouldn't go alone. Wait! I'll go with you!"

"No. It's okay–I'll be right back."

Abbie threw her coat on, slipping a pair of kitchen shears into her pocket. When she shut the door behind her, Aroya began to feel uneasy. He shook off the feeling and turned his attention back to the altar. Finally, he stabilized it. He draped it with the pillowcase, then set the broken teacup and candle in the middle. He studied the picture of Archangel Michael, brandishing a sword and surrounded by electric flames. Flipping it over, he saw some words on the back. He thought to himself, *Oh look! A poem in dedication!* Considering the awesomeness of the picture, he thought he might honor the Archangel by reciting the poem. He began:

> *"Archangel Michael, defend us in battle.*
> *Come to our aid with your celestial legions.*
> *Bring us protection and guidance, by the power of*
> *the Most-High.*
> *Fill us with your strength as we fight against the*
> *agents of evil.*
> *Come to our protection and be a refuge–against*
> *the snares of the devil, and all his wicked powers.*
> *Be our defense against all evil intentions, thoughts,*
> *and actions against us.*
> *May the divine fire of your sword, destroy every*
> *evil."*

Suddenly, Abbie's voice crashed through Aroya's skull, echoing with a scream born of sheer terror! In less than a moment, he found himself standing on the rooftop in the rain. Two men were accosting Abbie, pushing her toward the edge of the roof. Lightning struck, and it traveled up Aroya's leg–electrifying his entire body from within. The two men froze as Aroya grew 10 feet tall–radiating a blinding light. His features glowed with a golden hue, and his eyes shot fiery arrows, hitting the men in their feet. They screamed in agony, smoke rising from the tops of their shoes.

Terrified, the men released Abbie–scrambling away, moaning and weeping. When they had gone, the fiery electric current left Aroya's body, and he returned to normal size–collapsing on the rooftop.

Abbie ran to his side. He was unconscious, and his hot glowing skin was quickly fading back to a cool pale silver.

Abbie tried to wake him. "Aroya! Aroya!" she shouted. But he didn't respond.

She reached for his wrist to feel his pulse. Startled by tiny flashing lights beneath the skin on his forearm, she checked his carotid artery instead. Relieved to feel a pulse, she propped him up. The rain had stopped, and the storm clouds parted, allowing the bright moon to illuminate Aroya's face.

"Aroya! Come back! Come back!" Abbie pleaded.

Aroya's eyes opened slowly. "Abbie. Are you all right?" he asked, barely managing a whisper.

She released a sigh. "Yes. Oh, God–thank you!"

Still disoriented and weak, Aroya struggled to sit up.

"Do you think you can walk?" Abbie asked.

"Yes. I think so."

She helped him to his feet, and they made their way back to the apartment.

Abbie laid Aroya on the couch and began removing his wet clothing. He could barely move, but he wondered what she was doing.

She noticed his puzzled expression. "Relax," she said. "I'm a nurse, remember? I'll take care of you."

Aroya surrendered to her care, temporarily setting aside his self-consciousness–finally allowing her to touch his cold cellophane skin.

She wrapped him in a warm blanket and brought him hot tea. Then she lit a fire. Cuddling up in her chair, she watched him sip his tea–grateful that he was all right.

"For a moment…I thought I'd lost you," she said. Then she thought about what she'd seen. "Aroya–what *was* that? The lightning and the fire…how did you do that?"

"I don't know." He tried to recall what happened. "Abbie, the picture on your altar." He pointed to it. "Can you bring it to me, please?"

Abbie brought him the picture of Archangel Michael, then knelt beside him.

Aroya studied the picture, noting the fiery electric wings. Flipping it over, he studied the writing on the back. He read the title out loud: *"Archangel Michael's Prayer for Protection."* He laid the picture on his chest. "I've seen the word 'prayer' in poems, but I'm not sure I ever understood it. When I saw how it was written, I thought it was something like a poem…or a dedication."

"Not exactly," Abbie said. "A prayer is more like a call for help."

Aroya held up the picture of Archangel Michael. "I know a little about Angels…but what is an Archangel? Is it like a god?"

"No. It's a special type of Angel with extraordinary powers. We can pray to Angels if we need help." Abbie studied the picture, noticing a resemblance to the 10-

foot-tall, fiery Aroya on her rooftop. "Aroya! Did you say this prayer?"

"Yes. I recited it."

Abbie raised her eyebrows. "Could you have turned into an Archangel?"

"I don't think so. I didn't have any wings," Aroya replied. "I would've liked some wings," he said, smiling. He imagined what it might be like to have those glorious wings. "I don't understand. If an Archangel has extraordinary powers, and a god, with a little 'g', also has extraordinary powers...then what's the difference?"

"I think that Archangel's are closer to God, with a capital 'G'. I guess the other 'gods' have a little 'g'...because they're littler." She giggled. "Well, anyway...thank God, with a big 'G' for Archangel Michael...and for you. You saved my life tonight."

"You saved mine first."

"Me and the stone–I guess."

"That's right. It was my dream of you that saved me."

Abbie recalled her vision and remembered how Aroya had kissed her.

Of course, he read her thoughts. "That memory you have of me...from your vision. I was warm then. And that kiss you remember...it wouldn't be the same."

"You *did* look different in the vision."

Regaining his strength, Aroya sat up. "I was still living on the surface then. I wasn't processed yet."

"You really want to be an ordinary man again, don't you?"

"More than anything."

Abbie retrieved the chelation book from the shelf. Sitting in her favorite chair, she flipped through the pages. "According to this book, chelation can be risky."

"I'm willing to take the risk," Aroya said.

"But what if something goes wrong?"

"I don't want to burden you. Maybe I can do it myself."

"It says that silica works. I think silica is just sand. We've got a whole beach full of sand here. Oh, look, and cilantro! I have cilantro in my garden!"

"Good. Then tomorrow, I'll take some cilantro and visit the beach."

"I don't know... I think you should see a doctor." She thought it over. "I have a friend. He's a naturopathic doctor. He's very open-minded, and I trust him."

"If you trust him, then I trust him."

"Okay then. Tomorrow we'll go see him–but now, let's get some sleep. G'night, Aroya." Abbie turned out the living room light.

Aroya fluffed his pillow and nestled into the couch. On this night, they both dreamt...the same dream.

In their dream, the feathered Vision Maker came again. He held the stone and said, *let the moving waters of your desire...bring you to your destination.* The image of the feathered man slowly faded, and Abbie and Aroya found each other in the dream, once again. Aroya's skin was warm, in the dream, and flushed with passion. He took Abbie in his arms and kissed her. She melted like butter as the heat of Aroya's mouth engulfed her lips. And then–the phone rang.

Abbie tried to wake herself. She was reluctant to let the dream go. Finally, she answered the phone. "Hello? ...Oh, hi Millie. What's up? ...What? ...A fire? Oh that. ...Yeah, I know, but that's not what happened. No, they must be hysterical. Can we talk later? I'm taking Aroya to see Markus today. Yeah, for his skin. ...Yes, Millie, he's still sleeping on the couch. ...I've really gotta go. Okay. Bye."

Abbie wrapped herself in her robe and shuffled into the kitchen. Aroya was already sitting at the kitchen table with two cups of hot tea.

"Good morning, Abbie," Aroya said with an impish grin. "Did you sleep well?"

Abbie sipped her tea, suspecting he already knew how she slept. "I slept very well. Thank you."

"Did you have any interesting dreams?" he asked.

Abbie laughed. "What about you? Did *you* have any interesting dreams?"

"You know I did," Aroya replied, sipping his tea.

Propping her chin up, Abbie said, "Ya know, I'm starting to feel like this is all some kind of cruel joke."

"Cruel? You mean, you didn't enjoy it?" Aroya asked.

"You *know* I did," she said, smiling. She got up from the table. "How do you want your eggs–fried or scrambled?" she asked.

"Either way is good," Aroya replied.

While Abbie scrambled the eggs, she commented, "Millie called this morning. She heard the *craziest* story on the news...about a 10-foot-tall *monster* who came down from the sky last night, on a *bolt of lightning*!"

"Really? How interesting."

"Yeah. And it happened right here on our rooftop, while we were sleeping! Two unfortunate men witnessed it. They both had their feet *burnt to a crisp*! They're completely out of their minds now…raving on and on about the *monster*."

"You see…if I only had wings, they'd be calling me an *Angel*…instead of a *monster*!"

Abbie brought the eggs to the table. "You really want those wings, don't you?"

"Well, I'd rather be an Angel than a monster."

"Actually, I'm glad they think you're a monster…because *then* maybe they won't come back!"

7– MARKUS

2019

San Francisco

Timeline 1.0

Abbie and Aroya arrived at Markus' office. A sign on the door read, 'MARKUS KAZAN, N.D.'

"Hi, Liz. Has Markus left for lunch yet?" Abbie asked the receptionist.

"No. He's just finishing up. I'll tell him you're here."

They sat down, waiting for Markus.

Markus strolled into the waiting room–cheerful as ever. "Abbie! It's so nice to see you!" He gave her a big hug. "Is this your friend?" he asked, turning to Aroya.

"Yes. This is my friend Aroya."

Markus offered his hand, but Aroya just smiled–awkwardly shoving his hands in his pockets. Markus disregarded the gesture.

"Aroya. What an interesting name," he said.

"There's a reason Aroya doesn't shake hands," Abbie explained.

Markus examined Aroya's face. "Yes. I think I can see why." His cheerful expression turned to concern. "How long have you had this condition?" he asked.

Unsure of how to reply, Aroya turned to Abbie for support.

"Are you free for lunch?" Abbie asked. "It's kind of a long story, but if you have 30 minutes."

"Sure! I was just going downstairs to grab a sandwich. But I've got two hours, so we could go somewhere else, if you like," Markus suggested.

"How 'bout pizza?" Abbie said.

She took Markus by the arm, and Aroya followed at Abbie's side.

They ordered a large cheese and tomato pizza.

"Please don't tell my patients I'm eating pizza. I know it's pure poison, but it's such delicious poison!" Markus said.

Abbie laughed. Then her tone changed. "Markus? You might have a hard time believing my story…but you know I'd never lie to you," she said.

Markus raised his bushy eyebrows–bracing himself. "Of course." He glanced at Aroya for a clue, but Aroya turned away, pretending to take notice of events outside the window.

"What if I told you...Aroya was injected with technology against his will?" She turned to Aroya and asked, "You were injected, right?"

"Yes, I think so...but there was more to it than that," Aroya said.

"Injected with technology? Against his will? By who? And what type of technology?" Markus asked.

"Can you explain what they did to you–in the simplest terms?" Abbie asked Aroya.

Aroya was a little nervous. "They did something to me in a laboratory, and I lost consciousness. When I woke up, my skin was shiny and cold. They said they performed a process on me... to incorporate microscopic computers into my body to enhance my abilities."

Markus showed concern. "You were an unwilling subject of a trans-human experiment?"

"Something like that," Aroya replied.

Markus leaned back in his chair, pursing his lips. "Aroya, who did this to you?"

Aroya turned to Abbie, unsure of what to say next.

Abbie recalled something about the *Elite Guard*–but thought it best not to go there right now. "It was just some bad people," Abbie replied, "but he ran away...and he came to me for help."

"And you think I can help?" asked Markus.

"We were wondering about chelation to remove the metals from his body," Abbie said.

Markus pondered Abbie's idea. "Chelation. Yes, I do quite a lot of chelation. But I don't really understand what we're dealing with." He turned to Aroya. "Can you perhaps, come back to my office after lunch. I'd like to perform a full examination...if you don't mind?"

"Of course," Aroya replied.

The pizza arrived, and Markus' mood lifted. "Oh, look–isn't it gorgeous!"

Returning to the office, Markus took Aroya into an examining room. Although Abbie trusted Markus, she was still very protective. She sat in the waiting room, trying to relax. After a few minutes, she got up–pacing and checking her cell phone periodically for no apparent reason.

Finally, Markus came out alone. "I've asked Aroya to remain in the room, because I need to speak with you privately. Please have a seat."

Abbie was still fidgety, but she sat with Markus, trying to hide her concern.

"Abbie, where did you meet this man?" Markus asked. "I get the feeling there's much more to this story."

Abbie held her breath, hesitant to say more. "If I tell you, and you don't believe me, will you still help him?"

Markus titled his head, confused. "Why do you think I won't believe you?" he asked.

Abbie remained silent.

"I'm not sure what to do, exactly, but if I had more information, I might be closer to understanding what we're dealing with," Markus explained.

"What did you find during the examination?" Abbie asked.

"I found things I can't explain. If he was the subject of a trans-human experiment, then they've indeed come very close to turning Aroya's body into something...well...into something other than human.

I've never seen–I mean, I've never even *heard* of anything like this before."

"Now that you've examined him…maybe you'll be better prepared to hear the rest of the story."

Markus got up and locked the door. "Go on. I'm listening."

"My dear friend…what I'm about to tell you may challenge your ideas about what is possible. First of all, Aroya is very frightened…that's why he's so quiet. He doesn't know who to trust, and he's afraid you won't believe his story. I believe it because in a strange way, I'm part of it."

Markus leaned back in his chair, focusing on her every word.

"Aroya is from another time," she continued. "He's a *time traveler.* He escaped from the people who did this to him by using *time travel.*" Abbie waited for Markus' reaction.

Markus leaned forward. "I thought you were going to tell me something dangerous…like the military was involved, or a government agency…. But *time travel*–as incredible as it seems… Well, I assume it's not nearly as dangerous–at least, for you and me. Do they know where he is?"

"No. I don't think so."

Markus mulled over the situation. "I *do* believe it is possible. I've read that Nikola Tesla figured it out. But unfortunately, what I don't know is…if it's possible to remove what they put inside him. Chelation can be dangerous for even normal people–and he may not react like a normal person."

"He's desperate. If we can't help him, he'll try to remove the technology himself."

"C'mon," Markus said. "Let's go talk to him."

Abbie followed Markus into the examination room, where Aroya waited anxiously.

"Abbie told me about your time travel," Markus said to Aroya, "and actually, it explains a lot. She also told me you plan to remove the technology yourself if I can't help you."

"Yes," Aroya replied. "I'm sorry, I don't want to cause any trouble."

"Someday, I'd like to hear the whole fantastical story," Markus said. "But right now, here is what I'm proposing. First, we'll need to keep this very private–no matter what happens. The whole procedure must be done in secret. Second, I will need to examine your blood and other bodily fluids–and I should also scrape some tissue from the inside of your cheek. Third, we'll need to take the chelating procedure very slow. Because we have no idea how your organs will react if the technology suddenly breaks loose, flooding your system. Do you understand?"

"Yes. I understand."

"Then let's begin tonight. But not here. We'll do it at my house. Abbie knows where I live." He turned to Abbie. "Is 7 pm good?"

"7 pm is fine," Abbie replied. "Thanks, Markus. You truly are one in a million," Abbie said, hugging him.

Markus offered his hand to Aroya again. "C'mon, I've just palpated your entire body. You're surely not going to *shock* me now!"

Aroya smiled, shaking Markus' hand. "Thank you," he said.

Abbie and Aroya arrived at Markus' home at 7 pm. Markus drew his blood, scraped the inside of his cheek, and began running chelating agents through his vein.

The procedure continued daily for an entire week. It was a difficult time for Aroya, and his body did not tolerate it well. He never complained, but it was very apparent that he was becoming weaker by the day.

"Markus...are we making any progress?" Aroya finally inquired, after the 7th day.

"Honestly, I'm not sure," Markus replied. "Your lab results were highly irregular, right from the start...and they still are." He took Aroya's hand and pushed up his sleeve. "Abbie, come here," he called out. Abbie watched Markus run his fingers over Aroya's arm. "The unusual quality of Aroya's skin is due to the technology being situated mainly in the periphery, just below the skin. I suspect it runs all the way through him–but there's such a large percentage, just beneath the skin. I thought about using surface agents to draw it out, but–"

"I read about that," Abbie said, interrupting. "Some plants can do that...and even silica."

"Yes, silica...or Bentonite clay. But again, I'm hesitant." He turned to Aroya. "I'm afraid it's much too dangerous to continue," he said.

Aroya examined the skin on his arm. He ran his fingers over it and closed his eyes. "It's *blocked.* I can't see a *damn* thing," he said, frustrated.

"What did you expect to see?" Markus asked.

"I don't know. I just want it *out* of me," Aroya said. "What good is it for me to even be here, if I can't live like a normal human being?"

Aroya rarely got like this, but he was now despondent. He had 20 years of practice in keeping his chin up, but that was in 2050…a time of hopelessness, with nothing to look forward to–and almost nothing to lose. Now, however, he was in a time, and with a woman, that actually gave him hope…and losing that hope now was more than he could bear.

Markus sighed, looking at Aroya with sympathy. "Aroya…there are many people who don't look or feel normal. They find a way to still appreciate life, just accepting their lot. That might be your best option."

Abbie never expected Markus to quit so soon. "So, that's it, you're giving up?" she asked, surprised.

Markus felt terrible, but there was nothing more he could do. "Abbie, if I knew what to do, I would do it. But this is just *way* out of my league. It's like shooting in the dark. While we're trying to *save* him, we could be *killing* him–and I don't want to take that chance."

Aroya rolled down his sleeve and stood up. "You did your best. You're a good man, Markus. Thanks for trying." He walked out the door.

8–THE BEACH

2019

San Francisco

Timeline 1.0

That evening, Aroya sat on the couch, reading Millie's book about chelation. Markus may have given up, but he hadn't.

"How much cilantro do you have in your garden?" he asked. "Oh, and parsley–and maybe celery too?"

"I have lots of cilantro and parsley, and we can get celery at the market."

"Then I want to try it. Maybe I don't need the clay– if we can just get enough sand."

"Are you sure? But Markus said it might kill you."

Aroya closed the book, looking directly into Abbie's eyes. "I'm already dying, a little more each day," he said. "Every morning, when I look in the mirror, I see what I've become…and what's worse, I see what I'm *becoming*. It's progressing, Abbie. At night when I sleep, it crawls under my skin. It feels like tiny spiders spinning webs all over inside of me. It's reproducing. I'm not sure how much longer…I'll even be a man."

"Oh, my *God*. I didn't know. You never said anything."

"It's what I meant when I said, *what is worse—is what's inside of me*. And what's even worse than that—is to live an entire life in the absence of human touch."

Abbie's heart broke to hear the truth about how deeply Aroya was suffering. "I'm so sorry," she said. "Okay, I'll help you. We'll begin tomorrow. But tonight, we'll pray."

"Do you really think that's smart? If I recite another prayer, it might *reactivate—*"

Suddenly, a device began flashing in Aroya's forearm. He grabbed his wrist, trying to hide the colored lights, but it was too late.

"It's okay," Abbie said. "I've already seen it…that night on the roof. What is it?"

"It's a communicator…and a tracker. I can't believe it still functions here. I guess it will always be a painful reminder of where I come from."

"Some people have tattoos…yours just lights up. It only makes you more unique, if that's even possible," she said, smiling. "Are you ready to begin our prayer?"

"Yes. I'm ready."

"Okay. I'll say the prayer, and you can just ride along."

"I'll follow your lead."

There was a knock at the door. It was Millie. She unloaded a bag of items onto the table. There were pictures of Jesus and another Archangel, a candleholder, and a small copper bowl filled with sage.

"Wow, this is great stuff!" Abbie said. She picked up the picture of Archangel Raphael, flipping it over to read the prayer on the back. "Oh, this is perfect," she said.

"Yeah–well, I couldn't help but notice that Aroya's been looking exhausted lately," she said. "Those treatments with Markus must be taking a toll." She turned to Aroya, who was hiding in his book. "How are things going with Markus? Any progress?"

"Not really," Abbie answered for him. "Markus thinks it's too dangerous to continue."

"Oh, no... Well, that's disappointing." Millie approached Aroya. "I don't know the details about your condition, but personally, I think your skin looks kind of cool. And you should hear the girls at the café talk about you," she said, winking at Abbie.

"Thanks, Mil'," said Abbie. "We're both kind of tired after today."

Millie got the hint. "Okay. You guys rest. Tomorrow's another day." She blew a kiss, then shut the door behind her.

While Aroya continued reading the chelation book, Abbie arranged the new items on her crowded altar. She removed the broken cup that served as a candleholder, replacing it with a small glass votive decorated with a golden image of Mary.

Aroya lowered his book. "Do you know what kind of sand the beach has? The book says it should be very high in silica–they even call it *silica sand.*"

"I'm not sure about the beach–but wait a minute." She opened the door to her patio and brought in a small bag. "This bag actually says *silica sand* on it. I use it for my fire pit."

Aroya took the bag from Abbie and examined the sand. "It's very white. In my time, the sand isn't this color at all."

"I think the sand at China beach is kind of light-colored, but it's not as white as this."

"I suppose one bag is probably not enough," Aroya said.

"Probably not. But we can borrow Millie's car tomorrow and buy some more. I'll just lay you down on the beach, and pour the silica sand on top of you so that your whole body is covered. The natural beach sand probably has some silica in it too."

"Okay. Maybe that'll work." Aroya smiled at Abbie, encouraged by her enthusiasm. "I'm a little excited. I wasn't sure if I'd ever be normal again."

"Remember what Markus said…it's risky. We don't know what will happen."

Aroya closed his eyes, pointing to his head. "I can't see a damn thing. I'm totally blocked. Maybe the tech is threatened–and if the tech is threatened, that's probably a good sign."

"Well, let's pray on it." Switching off the lights, Abbie placed two cushions in front of the altar. "C'mon. Have a seat," she said, patting a cushion.

Aroya sat cross-legged on the cushion while Abbie lit a candle. She took two more matchsticks from the box. "Before we start, I wanna show you something." She lit both matchsticks, holding them in front of Aroya. "Look at the two flames on these matches," she said. "They're both about the same height. Correct?"

"Yeah. I guess so."

"Now, watch what happens when the two flames come together." She pressed the matches together, and the flames conjoined into one. "What do you see?"

"Now, I see just one flame."

"What about the *height* of the flame?"

"It's much higher than before."

"When we pray or meditate alone, our prayers are like the small flames on the two separate matchsticks. But when we join our energies in prayer, the flame rises higher."

"That's very poetic," Aroya said.

Abbie extinguished the matchsticks. "Do you ever write your own poetry?" she asked.

"No. None of us do. To write about beauty authentically, you must have experienced it. It's been so long for most of us, that we can only experience it through vague memories–and other people's poems. Sometimes, I'm not even sure if we understand what we're reading." He pointed to the picture of Archangel Raphael on the altar. "For instance, a lot of our poems talk about Angels, but I never really understood what an Angel was."

"Do you have a Bible?" Abbie asked.

"I remember religious people having Bibles, but my parents weren't religious...and all religious books were destroyed–even before the catastrophe. We only have our poetry books now, and we're lucky to have those because all books were outlawed after the catastrophe. Our books were buried in the basement of an old, crumbled-down house. My friend, Elijah, found them– and hid them away."

"Elijah? Did you know that the name 'Elijah' comes from a Bible story?"

"Elijah is like my brother. Can you tell me the story?"

"I don't know it well enough to recite it. I wasn't raised with religion either. I guess my church has always been my heart. But I *do* remember something about the story: Elijah was a good man. A man of God. He lived alone in the desert, and the crows brought him food to eat. He met a woman whose son died, and Elijah brought the boy back to life…." Abbie detected a tear in Aroya's eye.

"I was just 17 years old when Elijah found me," Aroya said. "He was five years older. We both lost our families in the catastrophe. When the Squad came, they took us both away." He wiped his eyes. "Who are we going to pray to? Are we praying to God?"

"Yes. And to Archangel Raphael. He's God's healing Archangel. It seems appropriate–since you really *do* need some healing. I'll say the prayers. You don't need to say anything."

"Yeah. I'd better not."

Abbie laughed. "Archangel Raphael is a totally different kind of Archangel, but still, it's probably best if I say the prayer. Of course, we'll also call to God– and our hearts are kind of like the phone we use to make the call…so when we pray, we need to focus on our heart."

"Should I close my eyes?" Aroya asked.

"Yes. Close your eyes."

Aroya closed his eyes. "Okay then. I'm ready."

Abbie held her hands above her head–then she rubbed her palms together briskly. She passed them through the electrified air, moving them down either side. Closing her eyes, she recited a protection prayer:

"Of and by the power, of the Lord, Jesus Christ, A living shell of white light is built up all around me, protecting me from harm. I am encased in a shell of living white light and positive energy, protecting me. In the name of the Father, and the Son, and the Holy Ghost. Amen."

Abbie opened her eyes, catching Aroya peeking out at her. She scooted closer to him. This time he kept his eyes closed while she repeated the protection prayer, moving her hands from the top of his head and down his sides. His legs trembled–not from fear but from the electric charge coursing through his body. Finished, Abbie rested her hands on Aroya's knees. The trembling ceased. Abbie faced the altar and began reciting prayers to God and Jesus. She took the picture of Archangel Raphaelle, and turning it over–she recited the prayer. Finally, she faced Aroya...taking his hands in hers. Abbie's touch surprised him, and when he opened his eyes, he saw her smiling, unaffected by his cold, plasticized skin.

"Are we done?" Aroya asked.

"Yes. How do you feel?"

"Amazing. Electric!"

"Good."

"Abbie, are you a mutant?"

Abbie laughed. "I dunno. Maybe."

The next day in the afternoon, they borrowed Millie's car. They picked up two large bags of silica sand from the store; then drove to China Beach, arriving at sunset. It was a small beach and not very well known. The few locals and tourists who visited that day had long departed–the chilly wind blowing through the Golden Gate, having chased them away. They sat in Millie's car, watching the sunset. Abbie had doubts about what they were about to do.

"Are you sure you want to do this?" she asked, worried. "Markus said you could die. What if you die?"

"If I die–then I'll die," he said.

"But what will *I* do?"

"I suppose you'll cover me with sand and go home. What else could you do?"

"I'm scared."

"I can do it myself. You don't need to stay."

"No. I'll stay."

It was cold and windy, and the beach was empty. They dug a deep trough in the sand, roughly the size and shape of Aroya's body. Abbie took one bag of pure white silica sand, spreading a layer across the bottom of the trough. Bundled up in a coat and a scarf, Abbie wondered if Aroya was cold.

"It's windy here. Are you cold?" she asked.

"No, the process altered my sensations. There are some things I feel mostly with my mind now."

"That's probably a good thing because you'll need to remove your clothes."

Aroya removed his clothes, standing before Abbie– awaiting further instructions.

Abbie was a nurse–she had seen naked men in all shapes and sizes–but Aroya's body was so beautiful that she couldn't help but take a moment, just to gaze upon him. She laid him down in the sand and poured more white silica sand over him, covering the surface of his body. Then she pushed the beach sand over it so that only his face remained exposed to the elements. She sat by his side, watching the sun disappear over the horizon. It was cold, but the sky was mostly clear–except for a few fingers of fog drifting slowly toward the beach. In the distance, a row of golden lights glowed like magic lamps–adorning the Golden Gate Bridge.

Abbie laid on the sand next to Aroya, looking up at the sky. Wispy ribbons of fog sailed overhead, and only a few stars dared to peek out; they winked off and on as if they found the joke of being a star in foggy San Francisco amusing. Abbie knew very little about poetry, but she remembered a line from an old poem she once heard. She recited it for Aroya: *"'Looking up at the stars, I know quite well–That for all they care, I can go to hell.'"* She giggled.

Aroya offered another line of the poem: *"If equal affection cannot be–Let the more loving one be me.* That was W. H. Auden," he said.

Surprised, Abbie propped her head up. "You really *do* know your poetry."

"In my time, poetry was even more precious than a good night's sleep," Aroya answered.

"Does that mean it was difficult to sleep in your time?"

"Yes. Very. All was chaos...especially at night."

"But it's peaceful here," Abbie said. "And the ocean waves sound so beautiful. But boy, do I have to pee! Can I leave you for just a moment?"

"Sure. I'll just wait right here," Aroya joked.

Abbie hurried down to the water's edge. Facing the ocean, she kicked off her shoes and waded into the water, just up to her ankles. It was already dark, but a lone street lamp shone from the road, helping her find her way. She pulled down her jeans, lowering into a squatting position over the water.

Aroya lifted his head, witnessing her beautiful round bottom, thinking to himself–*if I should die now…I shall die a happy man.*

When Abbie stood up to zip her pants, Aroya quickly lowered his head back into the sand, pretending he saw nothing. When she returned, she noticed something had disturbed the sand, and a few granules were on his face. Delicately, she wiped the sand from his cheek. She found it easier to touch him now–and brushed his hair away from his forehead.

"I think you're getting warmer," she said. She pressed the back of her hand against his cheek. "Yes, you are!" she exclaimed.

"Yeah. I am feeling kind of different," Aroya said.

Abbie touched his lips with her finger. "You still have a little sand…right here." She remembered when they first met, how she imagined kissing him.

Of course, Aroya read her mind. "I think my lips are still cold," he said.

That might have been true, but she still couldn't resist stroking them, just a bit more. "Shall I kiss you to find out?" she asked.

"Please," he said, closing his eyes.

Abbie laid down on the sand–over Aroya's body.

He pulled his arms out of the sand, embracing her.

"Am I too heavy?" she asked.

"No. You're as light as air."

Abbie moved her lips to his–teasing him, just barely touching.

His lips parted, and his breath quickened. "Abbie, I think something's moving under the sand."

Abbie thought he was referring to an erection. "Oh, really?" she said, smiling.

"No. There really *is* something moving under the sand. I can feel it on my skin, like something *crawling* on me." He squirmed.

It was dark, but Abbie saw something on his arm. Alarmed, she pushed the sand away from his chest. There were black sores everywhere!

"I've never seen anything like this before. I'm not sure if it's good or bad," she said.

"Let me assure you, it feels very bad…and my head is spinning."

"Then that's enough," Abbie said. She helped him to sit up, handing him his clothes. "Let's get you home."

Once inside the car, the light revealed ugly black sores everywhere. Aroya's body shook–his face drenched with sweat. Abbie laid her hand on his forehead. He was BURNING UP!

"You've got a high fever," she said. "Should I take you to the hospital?"

"No. It's too dangerous," he replied. "Besides, they wouldn't know what to do with someone like me."

Back at the apartment, Aroya's condition worsened. He continued to tremble and sweat, and the sores kept getting larger. On Abbie's small patio, she laid him on a blanket and lit her fire pit.

Lifting his head onto her lap, she cooled his forehead with a wet cloth. "I can't believe I'm actually trying to cool you down," she said.

Using tweezers, she dislodged dark wiggling fibers from his wounds–dropping them into the fire pit. The fibers burnt and fizzled, creating a foul-smelling smoke. She cringed and coughed, trying to avoid the fumes. Finally, she reached through the open door, pulling an air purifier out on the patio. Turning it on, she resumed her work.

"What is the machine for?" Aroya asked.

"It's an air purifier," she said. "It cleans the air. This stuff really smells bad, like burning plastic or something."

She continued working on Aroya's wounds, picking out all the particles and fibers until she could find no more. "I couldn't get them all," she said. "Some of them retracted back into the wound." She laid her hand across his forehead again. "You're still burning up. I'm afraid you're in *real trouble.*"

Aroya examined his arm. Then he called out, "Activate!" Abbie squinted at him, confused by his behavior. Again he called out, "Activate! Activate!" Nothing happened. "I think my tracker is gone!" he exclaimed, excited.

"I pulled out some long threads there," she said, pointing to his arm, "and a bunch of shiny particles."

"I think you pulled out the whole tracker!" he said, even more excited. "If they can't track me, then maybe I can go back for help!"

"Who will help you?" Abbie asked.

"The doctor who did this to me. He'll know what to do," he said. "He's an ambitious man. Maybe I can make a trade."

Aroya struggled to his feet. He peered through the patio door, searching for something.

"What do you need?" Abbie asked.

"I need the stone."

Abbie retrieved Aroya's jacket and searched his pocket for the stone.

Weak from the fever, he leaned against the balcony, trying to steady himself.

Abbie handed him the stone. "Can I help? How does it work?"

"You just focus on someone–then imagine being with them. Then you drop the stone from one hand to the other."

Abbie put her arm around him. "Here, I'll help you stand while you do it."

"No. You might get pulled in. You'd better stand back."

Abbie stepped back, fearful of being transported through time.

"I need to do this myself," he said, gazing at her worried face. "Thank you, Abbie. You've been a real dream come true…a *beautiful* dream come true. I'll return–I promise."

Abbie nervously watched as Aroya closed his eyes and dropped the crystal stone–from one hand to the other. The patio began to undulate like a boat on rough water. Aroya's body rippled. Suddenly, a powerful wave of energy rolled into Abbie's chest. She lost her balance, grabbing onto Aroya as she stumbled forward.

They fell and were transported together…forward in time.

9– THE REVERSION

2050

San Francisco

Timeline 1.0

Dr. Biegel was alone in his lab, working on another experiment. Suddenly, Aroya and Abbie appeared out of nowhere–tumbling onto the floor.

Dr. Biegel nearly jumped out of his skin! He cautiously approached–kneeling down to get a better look at Aroya's face. "What have you done? How did you get here?" he asked.

"I'm sick. I tried to remove the technology, but I failed. I need your help," Aroya said.

Dr. Biegel panicked. "You'll be tracked!" he exclaimed. "And who is this woman? Oh no, I can't help you!"

"My tracking is disabled." He held up his arm. "Here, scan me. Check for yourself."

Dr. Biegel glanced at Aroya's arm, then turned his attention to Abbie.

"She can't be tracked either," Aroya said. "No one knows we're here."

Abbie and Aroya helped each other to their feet while Dr. Biegel considered the situation.

"This is dangerous–very dangerous. For me, and for you!" Dr. Biegel said.

"If you want to know how I got here, then I'll tell you. I have a device. I used it to time travel. I'll give it to you if you help me."

"Hmmm…." Dr. Biegel considered the proposition. He noted the surveillance camera. "Wait! The holograms always confuse them," he whispered. He pushed a few buttons, and three holographic bodies materialized. "Shhh…" he said. "Be quiet." He motioned for them to follow.

Abbie and Aroya followed him into a back room. He double-locked the doors.

"If what you say is true, I might accept your proposition," Dr. Biegel said. "But *reversion* is dangerous. You may not make it."

"I'll take a chance," Aroya replied.

"And even if things go well, reversion is rarely complete. The truth is, you will never be normal again. But as much as you insist on denying it, you never really *were*, to begin with," Dr. Biegel said.

"What do you mean by it's 'rarely complete?'" Aroya asked.

"I can restore the feeling and appearance of an unprocessed man, but you may still retain some of the benefits," Dr. Biegel replied.

"Such as?" Aroya inquired.

"Such as heightened strength and endurance, and self-healing abilities. Your psychic talents will also remain accentuated." He waited for a reaction...but there was none. "In any case, we can't do it here," Dr. Biegel continued. "We'll need to go to the old hospital. It's archaic, but there's no surveillance there. Nobody must know...and that means I can't ask Betty to assist me."

Abbie spoke up. "I can help. I'm a nurse. I don't know anything about the *process* or *reversion*, but I do know my way around old hospitals."

"Very well. But first, you must show me the time travel device," Dr. Biegel demanded.

Aroya showed him the crystal stone.

"What's this? A *rock?*" Dr. Biegel asked, confused.

"It's a crystal...with unusual properties," Aroya answered. "You saw us materialize, didn't you? And the Squad couldn't locate me after I left."

"Yes. And they came here looking for you–with a very disagreeable man, named Wolfe," Dr. Biegel said.

"Klaus Wolfe. He was my trainer," Aroya said.

"Your trainer? Oh, *Elite Guard.* Well, that explains his attitude. He said he'd be back–and I believe him! We'd better work quickly!" Dr. Biegel said.

"I'm a fast learner," Abbie said. "Just tell me what to do."

"All right," Dr. Biegel agreed. "But on one condition: you not only give me the stone, but you also instruct me on how to use it."

"Okay. It's a deal," Aroya replied.

Dr. Biegel took a notebook from his pocket, preparing to write something down. "First: what is the name of the stone…and what gives it its special properties?"

"I don't know the name–" Aroya started.

"I know it!" Abbie interrupted. Aroya nodded, gesturing for her to continue. "The name of the stone is labradorite," she said.

Dr. Biegel jotted it down. "Now…step by step, tell me how it works."

"Step 1: You hold the stone in your right hand and visualize a person you want to be with, in another time," Aroya said. "Step 2: You close your eyes and see yourself *with* that person… while you drop the stone, from your right hand to your left hand."

Dr. Biegel finished scribbling in his notebook. "Is that all?"

"That's all there is to it," Aroya said.

"I find that difficult to believe–but okay. Now give me the stone," Dr. Biegel demanded.

"No. Not until you help me," Aroya said.

Dr. Biegel grabbed an old suitcase from under the table. "Follow me," he said.

As they left through the back door, Klaus Wolfe entered the lab, discovering the holograms rotating under the camera. Surveying the empty room, he angrily called out to the guards. *"TRACK HIM!"* he yelled. The guards stared at him, bewildered. *"THE DOCTOR! TRACK DR. BIEGEL!"* Klaus shouted louder.

Approaching the old hospital, Abbie recognized it. It was the same public hospital where she used to work. Although still operating, in a third-world kind of way— there was very little organization and no real doctors. Abbie knew this hospital like the back of her hand. She led the way to an unoccupied wing of the hospital, and they entered an operating room, locking the doors behind them.

"Lucky for you, that I'm an old guy," Dr. Biegel remarked. "I still remember the old procedures." While preparing the room, Dr. Biegel asked Abbie, "What is your name, and what year did you come from?"

"My name is Abbie, and I'm from 2019."

Dr. Biegel searched his memory. "Ah yes. The prelude to a fall," he said.

"The prelude to a fall?" Abbie asked.

"Yes. The beginning of the end, you could say." After a few mental calculations, he continued, "But there are still 11 years before the catastrophe brings everything down." Then, reconsidering, he added, "But, of course, the catastrophe would never have happened at all, if it wasn't for the fall."

"What sort of catastrophe?" Abbie asked.

"It was the 'higher-ups'…the 'elites.' Maybe it was their misguided technology—or maybe it was that crazy machine they built. But before that, they withheld food and water from the people…and then, there were the bioweapons. They're responsible for *all* of it." He shook his head, recalling the destruction. Turning to Aroya, he said, "If I'm correct, you must have been about 17. You remember, don't you?"

"I don't remember anything about a machine," Aroya replied.

"Oh, well–they made a machine. It was a colossus. They thought they were gods–playing with the very essence of energy and life itself." Again, he shook his head. "They were reckless. Nobody knows for sure how it happened…except for them, of course. But before that, they engineered the fall, the famine, the drought–and all the rest."

"Famine and drought? When did *that* happen?" Abbie asked.

"I guess you could say the precursors began in 2021–give or take a year…but it was the fall of culture that really kicked it into gear. No more ethics, morals, family, art, music…all of it, gone. Then they turned the people against each other, right before unleashing the bioweapons." Changing the subject, he said, "Aroya, please remove your clothing and sit on the table." Pointing to a basket, he said to Abbie, "Those look like gowns near the door." Abbie grabbed a hospital gown, handing it to Aroya. Dr. Biegel continued, "He'll need some fluids. We'll just piggyback the medications–" He reached into his suitcase and pulled out a bag of IV medication. Continuing, he said, "and we'll need to prepare for two blood transfusions."

"Two different transfusions?" Abbie asked.

"Yes, that's right." Dr. Biegel replied. "And with all these sores–you'll be lucky to find one clear vein. I suppose he'll need a central line. Better get a cannula…and the whole setup. Oh, and a tray for minor surgery. I'll need to remove his operating system."

"May I ask what to expect?" Aroya inquired.

"First, we'll need to chase the vectors with their attached technology–into your bloodstream…so that we can access it." Then to Abbie, he asked, "Can we get an ultrasound unit in here?"

"I think so. Sonography should be right down the hall. They should have a portable unit," she replied.

Turning his attention back to Aroya, Dr. Biegel explained, "After the ultrasound, we'll give you an antiparasitic to disable the vectors. Then you'll receive a blood transfusion, just for support, until your body resumes its normal functioning."

"Antiparasitic?" Aroya asked.

"That's how they get the technology into you…they use a common parasite. We're lucky to be stopping it so soon—because eventually, it would have completely commandeered your brain—and your entire nervous system. It's called the *process* because it is indeed an ongoing process. The vectors and the technology, continually multiplying—gradually invading all systems."

"Is that why I feel like something's crawling under my skin?" Aroya asked.

"Yes. It's proliferating," Dr. Biegel said. "The parasite and the technology, working together."

Abbie found what she needed in the cabinets. "Should I go check to see if the hospital still has a functioning blood bank?" she asked.

Dr. Biegel ignored her question. "We'll need the ultrasound unit before we do anything else."

"Okay. I'll go get it," Abbie replied.

Dr. Biegel explained further, "We're going to use the sound frequency, to chase the vectors from your brain, and into your bloodstream—and then from your kidneys, into your bladder. This should clear a large percentage of them."

"And after you've chased them into my bladder…then what?" Aroya asked.

"You'll pee them out!" Dr. Biegel replied.

"Oh, of course. I'll just pee them out." Aroya wasn't looking forward to that.

Abbie returned with a portable ultrasound machine. "I hope it still works. It doesn't look like anyone's been in that department for years!" She moved the unit near the procedure table. "I'm sure there's no usable blood in this wing. It's like a ghost town out there."

Dr. Biegel surveyed the room, and upon seeing a water dispenser, he pointed to a large bottle on the dusty floor. "Abbie, do you think that water is still clean enough to drink?"

She examined the bottle. "I suppose so. It's in glass, and the cap looks sealed."

"Then let's get a quart of water into him, by mouth," he said.

Abbie lifted the heavy bottle to the counter and broke the seal. Tipping it sideways, she poured the water into a large plastic container. Placing a drop onto her tongue, she said, "I guess it tastes okay."

Aroya took the water and began drinking.

Gloved up, Dr. Biegel prepared for the first procedure. "We'll need a bedpan–or something large to catch his urine," he said.

Abbie located a bedpan in the cabinet, handing it to Aroya.

"Gee, thanks," he said.

"Now, sit on the edge of the table facing the wall," Dr. Biegel instructed Aroya.

Aroya shifted his position while Dr. Biegel started up the machine. And voila! It still worked! He set the ultrasound unit at the desired frequency, then moved the transducer probe over Aroya's head–working his way down, to his lower back, then over his kidneys. "Now, lean back a little," he said, standing in front of him with the transducer.

Aroya held the bedpan. "Is it time?" he asked.

"Not quite yet." Turning to Abbie, Dr. Biegel instructed, "I'll place the central line when we're finished with this procedure. In the meantime, look for a good vein in his arm for his transfusion. Just run some saline for now–we can switch it out later. But be sure to avoid the sores."

"You want two lines?" Abbie asked, still confused.

"No, of course not. Just finding *one* clean vein ought to be a real challenge."

Abbie placed the line in Aroya's arm. "I'm sure the blood in this wing–if they have any at all–isn't any good," she said. "Should I go to the main hospital? What's his blood type?"

Dr. Biegel ignored her question again. Now, he was using the ultrasound probe over Aroya's bladder.

Aroya squealed a bit. "Oh, Jeez! I think they're getting ready to exit, Doc! "

"Then prepare the pan–and when you feel the urge, go ahead and urinate."

"I feel the urge!" he exclaimed. He peed in the bedpan. The sensation was not pleasant. *"Out, monsters! Out!"* he commanded.

Aroya completed his assignment. Dr. Biegel took the bedpan from him, dumping it into the trash. Then he moved the procedure tray next to Aroya. "Lay back, Aroya." He changed his gloves and began prepping Aroya's neck for a central line.

"Should I go look for blood now?" Abbie asked.

Dr. Biegel looked up. "There's no need to go anywhere, dear. Just move that gurney over here, next to Aroya." He postponed the central line, turning his attention back to Abbie.

Perplexed, Abbie moved the gurney.

"We just need you to lie down on the gurney now– and push up your sleeve," Dr. Biegel told Abbie.

"Why?" Abbie asked.

"The program will automatically quit, but the peripherals…" Dr. Biegel took a closer look at Aroya's arm. "Although, it does appear that you've removed quite a bit already–and Aroya's body is attempting to find its natural homeostasis, judging by his perspiration."

Abbie was still standing next to the gurney, confused. "Why do you want me to get on the gurney?" she asked again.

"Isn't it clear?" he replied. "When I disable the technology, he will need healthy human blood for support–just until he makes his own. His body is different than most, so it should happen rather quickly– but he will still need your blood."

"Wait a minute!" Aroya protested.

"It's only a little blood. She's a nurse–she understands," Dr. Biegel said.

"But do you even know his blood type?" Abbie asked.

"Of course, I know his blood type, but it doesn't matter because–"

"But you don't know *mine,*" Abbie interrupted.

"My dear girl, Aroya is a *mutant.* Didn't he tell you?"

Aroya raised his head. "Why do you keep calling me that?"

"The point is...his body does not react to viscous intelligent matter. If he doesn't react to the *VIM*, then I *promise* you, he will not react to a little human blood– no matter *what* type it is."

"Don't pressure her! She didn't volunteer for this. She's only here by accident," Aroya exclaimed.

"Well then, what a happy accident it is for you!" Dr. Biegel said, checking with Abbie. "Am I right?"

Nervously, Abbie climbed onto the gurney. She held out her arm.

Aroya reached for her hand. "Abbie, are you sure?"

"It's okay. It's just a little blood. It's *you* I'm worried about," Abbie replied.

While waiting for the blood to transfuse, Abbie got a few things off her chest. "How could you do that to people?"

"You mean the *process?*" Dr. Biegel asked. "I was forced into it as punishment. So was Betty. Most of the people working underground are there for punishment. They were simply too ethical to go along with their hideous experiments–but also too useful to exterminate." He lowered his eyes. "I'm afraid, over time–I lost the will to fight. It was easier just to go along with the program. But now it's all come to an end. I'll be turning 60 soon."

Aroya's ears perked up. "That's why you want the stone. You need a way out."

"Yes," Dr. Biegel said, nodding.

"What's turning 60 have to do with anything?" Abbie asked.

"My 60th birthday…it's my expiration date," Dr. Biegel replied.

"They kill people who turn 60?" Abbie asked.

"Not just people who turn 60–" Aroya added, "but anyone who's no longer useful…in their opinion."

"Yes, and I was hoping that you might consider taking me with you…back to your time," Dr. Biegel added.

Abbie turned to Aroya for his reaction.

Aroya appeared hesitant, but he agreed. "Okay. But only if the reversion is successful." Then he addressed Abbie. *"Promise me, if I die on this table–that you'll go back immediately–"* looking at Dr. Biegel, he continued, "by *yourself."*

"You know, Aroya…." Dr. Biegel responded, "those of us who live underground may live better than you on the surface…but the reality is, we're simply slaves to the Council…just like everyone else. We all know the *process* is wrong, and I'm old enough to remember a free world–but if we don't follow orders here, we get demoted…or worse."

"But why do they do it…the process?*"* Aroya asked.

"It's about control, mainly–and usefulness. In the beginning, they worked diligently to create more human-like robots, but they could never successfully replicate the human brain in its full capacity. Finally, they realized it was much easier to simply make humans more robotic–rather than the other way around. The *process* is a clever way to robotize human beings– to improve and strengthen their physical functioning while harnessing the untapped potential of their brains. They've been building legions of remote-controlled humanoid robots."

"You mean, legions of human slaves," Aroya added.

"Honestly, at this point, it's all just a cruel experiment," Dr. Biegel said. "Not all processing is successful. Many perish. And merging with the VIM…is just another deranged experiment. I'm sorry–but my job was to recruit. I just said what I was supposed to say."

"For those who don't perish after processing, what's their fate?" Aroya asked.

"The truth is–once processed, you become property of the Sky Council. They own you–because you're embedded with their patented technology. Your life is theirs 24/7–even your thoughts are theirs. Your personality might even take a back seat to another agent…inserted in your mind."

"They can insert other personalities into peoples' minds?" Abbie asked.

"Oh, yes," Dr. Biegel said. "The process eventually changes your DNA. It's like switching antennas. It allows for foreign agents to enter through the new frequency. Your DNA will no longer be your own, and another agent might take possession of your body and mind at any moment."

"Has my DNA been changed?" Aroya asked.

"It's likely begun. But at this point, I don't think it's irreversible–especially so soon after processing. I believe there's still enough of *you* remaining to recover your own original DNA, almost completely. And you still have control over your mind…thanks to Betty."

"You know what Betty did for me?" Aroya asked.

"Yes. She confessed–privately. Betty's always had a soft heart. That's how she ended up in the underground as my assistant. The truth is, Betty is an exceptionally brilliant scientist. As my subordinate, she's being punished for her soft-hearted conduct."

"I hope she won't be punished for what she did for me," Aroya said.

Dr. Biegel just shrugged.

"Will Aroya be completely free of the technology after the reversion?" Abbie asked.

"Mostly," Dr. Biegel replied. "The processing was never fully complete in him, anyway. We may even be able to re-establish full dominance of his original DNA. And I suspect his own unique mutation offered him some degree of protection. Mutants never seem to lose their innate specialness, even after they've been processed."

"You mean the VIM will still merge with me?" Aroya asked.

"Yes," Dr. Biegel said. "And what Betty did for you may have spared you from full VIM transformation. She bought you some time, and you used it well."

"Then I guess Betty saved me from becoming a god," Aroya said, smiling.

"Oh yes. You would have indeed become like a god—a very dark god...and you might have paid for it, with your very soul," Dr. Biegel said.

"They can take your soul?" Abbie asked, alarmed.

"Not the Council...but the VIM itself," Dr. Biegel replied. "Once it fully merges, the soul is captured. I know of no reversion procedure for that...except maybe prayer."

Abbie and Aroya were both stunned. The room was so quiet; you could hear a pin drop.

"I'd better get that central line started now," Dr. Biegel said, moving back to Aroya's neck.

Then suddenly, *BOOM! A LOUD EXPLOSION* blew open the door! Guards charged inside–with Klaus and Burk in tow. Burk carried two bottles of the VIM.

Shocked, Aroya and Abbie yanked out their IV lines, facing the guards.

"Get him back on the table!" Klaus shouted to the guards.

Abbie looked on helplessly while they overpowered Aroya–strapping him down to the table.

Burk set one bottle of VIM on the counter–handing the other to Klaus.

Klaus hung the VIM on the IV pole, then turned his attention to Aroya. "Feel like a *change,* Recruit Wallace? How about a *full transformation?"* Then he shouted to the guards, *"Bring in the chains!"*

From the hallway, more guards came through the door–hauling heavy chains. They wrapped the chains around Aroya, pulling them tight across his chest.

"Biegel! Start the VIM!" Burk ordered.

"No! Not without his consent! The VIM will not merge without his consent!" Dr. Biegel shouted back.

The guards tugged on Aroya's chains, preparing to fasten a lock.

Aroya's face turned beet red. He clenched his teeth and managed to whisper, "I can't breathe!"

Suddenly, Abbie rushed forward–grabbing the lock–and smashing it against the window. Glass showered down everywhere, startling the guards.

Klaus grabbed Abbie by the hair. "Maybe we should practice on *this* one first!" he hissed.

"No, you mustn't!" Dr. Biegel protested. "It will drive her mad!"

"Yes," Klaus replied, grinning, "and we'll all get to witness it!"

Aroya struggled to free himself. *"Don't touch her!"* He managed to shout, his voice cracking under the strain of heavy chains.

Klaus threw Abbie against the wall, turning his attention back to Aroya. "What did you say, tough guy?" he growled. He yanked the line from the saline bag, examining both ends. "Oh, I see how this works," he said. "You just take this end here...and you plug it in over here." He plugged the line into the VIM bottle, jeering at Aroya. *"Okay, mutant let's show your girlfriend how tough you really are. Do you think she'll still love you–after you've been turned into a fucking goo-bot?!"* Grasping the needle at the other end, he grinned at Aroya like a psycho. "Hmm...," he said, "maybe this part goes right *here!*" With a quick thrust, he jabbed the needle into Aroya's neck!

Abbie charged, yanking out the IV line. The entire bottle of VIM came tumbling down, smashing on the floor. Klaus stood frozen, stunned–his face spattered with VIM goo.

The guards backed away, hesitant and confused.

Burk motioned to them. *"Get back–don't touch him!"*

Klaus' eyes turned black, and his face contorted. He smiled wickedly, showing his blackened teeth–spitting putrid goo everywhere.

Burk and the guards panicked–pinned up against the wall, stuck between the VIM and Klaus–who was quickly losing his mind.

During the confusion, Abbie released Aroya from the chains. Before running, they called out to Dr.

Biegel–also trapped against the wall with Burk and the guards.

Dr. Biegel smiled at Aroya. "My time was up, anyway!" he said. "Run, Aroya! Run!" he shouted.

Burk grabbed a gun–aiming at Aroya. But Dr. Biegel fell on the gun as it fired, sinking to the floor–collapsing into the puddle of goo.

Aroya grabbed his clothes and ran outside with Abbie. He took the stone from his pocket.

Abbie wrapped her arms around him, pressing her face against his chest–as he dropped the stone from one hand to the other. In an instant…they were gone!

Still in her bathrobe, Millie was enjoying her morning coffee. Suddenly, Abbie and Aroya materialized out of thin air–tumbling onto her kitchen floor. Millie stared at them in shock.

"Sorry, Millie–I couldn't think of anyone else," Aroya said.

Millie was speechless.

"I know this looks weird. Just trust me," Abbie said. "I'll explain later."

Millie threw up her hands. "Okay," she responded. She watched Abbie and Aroya stumble towards the door, catching a glimpse of Aroya's bare ass peeking out of his hospital gown.

Once back in 2019, Aroya spent all day and a night resting and recuperating from the reversion process. Both of them were exhausted and slept right through lunch and dinner.

In the morning, Abbie shuffled out of the bedroom. She peeked in on Aroya, finding him in his usual place–on the couch with a book.

"Good morning. Are you feeling better?" she asked.

"Yes. Very much better!"

Abbie shuffled into the kitchen to put the kettle on.

From the other room, Aroya heard, *"What the hell?!"* followed by, *"Aroya, come here!"*

Aroya watched Abbie examining the teakettle.

"Look! Do you notice anything?" she asked.

"Yeah. The little bird is missing...no, the whole pot is different," Aroya said.

"Do you think someone's messing with me again? Why would they just switch my teakettle?"

Aroya scanned the room. "Is there anything else missing?"

Abbie set the teakettle on the kitchen table. "I don't know. I guess I should look around."

There was a knock at the door. It was Millie.

"I'm so glad you're here," Abbie said. "Maybe you can solve a little mystery for me."

"Me solve a mystery for *you?* How about *you,* solving the mystery of how you ended up on my kitchen floor yesterday?"

"Uh-oh," Aroya muttered as he retreated to the couch–burying his nose in a book.

"Okay," Abbie replied. "I *do* owe you an explanation."

Millie sat down. "Yes. You certainly do." She picked up the teakettle, examining it. "Something wrong with your teakettle?" she asked.

"That's what I wanted to talk to *you* about. I have no idea where this teakettle came from, and *my* teakettle is gone!"

"But isn't this your teakettle?" Millie asked, confused. "It looks like your teakettle."

"No. My teakettle has a little bird on the spout that whistles."

"Oh, really. Well, *I* gave you *this* one when you moved in here. Remember? I guess that means you have *two* teakettles?"

Abbie remembered receiving a teakettle from Millie as a housewarming gift, but it definitely had a little bird on the spout. She sat down at the table, looking at the teakettle–confused.

"Abbs'…are you all right?" Millie asked.

Abbie rubbed her eyes. "I guess I'm just tired."

"Yeah, I guess so. Teleporting into your best friend's kitchen must take a lot out of you."

"I'm sorry. Okay–let me explain. But promise me you won't say anything until I'm done."

Millie gestured, *zipping her mouth shut,* then she crossed her arms, waiting.

Abbie paused, searching for the right words. "Aroya is from another time," she said. "He's a time traveler from the year 2050. He escaped from some evil people who injected him with some kind of technology, against his will. That's why his skin was all silvery. He escaped from them…by using time travel."

Millie motioned for permission to unzip her mouth.

"Yes, of course," Abbie said.

"Well…why didn't you just say so?" Millie said. "This whole thing's been really weird, right from the start." She called out to Aroya, "No offense, Aroya."

She continued, "But that still doesn't answer my question about how you ended up in my kitchen."

Abbie let out a sigh. "We had to go back to Aroya's time to get him some medical help. When we returned– Aroya envisioned you in his mind to help us navigate back here."

"Sorry again, Millie," Aroya called out from the couch.

"Okay. I guess that explains things," she said. "But how did you manage to time travel in the first place? Do you have a machine or something?"

"No. We use the crystal stone," Abbie said. She retrieved her stone and set it on the table.

Millie squinted at it. "The rock? From the guy's hat?"

"Yeah. Aroya has one too," Abbie replied. "But he got his somewhere else."

"I knew there was something special about that rock–because of your dream!" Millie said.

"Yeah. Something special, indeed," Abbie agreed.

"Okay. I guess you put my mind at ease," Millie said. "But you know…even though I interview people who claim to be E.T.s and all…I'll still need time to digest this." Millie sighed.

"I understand," Abbie said.

Millie called out to Aroya again. "I'm glad you're feeling better, Aroya! I guess I'll see you guys later." She opened the door, then stopped in her tracks. Turning back around, she addressed Aroya again: "I just have one more question. Why were you wearing a hospital gown?"

Aroya hesitated, peering over his book at Abbie.

"I told you–he had a medical procedure," she replied.

"Well, yeah… I guessed that much. And by the way–Aroya, your skin looks great! I guess they have more advanced techniques in 2050. Maybe I oughta try it myself some time," she joked, shutting the door behind her.

"Well, that went well," Aroya said.

"Yeah. Just like when we told Markus…no shock or anything. It's weird how my friends just accept this stuff and then carry on, as if everything's perfectly normal."

"Maybe it's just *your* friends. I bet *normal* people wouldn't react that way," Aroya teased.

"Are you suggesting my friends aren't *normal?"* Abbie joked.

"I don't know… I guess that depends on what you call *normal."*

"Well. Millie does interview E.T.s–and Markus spends all his time thinking about government conspiracies."

"Maybe your friends *are* a little bit crazy, Abbie."

"Oh yeah. E.T.s and government conspiracies are *much* crazier than *time-traveling trans-humans."*

"That's exactly my point. It's *all* crazy…and it's all *true,"* Aroya said.

"Well, you know what they say; sometimes, the truth is stranger than fiction. And the more time that goes by…the stranger it gets," Abbie said.

"Speaking of Markus–aren't we supposed to see him today?" Aroya asked.

"Oh yeah. I better hop in the shower!"

While Abbie was in the shower–once again, Aroya used the kitchen sink and some paper towels to wash up. And the shiny pan lid to groom his hair. It was now a routine.

Abbie accompanied Aroya to Markus' office. She was hoping his bloodwork would finally prove he was free of technology.

Markus greeted them in the waiting room, surprised by Aroya's appearance. "Wow. What a change! C'mon in. Let's have a better look!"

In the examining room, Markus drew Aroya's blood. He prodded Abbie. "Okay…tell me the story."

"There's not much to tell, really," she said. "We just time-traveled to the year 2050 convinced a doctor to reverse the process–fought off the evil demon people– escaped the VIM goo…and then returned home to 2019. That's all." Abbie said, chuckling.

"I believe it!" Markus replied. "Every bit of it!" He examined the sores on Aroya's arms–mostly healed now, but still visible. "What happened here?" he asked.

"Oh. That happened when I tried to revert myself. Abbie cleaned most of it out before we left." Aroya replied.

Markus shook his head. "I don't know how you got back to 2050 for help, but it's a good thing you did." He filled a few tubes with Aroya's blood. "I'll call you with the results," he said, pressing a Band-Aid on Aroya's skin. "Be sure to keep track of his temperature. It's approaching normal, but he's still a bit icy." Turning to Aroya, he continued, "Something's been puzzling me. You clearly have the means to time travel, so why did you choose to travel back to 2019? That's only 31 years…and considering your age, you were already here once before."

"It wasn't really my choice," Aroya replied. "Actually, at the time–I wasn't sure where I'd end up."

"What do you mean?" Markus asked.

Again, Aroya turned to Abbie for help.

"We can't explain how it happened–but actually, I think it was *my* choice, somehow," Abbie said.

Markus tilted his head, waiting for more information.

"I'll make you a promise," Abbie said. "Just as soon as Aroya achieves his goal of 98.6 degrees, we'll tell you all about it over dinner."

Markus smiled. "Oh boy, I can't wait!"

Aroya remained on the couch, still convalescing from his ordeal in 2050. Relaxing, he read a book while Abbie unpacked a box of men's clothing in the living room.

"Are you sure he doesn't want them?" Aroya asked.

"He's been in Spain for three years. Last time he called, he said to give this stuff away–I just never got around to it." Abbie folded the clothing neatly on an empty shelf. "I'm glad it fits you. I thought it would because you're roughly the same size." Abbie lit the fireplace. "I've been thinking…" Abbie said.

"About?"

"About when you were in chains on that table. Why didn't you just turn into a fiery Archangel and escape?"

Somewhat amused, Aroya closed his book. "It didn't even occur to me. Do you think it would've worked?"

"I don't know. Maybe you should try it again."

"Why? You liked that? A 10-foot-tall fiery Archangel–with no wings?!"

Abbie giggled, then moved next to him on the couch. "You're really developing a complex about those wings. You know what they say–*Wings don't necessarily make the Angel.*"

Aroya put his arms around Abbie, pulling her close. "Is that what they say?"

Abbie rubbed the skin on Aroya's arm, observing the healthy color. His body temperature was now approaching normal, and the plastic feeling of his skin was completely gone. She knew that soon… she'd be inviting him into her bed. But not yet.

10– THE LAKE

2019

San Francisco

Timeline 1.0

In the days that followed, Abbie and Aroya noticed more and more how the seeds of a dystopian future were being sown: there were more homeless people on the streets, more drug dealers in the parks, more people beaten by thugs, more children going missing–and nobody did a thing to stop it. The news was regularly censored now, and when courageous people spoke out, they suffered threats and ridicule–or simply disappeared altogether.

Aroya's favorite bookshop owner received threats because of his political views and the type of books he sold. The relentless harassment caused him to seriously consider shutting down his business altogether. Despite

Abbie and Gina's heroic efforts to expose corruption at the hospital, reports about mysterious deaths continued, mostly involving the elderly and the poor. There were days when the city was so smoky that the air was almost unbreathable. Screaming sirens drowned out bird songs, buildings burned, and cops rarely responded anymore. Tragically, most people just stopped paying attention.

New Draconian laws and regulations passed, mostly without the public's knowledge or consent–only coming to light after bewildered citizens found themselves in handcuffs. Still, as terrible as things appeared (to those paying attention), the situation was not nearly as dark and hopeless as in Aroya's time. And because he had come from such a hellish future, he dearly treasured every hint of beauty still left in this world. He stubbornly held onto his optimism, even in the face of new atrocities. But one day, there was something so ugly that his heart could not bear it. It was a giant billboard, erected above Ray Widdle's bookshop, across from the café. The billboard advertised a free women's health clinic. Below the picture of a smiling woman, neon pink letters announced abortion services–now available for full-term pregnancies. In his mind, this very pleasant-looking advertisement for killing full-term infants was horrifying. He felt as if he were literally falling forward–into the black hole of 2050.

Together, Abby and Aroya watched the ugliness progress–like an infected wound festering more each day. There was no denying it–they were definitely witnessing signs of Dr. Biegel's *prelude to a fall.* Despite it all, they tried their best to keep their focus on beauty–knowing full well that in time, the world would eventually fall to ugliness.

One evening at sunset, they strolled along a bicycle path, overlooking a smelly polluted lake. The lake was once a source of clean drinking water, until a recent earthquake created a sewage leak, turning the lake into a stinky mess. Dead fish floated on the surface, along with other rotting debris–and sickly raccoons meandered through the shrubs, most of them losing their fur in great patches.

Abbie sat on a bench with Aroya, discussing the stench of the lake. She retrieved her crystal stone from her pocket–then playfully, she proposed a question. "Do you think it would be possible to take the lake back...to a time when it was still clean?" She held the stone and closed her eyes. "Tell me how to do it!" she said.

"Just focus on two points: the first being your desire to restore the lake's clean water. The second being the fulfillment of your desire–which is your goal. In your right hand is your desire–it holds the stone, and in your left hand is the vision of your goal, already achieved...it catches the stone."

"But when *you* did it...you said your desire was for me–*a person*. But this is a lake!"

"Yes, it is a lake...and lakes can't time travel," Aroya replied.

Although the lake was not a person, Abbie refused to let the idea go. "Maybe we should meditate for guidance," she suggested.

"For guidance?"

"Yes. That's how I first saw you in the vision."

"Abbie, I don't know how to meditate," Aroya replied.

"Well…it's a bit like dreaming, but you're not asleep," she explained. "I once heard someone say that praying is how we call God, and meditation is how God answers. It just takes a little patience and practice–but sometimes, you can find answers that way." Abbie straddled the bench. "Here, I'll show you. Sit like this, across from me. Remember those matches–when we were praying? How the two flames rose higher together? It's the same way for meditation."

Aroya straddled the bench, facing Abbie. Abbie took his hands in hers. "Close your eyes," she instructed. "And in your mind, see our *two* hearts…beating as *one*. Listen to my breath–and let *your* breath fall into sync with mine. I will take you with me–and when you feel you are no longer here, in this place or time, that is when you ask your question. Then you simply wait…and watch. Sometimes you will see something or hear something that leads you to an answer."

They sat quietly, facing each other–eyes closed, holding hands. Gradually, their two breaths fell into sync. The smell of the pollution was distracting, and it was difficult for their minds to focus–but finally, they entered a deep meditative state together.

"I see the lake…and she's a lady," Aroya whispered.

Abbie opened her eyes. "Uh-huh. She's a lady. Now what?"

Aroya's eyes were still closed. "Maybe Lord Byron can help."

"Lord Byron?" Abbie asked.

"A poem." He recited a few lines:

"A brow like a midsummer lake,
Transparent with the sun therein,
When waves no murmur dare to make,
And heaven beholds her face within."

Aroya opened his eyes. "The poem says, *her face within.* If we see the lake as a lady–then the fulfillment of our desire would be *transparent with the sun therein."*

Abbie handed him the stone. "Here. Drop the stone and make it happen." Her eyes twinkled with excitement.

"Okay." He closed his eyes, holding the stone in his right hand. "My desire is for these waters to be healthy and clear...*transparent with the sun therein...*for this Lady, who is the lake...and *her face within."* He envisioned himself beside the cool fresh waters–then he dropped the stone from one hand to the other.

When they opened their eyes, it was dark. They detected no change in the lake.

Abbie held her nose. "It still stinks," she said. Then, the ground suddenly rocked back and forth. *"Oh, God– it's an earthquake!"* Abbie exclaimed, jumping to her feet!

Aroya stood up, looking around. "Maybe it was the stone," he said.

They peered into the water, but they could see no change.

On the way home, they discussed their dreams for a better future–knowing full well what the future actually held.

Abbie wondered if the world's problems grew worse as a consequence of people's resistance to confront the ugliness growing around them.

"They won't look at the darkness. They're not even interested in shining a light," she said.

Aroya replied, "It's just like Plato said: *The real tragedy of life is when men are afraid of the light."*

Maybe because he came from a time of hopelessness–and was so impressed with the beauty still alive in 2019–Aroya remained patient and optimistic. Even in 2050, he and his friend Elijah held onto their sense of humor. That–and the poetry–carried them through the harshest of days and the grimmest of nights.

Abbie, on the other hand, was becoming jaded. She had only visited 2050 for a brief period, never experiencing the full desperation of zone 9. In Aroya's optimism and sense of wonder, she somehow found remnants of her own hope. He made her smile, and before his arrival, she hadn't smiled in a very long time.

For Aroya, witnessing Abbie's natural beauty and determination only reminded him more–of why he wanted to be fully human again. Yes, he was falling in love with Abbie–but he was also falling in love with the year 2019…a time that still held so much beauty and hope.

11– THE HEDGE-ROSE OPENS

2019

San Francisco

Timeline 1.0

The following day, Abbie and Aroya had breakfast at the café. Aroya peered out the window while sipping his tea. A new sign in front of the bookshop read: USED BOOKS $1–CLOSING SALE.

"Ray's closing the shop!" Aroya exclaimed.

"I guess the pressure was finally too for much him," Abbie replied.

They left the café, walking across the street to the bookshop. Pushing open the door, a little bell jingled–catching Ray's attention.

From behind the counter, Ray hollered out, "Hey, Aroya! I've got something for you!"

Finishing with a customer, he reached under the counter. His tidy bookshelves were now dismantled; stacks of books were piled high around the shop, and signs everywhere read ALL BOOKS–FINAL SALE.

"This is my friend, Abbie," Aroya said.

Ray smiled. "Oh, I didn't know you had a girlfriend. Hi Abbie. It's nice to meet you."

Abbie returned the smile. "Nice to meet you too."

"You know…one of the saddest things about closing the shop is that I'll miss my favorite customers, like Aroya," Ray said. "Here you go. A parting gift," he said, handing Aroya a book. Then he addressed Abbie. "You must be good for him." He pointed to Aroya's face. "He's looking much healthier these days!"

Ray was right. Aroya was looking healthy, and he was feeling much more alive. His skin had become completely normal, and his temperature was quickly approaching 98 degrees. Abbie wandered around the store while Aroya and Ray shot the breeze.

Delighted with his new book, Aroya began leafing through the pages.

"It's Sufi poetry," Ray explained. "You seem to like the theme of beauty, and Sufi poetry is all about beauty." He reached over the counter, pointing to the top of a page. "See here? It says 'Love, Harmony, and Beauty.' Some people consider the author a saint."

Aroya struggled to read the author's name, *"Hazrat Inayat Khan."*

"I believe the 'Hazrat' part is an honorific," Ray said.

"Thank you, Ray. I can almost feel the beauty inside these pages."

"Actually, I think he's more like a spiritual teacher...but also a poet. He says, *Poetry is something that does not belong to this earth: it belongs to heaven."*

Aroya examined the cover again. "But...what is a Sufi?"

"I'm not sure about all Sufi's...but this Sufi is a mystic who sees the Divine in all Beauty." Ray pointed to the book. "I marked a page for you with my card."

Aroya found the page and read the passage: *"In Beauty is the secret of Divinity."*

The little bell on the door chimed loudly. An older couple entered the shop. They glanced at piles of books stacked high on tables, then approached the counter. "Would you be interested in selling the whole lot?" the man asked.

Aroya didn't want to be in the way. "Goodbye, Ray," he said. "Thanks again, and good luck!"

Aroya and Abbie left the shop while Ray conducted his business.

Walking away, Aroya turned to look one last time. "I'll miss Ray," he said.

They returned to the apartment, and Aroya cuddled up on the couch with his new book.

Abbie opened her laptop. "It's so nice to use my computer again. I guess you and Saint Michael scared all that bad juju out of it."

Aroya lowered his book. "Saint Michael?" he asked.

"Archangel Michael. Some people call him '*Saint* Michael.'"

Aroya turned to the author's picture at the back of the book. "Ray called *this* man a saint," he said. "Abbie, what is Divinity? The word is capitalized."

"It means something divine–something close to God."

"I used to hear about God as a child…but we aren't allowed to say that word in *my* time. Even before the catastrophe, they outlawed that word. But for some reason, we're still allowed to say, 'a god,' or 'gods,' or 'goddess'–just not *'God,'* with a capital 'G.' But then I hear *you* say it all the time–especially when you're excited: *Oh, God! –Goddammit! my God!"* he teased.

"I can't believe a man who once embodied the power of Archangel Michael is asking *me* about Divinity and God!" she joked.

"I suppose I'm just an ignorant vessel," Aroya said, turning a page. He offered another quote: *"When beauty is produced in the heart, then all that breaks the heart vanishes and the whole universe becomes one single vision of the sublimity of God."* Aroya sighed. "That sounds nice, but I'm not sure I understand it." He closed the book.

Something on Abbie's computer excited her. *"Oh, my God. Aroya! Come here, quick!"*

Aroya glanced at Abbie's computer screen. He read the title: *"Lake Merced Sewage Spill Mysteriously Disappears!"*

Abbie played the video: *San Franciscans want to know who to thank for the miraculous clearing of sewage from Lake Merced overnight! Environmentalists are celebrating, while scientists are at a loss for words! The formally clear water of Lake Merced was heavily polluted after the earthquake last month, which caused the wastewater treatment plant to overflow...dumping sewage into the lake and surrounding neighborhoods. But today, you'd never know it! Environmentalists are now hopeful that the local wildlife might make a full recovery.*

Abbie stopped the video, staring at Aroya, dumbfounded. "It worked! Oh my God, I've got chills."

"How interesting," Aroya said. "And I thought it was just for time travel."

Abbie wore a smile stretching from ear to ear. "Maybe there's hope, after all!" She grabbed her coat–reaching into the pocket. "And this time, it was *my* stone!" she said, holding up her crystal stone. "Whoa–I wonder what else it can do?!"

Aroya joined in her enthusiasm. "Maybe we should meditate about it–or pray on it. Which one?"

"Tonight, we'll meditate! Oh my God, I can't wait to tell Millie!" She grabbed her phone to text Millie. There was a knock at the door. "I bet that's Millie," she said.

Millie seemed to have a sixth sense about these things. "Did you guys hear about the lake? There was some kind of miracle last night! They say it's pristine now! Isn't that weird?"

"Yeah, weird," Abbie said facetiously. She smiled, glancing at Aroya–then back at Millie again.

Millie caught on. "This has something to do with you two, doesn't it?"

"Maybe."

"What?!" Millie exclaimed. She sat down at the kitchen table. "Okay–tell me everything."

"It was the stone," Abbie said. "We were just messing around. We didn't know it would actually work!"

"Wow. You guys really are something, aren't you?" Millie responded. "I sure wish I could report this on my show. But then again, I guess nobody would believe me."

"That's for sure," Abbie said.

"It's probably better that we keep a low profile anyway…considering the time travel and all," Aroya added.

"Yeah, I guess you're right," Millie replied, heading out the door. "Now, you two behave yourselves. Or at least, stay out of trouble," she said, playfully wagging her finger.

Abbie closed the door behind Millie. "Tonight, we celebrate!" she announced.

In the evening, they visited Abbie's rooftop garden. "I haven't been up here much…since the Archangel thing happened," Abbie said.

"I know… It still feels kind of weird to me," Aroya said. "I think I died–" he inspected the spot where he collapsed, "right here." He turned to Abbie, smiling. "But then a beautiful Angel came, named Abbie–and she resurrected me."

Aroya was feeling stronger now, and even more amorous. At times, his desire for Abbie was almost more than he could bear.

Abbie perused the garden, selecting a perfect rosebud, just beginning to open. She clipped it, lifting it to her nose, sniffing the perfume. Walking over to Aroya, she held it under his nose, teasing him–moving the rose closer, then farther–then close again. It was apparent her attitude toward him was evolving–from a deep affection to something else.

Later, she prepared her altar–while Aroya read his book on the couch. He was back to reading his romantic poetry again; this time, it was Alfred Noyes.

"Are you ready?" Abbie asked, finally satisfied with the altar.

"I suppose so. What should I do?"

Abbie tossed two cushions on the floor. "Sit here," she said. She turned down the lights and took two matchsticks from the box. Lighting the matches, she held them in front of Aroya. "Where two or more are gathered," she said. She moved the matchsticks together until the flames conjoined–rising higher–then she lit the candle on the altar and settled down on a cushion next to Aroya. She closed her eyes–and Aroya also closed his eyes.

Abbie recited her protection prayer while using her hands to spread energy around her body–from the top of her head to her feet. Then she turned to Aroya, doing the same for him. Finally, she recited the 'Lord's Prayer'–the only prayer she was taught as a child. Then afterward, she composed her own special prayer:

> *"Oh, God, Creator, Source of All…hear these prayers, listen to these prayers, and if it be your will, manifest these prayers. In the name of Jesus, forgive my sins. I am not perfect, but I am always working toward perfection, in your eyes. Tonight, I ask for understanding and guidance, in the best way to use the crystal stone. On behalf of myself, and my dear Aroya, I ask for protection, healing,*

and inspiration. If it be God's will, then let it be done. Amen."

She adjusted her position, turning towards Aroya. He recognized that she was preparing for meditation, and he also turned, facing her.

She said to him, "Before we begin, let's take a moment for purification." Aroya opened his eyes. "Keep your eyes closed," Abbie instructed. "Now...in your mind, see the floor beneath you as green earthen soil–and see the Earth's rainbow colors swirling around your feet. When I say, 'breathe-in'–see the rainbow colors rise up through your body, and at the same time, see the pure light of Heaven, rush down through the top of your head. The colored light from Earth and the white light from Heaven, meet in your heart as you inhale them both, simultaneously. When I say, 'breathe-out'–see your heart as a multifaceted crystal...exploding with rays of light and love, out to the world. Okay, let's do it together–slowly, three times. Ready? Breathe-in from Earth and Heaven," then about 3 seconds later, "breathe-out, light and love–" she said, exhaling. She continued, "Breathe-in...breathe-out. And one last time, breathe-in...breathe-out. How do you feel?" she asked.

"Like an air purifier," Aroya replied.

"Me too," Abbie said, laughing.

Now she took Aroya's hands–holding her palms against his, she rubbed vigorously. Immediately, intense heat filled the center of his palms–his hands buzzed with vibration. While placing her right hand on Aroya's heart–she also placed his right hand on hers. She closed her eyes, lowering her head in silence for a moment. "Let the two flames of our hearts join together as one. Now, follow me on this journey," Abbie instructed. She lifted her head, straightening her spine–then she laid her hands on Aroya's knees.

Imitating her, Aroya also placed his hands on her knees.

"Listen to my breath," Abbie said, "and bring your breath into sync with mine."

They sat quietly–focusing on their breath.

"Now, see the jaguar–a big spotted cat. Watch him turn and walk away. Follow him," she instructed.

Aroya's mind was free and creative, and the image of a jaguar came easily.

"Whatever happens, just go with it–but say nothing until we're done. Just follow the jaguar and see where it leads you. Stay alert and pay attention to detail."

Aroya studied the jaguar–watching and waiting. Then it turned, walking away. He hurried behind it, following closely, while it wound its way through a thick jungle of vegetation. Large tropical leaves slapped Aroya's face as he pressed onward. Then he lost sight of the jaguar. Finding an opening in the trees, he parted the leaves–stepping through. An unusual vibration suddenly filled his body. Then he saw him...not the jaguar, but the feathered man–the Vision Maker.

In a thick Brazilian accent, the Vision Maker spoke to Aroya: *Watch and listen.*

Abbie and Aroya were not aware of each other, but they were both experiencing the same vision at the same time. They saw Lake Merced–clean and clear. The sun shone down on the water, revealing a woman's face on its glassy surface. They heard the woman speak: *And heaven beholds her face within.*

Now the scene changed. They saw San Francisco in 2050–a dark and desperate place, lost in the chaos of maddening destruction. Next, they saw a large bearded man–sitting by the fire of an old open furnace. It was Elijah. He was reciting a poem by Lord Tennyson:

> *"Of old sat Freedom on the heights,*
> *The thunders breaking at her feet:*
> *Above her shook the starry lights:*
> *She heard the torrents meet.*
>
> *There in her place she did rejoice,*
> *Self-gather'd in her prophet-mind,*
> *But fragments of her mighty voice*
> *Came rolling on the wind.*
>
> *Then stept she down thro' town and field*
> *To mingle with the human race,*
> *And part by part to men reveal'd*
> *The fulness of her face–"*

There were tears in Elijah's eyes as he imagined the full face of freedom returning to the world.

Then the scene changed. Now, Abbie and Aroya saw another version of San Francisco–hardly recognizable. It was a bright and bustling modern metropolis, with clean streets and freshly painted houses. Happy people were busy everywhere, creating beauty in their daily lives and helping others to achieve the same.

Abbie and Aroya heard the Vision Maker's voice again: *Let the moving waters of your desire…bring you to your destination.*

Abbie became aware of her surroundings. She opened her eyes, lifting her hands from Aroya's knees. He too, opened his eyes–his cheeks wet with tears.

Aroya breathed a heavy sigh. "Abbie...what was that?" he asked.

"Did you see the Vision Maker with feathers on his head...and the bearded man, reciting a poem?" she asked.

Aroya wiped his eyes. "The bearded man...he was my friend, Elijah." Aroya's face filled with emotion. "He was reciting Lord Tennyson. I used to think it was a poem...but now I think maybe it was a prayer."

"Aroya, are you okay?" Abbie asked.

"I feel warm and vibrating–like my whole body is filled with electricity," he replied.

"Me too. Let's go for a walk to even things out," Abbie suggested.

Walking out to the street, they strolled down the block–still a bit spaced out from their powerful meditation. Homeless people camped out on the sidewalk in front of Ray's bookshop, some smoking crack on the curb. A large woman dropped her pants and defecated right in front of their favorite café.

Abbie and Aroya, still in a very sensitive state, found this harsh reality overwhelming. Turning away, they headed back home.

Taking the elevator to the rooftop–their hearts were consumed by emotion, both good and bad. From their perch atop Abbie's building–they surveyed the city, breathing in the crisp, cool air. Abbie thought of Gina and her unborn baby–and Tulio Guterres. She didn't understand time travel, but she wished that somehow she could travel back and save them both. Heavy clouds pressed down from the sky, blocking out the stars, threatening rain. It was cold outside but somehow refreshing.

"From up here, one would never guess that such ugliness existed down there," Abbie said.

"It was like that in my time, too. That's why the Sky People rarely came down. They preferred their safe and clean fantasy world, up in the sky–while us surface dwellers, scratched in the dirt and ran from the shadows."

"In our meditation, the Vision Maker instructed us to use the stone to change the future. Do you think we can do it?" Abbie asked.

"I think we must," Aroya replied.

The clouds finally burst, tossing sheets of rain onto Abbie's rooftop garden.

"C'mon. Let's go inside and listen to some music," Abbie suggested.

Returning to the apartment, Aroya stuck like a magnet to his spot on the couch. Abbie lit the fireplace, selecting relaxing music to help them wind down.

Reading a Noyes poem about a rose, Aroya's attention turned to the vase on Abbie's altar. Retrieving the rose, he brought it back to the couch with him. While reading, he stroked his cheek with the soft petals–pretending they were Abbie's tender fingertips.

"I'm just gonna take a quick bath," Abbie announced.

Aroya relaxed on the couch, enjoying the music, watching the raindrops scatter across the windowpane. The music's soft drumming reminded him of his dream circle–back at the warehouse in 2050. He detected a wave of feminine perfume drifting in from Abbie's bath, like the scent of flowers on a summer's breeze. For the hundredth time, he let his mind wander back to his dream of kissing her. The sensuous memory quickly carried him off to sleep.

He awoke to the feeling of something brushing against his arm. Opening his eyes, he saw Abbie standing there–her silk robe parted, her bare leg lit by the warm glow of the fire. She studied his face, smiling–then turned, dropping her robe to the floor. It was like the raising of a velvet curtain, presenting him with the grandest show on Earth–two round buttocks, as fair as a full moon–the same as he witnessed during that night at the beach. He held the rose in his hand, gliding it across her skin, tracing her curves–while reciting Noyes: *"How passionately it opens after rain."*

He dropped the rose, planting tender kisses, one after the other, over her skin. Standing behind her, he slowly brushed her hair away–kissing her neck. Then he whispered, "Don't move."

He studied her silhouette against the firelight, removing his clothes. "Come closer to the fire," he whispered.

He guided her to the hearth, where her entire form was illuminated in the flame's flickering glow. Her skin was smooth, and her curves so perfect–that Canova's Cupid might have abandoned his fair Psyche in favor of this sumptuous beauty.

Abbie stood perfectly still–her eyes remained shut, and her breath quickened.

Aroya moved to her front. Before this moment, lovemaking was only a theme in poems...poems recited so many times that he knew them all by heart. Now, he followed their enticing imaginations–as if they were sacred instructions, annotated in detail, and written solely for this occasion.

"I want to look at you…just for a moment," he said softly.

Stepping to her side, he stood silently–surveying her exquisite form by the firelight.

Finally, moved by emotion, he confessed, "I've never gazed upon a woman's body. I could never have imagined such beauty. You're like the goddess of a poem…or a lavish buffet laid out perfectly, from head to toe. I hardly know where to begin."

Abbie observed Aroya, lost in his rapture, taking in her every detail. His eyes were tender and moist–as if he were viewing the most exquisite masterpiece. She never realized how beautiful she was…until she witnessed it through his eyes. Watching him, watching her–excited her. Before they even touched, their breath found sync.

Aroya stepped closer, causing Abbie's heart to flutter. From the very beginning, he was a mystery–and now, each moment forward, filled her with that same sense of mystery.

He placed a tender kiss on Abbie's forehead. "I feel as though I'm about to embark on a wondrous adventure," he said. "Abbie, may I begin?"

"Yes," she whispered.

Aroya stroked Abbie's hair, as though it were a silken ribbon. His finger followed it down, and he brushed it back, revealing her bare shoulder.

Abbie studied his face, hoping to discover a subtle expression that might divulge the extent of his pleasure.

"Close your eyes," Aroya whispered.

He tenderly traced the outline of Abbie's lips with his finger. Then he spotted her ear lobe peeking out between two strands of hair. Even this, so small a thing, captured his imagination. He brushed her hair aside and tasted her ear lobe–holding it between his lips, savoring its sweetness. Catching her musky scent, he followed it down to her neck, nestling his nose in her nape–breathing in the natural perfume of her warm body. Now, more than ever, he needed to kiss her. He studied her face: her eyes closed, still holding patiently in a state of glorious anticipation. Lifting Abbie's chin with one finger, he paused for a moment to remember how she brushed her lips against his, that night on the beach. Now it was his turn. He touched his lips to her mouth, ever-so-slightly–periodically surrendering a tender little kiss.

Outwardly, Abbie remained still–but inwardly, waves of sensation engulfed her. Aroya's breath warmed her mouth–and her lips fell open. He moistened them with his tongue–then kissed her deeply and passionately.

The room fell away, and images from his dream flashed in his mind. He wanted to caress her and bring her tightly against him, but he knew that once he did–things would move quickly toward an end. Instead, he pulled away–forcing a pause–allowing Abbie to finally catch her breath.

Beholding her breasts, now golden in the fire's glow, he watched them rising and falling with each breath. He took them in his hand, tasting them and caressing them–as though they were the sweetest and rarest of all delicacies. The sensation was beyond imagination, and although he tried to compare them to luscious fruit, he once read about in a poem–he knew they were beyond compare to even the most beautiful of poems.

Abbie's knees were growing weak, and she wondered how long she could remain standing. Aroya sat on the stone hearth. Using one finger, he traced her curves–marveling at their grace. Blowing his warm breath over her belly–he slipped his hands between her thighs. "Abbie…open your legs for me," he said.

Lost in sensation, Abbie could barely move–but she managed to spread her legs just a little. Aroya held her thighs apart, studying her secret flower–imagining the moist lips to be velvety petals of a rose. He stroked them–and Abbie's legs trembled. Her scent beckoned to him–and again, he recalled the poem by Noyes–reciting it while parting her perfumed petals:

> *"See the imploring petals, how they part*
> *And utterly lay bare*
> *The perishing treasures of that piteous heart*
> *In wild surrender there."*

Abbie released a breathy moan.

Amazed by the feminine nectar wetting his fingers–Aroya savored it like sweet juice from a ripened peach. The lush garden between Abbie's thighs had never been written about in any way–that truly described its actual splendor.

Aroya's enthusiastic escapade was almost more than Abbie could bear. She bent her knees, cradling his head in her hands, pleading, "Lay me down. Please lay me down."

Aroya guided her down to the silky Persian rug, setting her hips gently over a cushion.

"I'm ready," she said, between quick breaths. "Take me, take me now."

Aroya opened Abbie's legs, easing himself inside.

She gasped, then began moving rhythmically–taking him in at her own speed and depth.

Aroya moved with her, watching her face while she moaned with pleasure.

She wrapped her legs around his back as he held her hips with his strong hands, venturing deeper. Ever since the *processing*, Aroya's unusually large erection had been a challenge. He studied Abbie's face for feedback, concerned that he might hurt her.

Abbie sensed his hesitancy. "It's okay," she whispered.

Finding their rhythm, they moved together–gasping and moaning with pleasure. Abbie rarely orgasmed this way–but this time was different; Aroya filled her so completely that every pleasurable part of her body was responding.

The momentum grew–their quick breaths rising and falling, in unison. This was Aroya's first–and it was Abbie's best. Approaching climax–their eyes locked...joining in that sacred space reserved only for the most fortunate of lovers. Overwhelmed by the intense intimacy–hot tears fell from Aroya's eyes, landing on Abbie's fair breasts. They grasped each other, caught up in the desire to unite wholly under one skin–sailing into an undulating climax that seemed never-ending.

Aroya settled down onto Abbie's wet body. Then, worried he might be too heavy, he lifted his weight–but Abbie stopped him, saying, "No–stay."

Aroya relaxed. He didn't want to leave just yet–
imagining he might, somehow, stay inside her forever.
Spent and satisfied…they surrendered to sleep.

12– THE WISH LIST

2019

San Francisco

Timeline 1.0

While at the café the next day, Aroya reflected on his good fortune; to have been given the stone, to have met Abbie, and to have had his human-ness restored.

"For the first time, since the catastrophe, I'm beginning to remember what happiness feels like," he confessed to Abbie. "It's like I've been given a second chance."

"Me too," Abbie said.

Aroya peered out the window. Now drenched in urine and littered with used needles–the bookshop storefront was surely succumbing to the fall. "The problem with time travel is we know what's coming,"

Aroya said. "We can already see the clues all around us."

"I know," Abbie agreed. "In the streets, at the hospital, in the government–it's everywhere. And people just go about their lives, oblivious to it all…like those nurses at the hospital who joked and carried on, while an endless train of patients rolled past them in body bags."

"I guess all we can do is focus on the good things," Aroya said. "There's still so much good left in the world."

"What about the catastrophe? Did Dr. Biegel say we had 11 years?" Abbie asked.

"That's right. It happens in 2030."

"11 years isn't much time."

"Actually, things get a lot worse, even before that happens." Aroya's mood shifted. "Dr. Biegel's, *prelude to a fall*, probably began in 2025. I was still just a boy, but I remember the hunger and the suffering."

"Did anyone see it coming?"

"Probably. There were plenty of signs…just like there are now. Some people just don't understand until they've reached the end. But it's not the end yet. So let's enjoy the beauty while we still can."

Abbie sighed. "I understand your appreciation for beauty–and why you prefer to immerse yourself in it. I think beauty feeds our soul, and we need that kind of nourishment–especially right now. But if we turn away from the ugliness, aren't we just as bad as those people who joke and carry on while everything crumbles around them?"

"Maybe," Aroya replied. "That Sufi book says *some people look for a beautiful place, while others make a place beautiful.* I guess I'm the kind who looks for beauty."

"But what if, instead, we could make a place beautiful?"

Coming from such a hopeless time, Aroya wasn't used to thinking in those terms.

"I can see how you're able to do that...especially in your home," he said. "Out on the street, there's filthy concrete–a putrid by-product of human suffering. And then above that, there's nothing but tall buildings made of glass and stone. But inside your little home, and even on the rooftop, you make things beautiful." He smiled. "Who would ever guess that high above all the dirt and stench–are those beautiful roses."

"I guess that's just how I cope. Maybe I use beauty like a bandage," Abbie said. "The only problem is, the wound inside continues to fester. I wish I could heal it instead of camouflaging it."

"Remember the lake?" Aroya asked, feeling a sudden spark of inspiration. "We *changed* that lake, Abbie."

Abbie considered what Aroya was implying. "Do you think it's also possible to change the future with the stone?"

"I don't know. But maybe it's worth a try."

"God. I wouldn't even know where to begin," Abbie replied.

"It all begins with a desire. What do you desire, Abbie?"

"Oh my God...that's a long list!"

"C'mon. Let's go upstairs and see if we can work it out on paper."

They sat at the kitchen table with a legal pad and a pen. Aroya held the pen.

"So, what *is* it–that you desire?" he asked.

"But this is different because this depends on people. There needs to be a change, but first, there needs to be awareness. The thing that confused me most at the hospital was how unaware people were."

Aroya began writing. "Then let's begin at the hospital. What do you want those people to be aware of?"

"That those patients, in those beds, and in those body bags, are somebody's mother–father–sister brother–or child…and they are *loved* by somebody. I'm not sure if it's right to change a person without their consent, but maybe we could influence their awareness somehow."

"What do you think happened that made them so unaware?"

"I think it happened gradually. People used to be different in my grandparents' time. Morality shifted, and certain things that used to be absolutely unacceptable–slowly became absolutely acceptable."

"How did that happen?"

"Maybe popular culture did it? Like our choices in music…movies…TV…. "

"That's the first thing I noticed about your apartment when I arrived. You didn't have a TV. When I was a child in 2019, everyone had a TV."

"I could see the ugliness creeping in on TV, and it made me feel sick. It's weird that nobody notices…just like the body bags."

"What if it was different? What would *make* people more aware?"

"I don't know... Maybe if certain influences just stopped for a while? If people got a break from it all, maybe it would free their minds."

"Is that your desire?"

"No. Because *how* that happens might not be very desirable."

"You're right about that. The catastrophe accomplished all those things...except it wasn't for just a little while."

Abbie considered the question more deeply. "I think there needs to be something more. Things have to come to light–but maybe in a shocking way. I think people need to be *jolted* out of their trance."

Aroya already had a long list of things written down. He held the pad up, reading it aloud: "Number 1–the problems of the world won't change unless people change; number 2–the change needs to be in their awareness; number 3–their awareness won't change because of some sort of programming from TV, movies, news, popular music–"

Abbie interrupted, "The schools too, and all the big institutions...crimes against humanity...the hospitals and medicine...and corporations–well, the corrupt and perverted ones, anyway."

Aroya continued, "Okay. And the schools, and other corrupt and perverted people and institutions; and number 4–all this corruption and crime needs to come to light, to shock people out of their trance. Is that all?"

"No. Balance and unity need to be restored," she said. Laying her head back, she stared up at the ceiling. "What if, one day, all the people of the world finally knew the truth?" She paused again to think. "What if, because of this new awareness, humanity was finally free everywhere–and nations actually prospered, without the unseen hand of control?" Abbie stopped. She turned to Aroya. "So tell me...what sort of 'lady' is this, that we desire?"

"I don't know. But whoever she is, she sounds very complicated."

"You're right. I wish there was somebody..." She sat straight up. "Why didn't we think of that *before?!*"

"What?"

"The stones–the dreams–the visions–"

"–The feathered man," Aroya replied.

"Yes! The Vision Maker!"

13– GOING HOME

2019

San Francisco

Timeline 1.0

Abbie and Aroya rode on the BART train on their way to see the Vision Maker. An announcement over the intercom stated: *this train will not be off-boarding at 24th and Mission, due to police action in the area. Passengers may transfer to MUNI at Glen Park Station.*

"That's okay," remarked Abbie. We've got 2 hours. We'll just hop on the 'J' train at Glen Park."

At Glen Park Station, they caught the 'J' train. Aroya gazed out the window, watching the scenery pass…then something caught his eye.

"I know this place," he said. "Abbie, can we get off here?"

"Sure. We've got time."

The train stopped in front of a row of brightly painted Victorian houses. A few people strolled by– some with children, others with dogs. Aroya was like a bloodhound who caught the scent of something exciting. Abbie followed his lead until he came to a sudden stop. Zeroing in on one particular house, he watched a woman watering her flowers. A small boy on the steps played with his toy cars.

"What's going on?" Abbie asked.

"That's my mother," he said. Then he pointed to the little boy. "And that's me."

"Whoa. This is weird. What're you gonna do?"

"I don't know."

The woman noticed Aroya staring and took the boy inside.

"What would I even say? Should I tell her to leave the city, to move somewhere safer?"

"Where would be safer?"

"Somewhere without earthquakes," Aroya said, reflecting on sad memories. "My mother was in the basement when the house fell." He pointed to the top story window. "I was in my bedroom, up there. I just turned 17."

Abbie could almost see Aroya at 17, looking down from the upstairs window.

"After the shaking stopped, I crawled out from the rubble...but I couldn't find my mom anywhere. It was just me and her. My father got a job in another state, and she didn't want to leave–so eventually, he just left without us." Aroya took a breath, recalling the trauma. "For days, I never stopped searching for her...my hands got all bloody and infected–digging through the splintered wood and broken glass. I never found her."

"You had to travel back in time to find her. Maybe you should take a chance now."

"Yeah, maybe I should. Do you mind waiting? I need to do this alone."

"Sure, I'll wait. I'll be at the coffee shop over there when you're done." She pointed down the road.

"Okay. I won't be long."

Aroya approached the house while Abbie went to the coffee shop, glancing back every so often.

He rang the doorbell and could hear the family dog, Millie, barking in the backyard.

26-year-old Catherine Wallace cracked the door open. "Yes? Can I help you?"

"Good afternoon," Aroya said, noticing his own voice crack. "Mrs. Wallace? Catherine Wallace?" he asked, knowing full well who she was.

"Yes. That's me," she answered with hesitancy.

"I'm sorry to disturb you. I'm an old friend of the family, and I just wanted to–"

"What's your name?" she interrupted.

The little boy poked his head out.

"Aroya," he replied.

"You know my son?" Mrs. Wallace asked, confused.

"I know your whole family: your husband, Brady; your sister, Peggy; her children, Michael and Shannon; your brother, Bobby; my Grampa–I mean your father, Joseph. And even your best friend, Mary Parker."

"I don't understand. How could you know all of them, but I don't know you?"

"We've lost touch over the years. But when I was a boy, I used to spend time at this house…with your family."

Mrs. Wallace tilted her head, examining Aroya's face.

"When you were a boy? That must've been when my parents lived here."

"Oh…maybe you're right. I remember there was a picture on the piano of Gramma and Grampa. And there was a big painting over the fireplace, of Yosemite…and upstairs in the hallway; there was a whole wall dedicated to the family pets."

Mrs. Wallace's demeanor shifted. "Who are you?" she asked.

"I have a message for you."

"Okay. Then what is it?"

Aroya took a deep breath. "Please, Mrs. Wallace, can you come out here and talk with me? It's a long story."

"Okay. But give me a minute." She closed the door.

Aroya sat on the steps, waiting. The door opened, and Mrs. Wallace stepped out with her dog on a leash and the little boy in tow. The boy played shy, tugging on his mom's jeans. When Millie the dog got a whiff of Aroya, she went nuts–pulling on her leash and whining.

Mrs. Wallace scolded the dog. "Millie, get back! Lay down!" Millie laid next to Aroya, licking his hand incessantly.

Mrs. Wallace found the dog's behavior curious. "I'm sorry. She's not usually like this…especially with strangers."

"My dog really likes you," the little boy said, giggling.

"I really like her too," Aroya replied.

"You said you have a message for me?" Mrs. Wallace reminded him.

"Yes, I do," Aroya said, hesitant, searching for the right words. "Remember what Grampa Joe used to say about Angels?"

"Hey! You know my Grampa?" the little boy interrupted.

Mrs. Wallace pulled the boy back. "Yeah, I remember what he used to say. He used to say, *always be kind to strangers because you never know when one might be an Angel–*" smiling, she continued, *"bringing you a message."*

Aroya smiled back, nodding.

"Are you an Angel?" she asked.

"Let's just say I'm acquainted with one," he replied.

Mrs. Wallace liked this unusual man, but she was still confused. "I came out here to talk with you because your face seems familiar. In fact, you're the *spitting image* of my brother *Bobby*. But what's your message?"

Aroya took a deep breath. "Please, listen carefully. There will be a time soon–when Mr. Wallace gets a job offer in another state–"

"He just *got* a job offer…in *Omaha,"* she interrupted.

Aroya nodded. "I know you don't want to leave your family…and right now, you're trying to decide what to do. My message is, please consider going to Omaha with your husband. If it's nice there, maybe your family will follow you."

"Follow me to Omaha? What for? Besides, Peggy's kids are all in school now–and Bobby would never leave San Francisco. And my father…." Mrs. Wallace took a closer look at Aroya's face. "Why do you keep calling my father *Grampa?*" She paused to calculate Aroya's age. "Forgive me if I'm wrong, but I'm guessing you're about ten years older than me. I was born when my father was only 23 years old–so I'm sure that's impossible."

"Where I come from, time is different," Aroya replied.

"Oh yeah, I forgot...*Angel time,*" she said, amused by his story. "Ya know...nobody knows about Brady getting that job offer but me. We haven't told anybody–not a soul." She took a moment to formulate her next question. "I'm trying to think of something else that nobody else would know...except maybe an Angel."

Aroya searched his memories, too–for something that would convince her to listen to him. Then he looked at the little boy and playfully began singing: "*I went to the animal fair, the birds and the bees were there–a big baboon, by the light of the moon, was combing his auburn hair. The–*"

Little boy Aroya joined in: "*The monkey he got drunk and fell on the elephant's trunk. The–*"

Now, Mrs. Wallace joined in: "*The Elephant sneezed–and fell to his knees–and what became of the monk, the monk–what became of the monk?!*"

They all laughed.

"Well, there are only two other people in my life who would know that song–and that would be my dad and my little boy," Mrs. Wallace said.

"Do you trust me now?" Aroya asked.

"I think so."

"Good. Now, I'm going to tell you about something that's going to happen in the future."

Both Mrs. Wallace and the boy were seriously listening now.

"It won't happen for many years, but if you don't leave now, your life will become much more difficult, with each passing year...until it happens."

"Until what happens?" Mrs. Wallace asked, alarmed.

"There will be an earthquake. And not just one, but many. They will go on for years, and this whole city will fall to the ground. It won't just happen in San Francisco–it will happen all over the world–all at the same time. But the cities on the coast will get the worst of it."

"When will this happen?" Mrs. Wallace inquired.

"In the year 2030."

She relaxed–letting out a sigh of relief. "Well...I guess we have some time, then," she said.

"Yes, there's still time. But before that happens, things will get worse in many other ways. If you stay here, alone–you won't be able to get out later...because you won't have enough money."

Mrs. Wallace grew quiet, seriously considering Aroya's prediction.

"It's a big decision," Aroya said. Then, he remembered what Abbie would say: "Maybe you should pray on it."

Mrs. Wallace smiled, a little embarrassed. "I haven't prayed in years," she said.

"But you used to pray?" he asked.

"My mother wasn't a big fan of the church, so there wasn't much religion in our house...but my father used to pray with me at bedtime–every night, dutifully."

"Do you remember how to pray?" Aroya asked.

Mrs. Wallace closed her eyes for a moment. "Yes. I can still hear the words," she replied.

Aroya stood up. "I think I'd better go now."

Mrs. Wallace also stood. "What did you say your name was again?"

"Well...some people call me Roy," he said.

She studied his face again. "I know this is weird, but I feel like I've known you forever. Can I give you a little hug?"

Aroya's heart melted. He never thought he'd ever feel his mother's arms around him again.

Mrs. Wallace gave him a hug. Smiling, she said, "Thanks, Angel Roy."

The little boy tugged on his mother's jeans, whispering loudly, "But Mom–he can't be an *Angel*...'cause he doesn't have any *wings!*"

"How do you know?" Aroya teased. "Maybe they're under my jacket." They both giggled.

Waving goodbye, Aroya headed toward the coffee shop where Abbie waited.

14– THE MISSION

2019

San Francisco

Timeline 1.0

They arrived at Carlos' house for their appointment with the Vision Maker, and Carlos welcomed them inside.

"Boa tarde!" Carlos said, kissing Abbie on the cheek and shaking Aroya's hand. "The Vision Maker is in meditation, so we need to be quiet. Follow me," he said. Carlos led Abbie and Aroya into a bright room. "Please sit. Would you like some coffee?"

"No, thank you," Abbie said, surveying the room. There was a picture of Jesus on the wall.

Carlos noticed her curiosity about the picture. "You like my picture?" he asked.

"Yes. But I'm surprised to see a picture of Jesus here."

Carlos chuckled. "Why wouldn't Jesus be here?"

"I didn't mean it like that–it's just that–" Abbie hesitated, a little embarrassed about how that came out.

The Vision Maker entered the room. "Hello," he said, in his thick Brazilian accent. Turning to Aroya, he presented his hands. Aroya offered his own hands. The Vision Maker took them, closing his eyes, reciting a prayer in his tribal language.

Carlos bowed his head, noticeably moved by the prayer.

The Vision Maker finished–sitting across from Abbie and Aroya, studying them, in turn.

Carlos whispered to the Vision Maker, and they both laughed. "Jesus!" the Vision Maker stated, pointing to the picture. Then he turned to Carlos, saying, "Por favor explique."

"He wants me to explain something," Carlos said. "I will translate." The Vision Maker spoke to Carlos, and Carlos translated. "In the beginning, the Creator gave us the force of the sun, the water, the fire, the earth–and all the animals. Later, Jesus came–and he spoke about the force of heaven. We had our own ideas about that, but we also liked his ideas. He said God, the Creator, lived in the heart of all men–he is as close to us as our heartbeat."

The Vision Maker spoke again. "Agora, você compreende porque você vê Jesus, e também Mãe de Deus, em sua visão?"

Carlos translated, "Now, do you understand why you saw Jesus, and Mother of God, in your vision?"

"I think so," Abbie replied.

"Força da terra e do céu juntos–em harmonia," the Vision Maker said.

Carlos translated, "The force of earth and heaven together–in harmony." He continued, "We mix the best of both traditions. It's okay." He smiled at Abbie, looking for understanding.

Abbie nodded. There was something about the idea that felt satisfying.

Then the Vision Maker's demeanor changed, and his eyes pooled with emotion. He addressed Aroya. "Amigo do futuro, obrigado, obrigado. Ela é uma mulher com um coração gentil, mas é forte. Juntos vocês restaurarão o futuro para os filhos de todos os humanos."

Aroya could already hear the translation in his head. "Yes. I understand," he replied.

"What did he say?" Abbie asked.

Carlos translated for Abbie. "He said, 'Friend from the future, thank you.' Then about you, Abbie–he said, 'your heart is gentle, but you are strong.' He said, 'together you will restore the future for the children of all humans.'"

"That's why we're here," she said. "We've come to ask–"

"We know why you are here," Carlos interrupted. "We have been waiting for you."

Abbie noticed a package on the floor near the wall. The name Mr. Guterres was written on it. She figured 'Guterres' must be a common Brazilian name, but it still brought to mind Tulio Guterres from the hospital.

"We saw you in a vision," Carlos said. "We saw you with my brother Tulio when he transitioned." Abbie's mind raced back to that day. Filled with emotion, she struggled to hold back tears.

"We saw you fighting for Tulio. You are a good woman...good and strong," Carlos continued.

Abbie listened–silent...tears streaming down her cheeks.

The Vision Maker spoke again. "Vimos o futuro. Fizemos um plano para restaurar o futuro. Toda a nossa tribo está em ritual - em meditação para ajudar."

Tears welled up in Carlos' eyes. He translated, "We saw the future, and we made a plan. All of our tribe is in ritual–sitting in meditation to help."

"But we don't know what to do. The problem is so big," Abbie said.

"And so complicated," Aroya added.

The Vision Maker spoke to Carlos. "Explique para eles."

Carlos listened to the Vision Maker intently–puffing on his pipe. Then he translated: "Listen well. Do what you did before, and it will happen. And after...you will need to go to that time, to confirm the change. That is step number 1. You will see a person you never met, but you will know this person very well. You will learn about music and prayer. This brings step number 2. You will need another confirmation to make the change *real* in your mind. But it is not finished yet. Next, you need to return to the year 2019 and complete your mission–to make the new future solid like stone. Remember...you need to come back. If you are successful, the future will look wonderful. Maybe, you will want to stay–but you cannot. If you don't come back, then our world is lost for a thousand years. We depend on you to bring the two worlds together: this world and the new future. You have been specially chosen–and when you return, you must dedicate your life to fulfilling your mission."

"What is our mission?" Abbie asked.

"Your mission is to connect others to the vision of our new future. The more connections you make, the more the two worlds will pull together, to become more solid."

The Vision Maker whispered something more to Carlos and chuckled. Carlos continued, "The Vision Maker said, you are preparing for a sacred voyage. We will all be in ritual–you and us, together. During ritual, there is no sex. We need to focus all our energy on connecting to God–and on the sacred voyage. Our tribe in Brazil will separate the men from the women, to help them stay focused. They will remain in ritual for three months. Because you cannot separate on your mission, you must be very strong. You must stay focused. Do you understand?"

"Yes. We understand," Abbie and Aroya replied.

"After you return...you can enjoy each other," Carlos said, smiling.

The Vision Maker approached Abbie and Aroya. He placed a necklace of red seeds around their necks, then bowing his head, he prayed in his tribal language. There was so much emotion in his words that the literal meaning did not matter–the energy spoke directly to their hearts, and all were moved to tears.

"Now, the Vision Maker is finished with his work here," Carlos said. "He will return to Brazil tomorrow to lead our tribe in ritual. Wait three days, then begin your voyage." Carlos stood up. "Okay. It is done," he said.

Abbie and Aroya said goodbye to the Vision Maker. He took their hands, offering them blessings.

Carlos gathered the package from the floor and walked them to the door. He handed the package to Abbie. "This is for you. Open it when you return." Shaking Aroya's hand and giving Abbie a kiss on the cheek, Carlos said, "Tchau meus amigos. Boa viagem."

Abbie and Aroya returned to the apartment. The day had been unusually warm, and the apartment needed airing out.

Abbie opened the patio door and switched on the air purifier. "It's kind of stuffy in here," she said. Hauling a pillow and blanket from the closet, she set them on the couch.

Aroya walked over to the altar, picking up the picture of Archangel Michael. "My mom thought I was an Angel today...but little 6-year-old Aroya doubted her."

"Why did he doubt her?" Abbie asked.

Aroya smiled, pointing to his back. "Because–no wings."

"Here we go again with the wings," Abbie joked. She checked her cell phone. "I got a text from Markus. He's inviting us for dinner tomorrow at his place."

Aroya yawned. "I'm glad it's not tonight because I'm tired."

"Yeah, me too," Abbie said. She pointed to the couch. "I guess it's just books and bed for us tonight."

"Books and *couch* for me."

Abbie kissed Aroya on the head. "Our sacrifices now will reap benefits later."

"If we don't sacrifice now, there might not *be* a later," Aroya responded.

"At least we don't have to wait three months–like the Vision Maker's tribe."

"Abbie…" Aroya said, "I waited 37 years for you. I think I can manage a few more days."

Abbie smiled. "Do you need anything before I get into the bath?"

"No. I'm fine."

"Yes, you *are,*" Abbie joked.

While Abbie bathed, Aroya enjoyed the fragrance of her soaps and lotions, filling the apartment with flowery perfume. He switched off the light and closed his eyes, reimagining his very first dream with Abbie…the one that ultimately saved his life. Soon, he drifted off to sleep.

Abbie finished her bath and donned her silky robe. Noticing Aroya fast asleep on the couch, she quietly turned off the air purifier. Aroya cracked an eye open, watching her silhouette against the pale blue patio light.

Shutting the door, she heard Aroya reciting:

> *"She walks in beauty, like the night*
> *Of cloudless climes and starry skies;*
> *And all that's best of dark and bright*
> *Meet in her aspect and her eyes."*

"Lord Byron, again," Aroya added.

Abbie sat down next to Aroya. "Thank you, Lord Byron," she said, "and thank you, Aroya."

"Good night, my beauty," Aroya sighed.

"Good night, my mysterious prince," Abbie replied.

She left Aroya's side to sleep alone in her big empty bed. Once a place of calm refuge, it was now a place of sweet torment. She knew she must quiet her sensuous impulses, but with Aroya in the next room and the memory of their lovemaking so fresh–she lacked the discipline to silence her mind. She drifted off to sleep, surrendering to the steamy memories of their first carnal encounter.

In the morning, when Abbie shuffled into the kitchen, she found Aroya reading a book and sipping tea at the kitchen table.

"Good morning. Did you sleep well?" Aroya inquired with a mischievous grin.

Abbie was still half asleep and kind of grumpy after her restless night of sacrifice. "No. I did *not* sleep well. The truth is, I spent the whole night entertaining fantasies about seducing you."

Aroya laughed. "Me too. Controlling the mind is a major challenge, isn't it? Just like wild horses."

"Wild horses?" Abbie inquired.

Aroya turned a page in his book. "Listen to this: *The mind of the average person may be pictured as an unruly horse that jumps and kicks and throws anyone that tries to ride it... The mind is just like a wild horse, and the will is the only thing which can catch it.*"

"How about yogurt and fruit for breakfast?" Abbie asked. "I'm not really up to cooking."

"Sure," Aroya replied, turning another page. "I really miss the bookshop...and my friend, Ray."

Abbie sat down, arranging two bowls of yogurt with fruit on the table. She sipped at her tea, then remarked,

"I think I've heard that somewhere before–about the wild horses. I thought it was about emotions, but I guess the mind is the same thing." She searched her memory. "Emotions are like a wild horse, beautiful and magnificent. But you can't accomplish much with a wild horse because it carries you off in all directions. To accomplish anything, you must train the horse. In other words...to accomplish anything, you must master your emotions."

"That's true," Aroya said, nodding. He turned another page. "I found something else in here...about your prayer." He located the page: *"The soul of man is the spark of God. Though this spark is limited on the earth, still God is all-powerful; and by teaching the prayer 'Thy kingdom come, Thy will be done on earth as it is in heaven,' the Master has given a key to every soul who repeats this prayer; a key to open that door behind which is the secret of that almighty power and perfect wisdom which raises the soul above all limitations. "*

"Whoa. That gave me chills," she said. "He's a Sufi? I always thought the *Lord's Prayer* was a Catholic prayer."

Aroya put his book down. "You know...my mother said she hadn't prayed since she was a child. She said her mother wasn't a big fan of the church."

"It was like that in my house too, because of my father–but my mom taught me to pray. Personally, I never liked the rigid dogma of churches, and I never thought we needed a priest to intercede for us. I guess my connection has always been pretty direct, even as a child."

"I have vague memories about Jesus," Aroya said, "but that's another name they outlawed in my time. Did your mother teach you that Jesus prayer you always recite?"

"The protection prayer? No, she didn't. Actually, an unusual old man taught me that prayer. He was a retired Catholic priest, but he spent years following a spiritual teacher around in India. I was just a teenager at the time, and I saw horrible demonic faces every time I tried to meditate. I'm told I have a 'gift' for seeing demons...but I'm not sure I'd call it a gift! Anyway, that old priest gave me the protection prayer."

"What about the other prayers?"

"I picked them up as I needed them, from other places. Some of them are considered Catholic, like the Archangel prayers. Even though I don't care for the Catholic church, those prayers go *way* back. They have very little to do with the current church...and they're very powerful."

"Yes...apparently," Aroya agreed.

"Especially when *you* say them," Abbie teased.

"Maybe I can learn to tone it down a notch," he said.

"Yes. Just a notch," Abbie joked, smiling.

15– QUANTUM PHYSICS

2019

San Francisco

Timeline 1.0

In the evening, Markus hosted Abbie and Aroya for dinner. After finishing their meal, they moved into the living room for tea.

"The salmon tasted just like fresh catch!" Abbie said, licking her lips.

"It did! I really enjoyed it!" Aroya agreed.

"Do they still have salmon in your time?" Markus asked.

"I don't know, but we certainly don't have it in zone 9. We mostly have surf fish–or crabs, from under the bridge."

"Aha! That would be...the Golden Gate Bridge?" Markus asked.

"Yes. Well, what's left of it."

"So, I guess the bridge didn't make it then. Ah, that's too bad." Changing the subject, Markus said, "I hope you don't mind that it was just *us* tonight. I was hoping we could talk more about time travel, and I thought our conversation might be a little too *out there* for virgin ears."

"What would you like to know about time travel?" Abbie asked.

"Well, I don't know. Maybe how it works?" Markus inquired.

"Honestly, we're not sure how it works. We just use the stone," Abbie replied.

"A stone, you say? What do you do with it?" Markus asked.

Abbie turned to Aroya, hoping he would explain.

"It involves two things–" Aroya said, "your desire, and the fulfillment of that desire. You hold the stone in your hand and focus on your desire. Then you focus on the fulfillment of that desire, while dropping the stone from one hand to the other."

"That's it? No fancy Tesla machine or DeLorean DMC-12?" Markus asked, confused.

"I don't anything know about those things. All we use is the stone," Aroya replied.

"What *kind* of stone?" Markus asked.

Abbie reached into her pocket, pulling out her crystal stone. "It's called labradorite…it's some kind of crystal, only it's dark–with swirling colors." She handed the stone to Markus. "Here, have a look."

Markus examined the stone. "Hmm…interesting rock. Maybe it's the method."

"Maybe. But it can do more than just time travel," she said, with a twinkle in her eye. "Remember the reports about how Lake Merced miraculously turned pristine overnight?"

Markus nodded, then his jaw dropped. "Oh, no...don't tell me. You did that?!"

"Us and Lord Byron," Abbie said, smiling at Aroya.

"Lord Byron? What's he got to do with it?" Markus asked.

"We used a poem to inspire us. We stated our desire–then we dropped the stone while saying it was–I mean *'she'* was–clean and clear," Abbie said.

Aroya recited the poem: *"Transparent with the sun therein, When waves no murmur dare to make, And heaven beholds her face within."*

"A time-traveling trans-human who recites poetry! Now I've seen everything!" Markus said, flabbergasted.

"Uh...I'm no longer a trans-human," Aroya said, correcting him.

"I'm sorry," Markus said, apologizing. "Yes, of course. And how are things going with your health? You look great! How is your body temperature and everything else?"

"Everything seems pretty normal now–in perfect working order, actually." Abbie blushed while Aroya continued, "I've even begun shaving again."

"Really? That's amazing!" Markus replied.

"Now I know what happened to my razor," Abbie joked.

"Sorry. I meant to tell you," Aroya said, feigning guilt.

Markus rolled the stone around in his hand, taking a closer look at it. "It's very pretty–all the colors...but something tells me it's not the rock." Then he stared up at the ceiling, thinking. "Tell me...how did you learn to use it," he inquired.

Abbie and Aroya smiled.

"It was in a dream," Aroya said. "A man with feathers on his head told me I should let my desire be like a *wave* of water...then, while I release the stone, he said I should let it flow into the solid form of my goal."

"Aha! A *wave!* That's quantum physics!" Markus exclaimed.

"Quantum physics?" Abbie asked.

"Yes. Waves and particles. In your case, the desire would be the *wave*...the swirling electrons of uncertainty, representing all possibilities. And then your goal would be like the particle...a particular probability, with enough weight to achieve a solid state, or at least, appearing to. I'm not a physicist, so I may have a few details wrong–but that's how it was explained to me."

"I guess that's possible," Abbie said, shrugging.

"Or *probable*...with enough weight," Markus replied. Turning to Aroya, he held up the stone. "How did you get this stone?" he asked.

"That's Abbie's stone. You'll have to ask her," Aroya said.

"You *both* have a stone?" Markus asked, surprised.

"Yeah." Aroya dug into his pocket and pulled out his stone.

"Aroya, you go first," Markus prodded.

"A tall man, with light blue eyes and white hair, came a very long way one night–to trade it for a few lines of poetry...in the year 2050, of course."

"Mine fell out of a juggler's hat in the Haight," Abbie said, with a giggle.

"I get the feeling that this phenomenon…is peculiar to just the two of you," Markus said, perplexed.

"I think you're right, and honestly, I still don't understand it myself," Abbie said.

"Incredible," Markus replied, "…and yet, Aroya is here, back from the year 2050…and he was once a silvery trans-human–a condition apparently achieved by methods currently unknown to science."

"That sounds about right…" Aroya agreed, "but again, I might add that methods currently unknown to science also *reversed* the process."

"Yes, thank God," Markus said. "But I *did* try my best," he added–a bit embarrassed that his treatment didn't work.

Abbie sympathized with Markus. "We're grateful for your help, but I think we can all agree that *trans-humanism* is kind of outside your specialty."

"Yes, that's true," Markus replied. Then, leaning forward, he showed a revived interest. "So tell me…when you returned from 2050, this *last* time–did you notice anything different? Did something seem to change while you were gone…something that shouldn't have changed?"

Abbie and Aroya shook their heads…then Abbie gasped, "Oh, yes! There *was* something! *My teakettle!* I had a whistling teakettle–you know, the kind with the little bird on the spout? When we got back, the bird was gone, and the whole teakettle was different!"

"We thought someone was playing a trick," Aroya added.

Markus smiled, recognizing the strange phenomenon. "Some people call it the *Mandela* effect," he said. "It kind of follows another theory about timelines. The theory suggests that if we time travel, we can never truly return to the same timeline that we left. Things may *seem* exactly the same–but there're likely to be some differences, however slight."

"Does that mean we're not in the same timeline as when we left?" Abbie asked, uneasy at the thought.

Aroya shifted in his seat, equally uncomfortable.

"Well…according to the *theory,* you've actually returned to another *version* of your reality–a version that is nearly identical. The main events may be the same–those really *big* things that cement our reality–but some trivial things might change…like teakettles, for example."

Abbie's brain felt like a twisted pretzel. "Then are *we* the same people–as when we *left?"* she asked.

"Now, that's an interesting question. I don't know," Markus replied.

All three of them fell silent–contemplating the possibility.

"Originally, Aroya traveled to our time by using an image of me in his mind," Abbie said, "an image of how I look *now*. If he had instead, visualized me as a small child or an old woman, would he have traveled to another time, where I appeared that way?"

"I suppose the answer would be yes," Markus replied, "which makes it even more complicated to travel to a specific time if you have no connection to any particular person to guide you…unless you're a psychic."

Abbie smiled at Aroya.

Markus noticed. "Oh, don't tell me...Aroya's also psychic?"

"Something like that," Abbie replied.

"I'm working on better control," Aroya added.

"Well, if you *do* use your psychic abilities for time travel, you had better be very confident about your accuracy," Markus said. "For example, if you use a picture of George Washington to help you navigate, then you'd better not imagine him on horseback, with his sword drawn–or upon your arrival, you could be dodging bullets!"

They laughed, but also considered the real possibility.

"What about when we cleaned the lake?" Abbie asked. "Why didn't that happen until the next day?"

Markus thought about it. "Hmmm. Maybe it was the words you chose–"

"Transparent with the sun therein," Aroya interrupted. "It happened the next day because that's when the *sun* was shining down on the water. Correct?"

"Yes. That's possible," Markus replied.

"I'm still thinking about what you said about not returning to our original timeline. That really freaks me out," Abbie said, wrinkling her forehead.

"And your suggestion, Abbie–that you may not even be the same people when you return is even *more* worrisome!" Markus exclaimed.

"Hold on! That wasn't *my* suggestion!" Abbie countered. "I was just saying 'according to the *theory!*'"

"Yes, well–it's just a theory, anyway. But you two are the *real deal*. I sure hope I show up in every one of your timelines because I'm looking forward to the *updates!* I *do* find it all so *fascinating!"*

16– CHANGING THE WORLD

2019

San Francisco

Timeline 1.0

The next day, Abbie and Aroya sat at the café, in their usual spot near the window.

"So…I guess tonight's the night," Abbie said.

"Yep. Are you ready?" Aroya asked.

"Honestly? I'm a bit nervous," she replied.

Spotting them through the window, Millie entered the café. "Hi, guys…I haven't seen hide nor hair of you in days! I thought you were off on another adventure!"

"Nope," Abbie replied. "We've just been staying in. But we'll be taking another trip soon."

Millie pulled up a chair. "Oh yeah? So, what's up? Going back to Aroya's time again? What year was that?"

"2050," Aroya replied.

Millie cringed. "I bet things are really screwed up by 2050. I mean, just look at how bad things are now. It must be a dystopian hell."

"Yeah. I guess you could call it that," Aroya replied.

Abbie leaned forward. "Millie, you know that you're my best friend...so I'm gonna tell you why we have to go back–"

"You're going back to save the world. I mean the future world, right?" Millie interrupted.

"Yeah. How'd you know?" Abbie said, surprised.

"Abbs'...ever since I met you, I knew you were special–that you were destined to do something amazing!"

"Thanks, Millie. I guess it is pretty amazing...but I don't feel very special right now. Actually, I'm kind of nervous."

Millie patted her on the arm. "Something tells me you're gonna be just fine...both of you." She gathered her things, then winked at Aroya, whispering, "Hey Aroya, give my regards to Archangel Michael." Waving goodbye, she left the café.

Abbie raised her eyebrows. "Do you think she knows?"

"Abbie, she's known for a long time," Aroya replied, smiling.

Preparing for their mission, Abbie and Aroya were still unsure about how to proceed. Time travel was easy compared to changing the world. From this point onward, Aroya would be searching for the perfect poem, and they would both be racking their brains, trying to understand what exactly needed to be done to get humanity back on track.

In the afternoon, Abbie placed a fresh rose in her vase, and rearranged a few items on the altar–while Aroya shuffled through his Sufi book.

"I don't know if there's anything in here quite right for what we need," he said. "But there *is* a passage that suggests we might have left something out." Turning the page, he said, "Listen to this: *The solution to the problem of the day is the awakening of the consciousness of humanity to the divinity within.*"

"How does one awake humanity to the divinity within?" Abbie asked.

"I'm not sure that we have to figure that out," Aroya replied. "When I focused on my desire to be with you, I didn't need to figure out *how* it would happen. It was more like an unseen power took my request and just made it happen."

"Hmmm. Maybe it's like ordering at a restaurant," Abbie said, "you don't need to *know* how the meal's prepared. You just trust that you'll get what you ordered." She paused, then had an idea. "*Trust!* That might be important!"

"Yeah. Maybe the more we analyze things–the more we muddy things up," he replied.

"But it's all just a big a guessing game, at this point. We're really in uncharted waters here," Abbie said, shaking her head. She was beginning to feel uneasy.

"You're right," Aroya agreed. "Do we dare try to change the future when we don't even understand the nature of time?" He gazed at the altar, reciting a few lines:

"Do I dare Disturb the universe?
In a minute there is time,
For decisions and revisions…
which a minute will reverse."

"T. S. Eliot said that," he added.

"Sounds like T. S. Eliot was a time traveler," Abbie replied.

Aroya shrugged. "Maybe." Then he pulled out the wish list. "If we could condense what you wished for into just a few simple words–then which words would be the most important?"

Abbie reviewed the list. "You mean…without any explanation? Just the *words?"*

Aroya nodded.

"Okay. Then number 1 might be; Civility. Number 2; Community. Number 3; Freedom–although maybe that should be number 1. Well…Liberty, and Justice, and Prosperity–in sufficient degrees. And then, of course, Truth and Beauty. I think everything else probably depends on all those things," she said.

"That reminds me of the Tennyson poem, the one Elijah recited during our meditation," Aroya said, trying to recall it. "That was always one of Elijah's favorite poems, but I never really took it to memory myself. I wish Ray still had the bookshop, because I'm sure he'd know it."

"Maybe you can find it on the Internet, or–" she pointed to his bookmark, "you could call him." She smiled, knowing how much Aroya would love an excuse to talk to Ray. "Maybe the phone number still works."

Aroya held up the business card. "Should I?"

Abbie just smiled again.

"Yes, of course!" Aroya exclaimed, excited for a chance to speak with his friend.

Abbie handed him her phone. It took him a moment because, of course, he wasn't used to using a cell phone.

He placed the phone against his ear. "Hello, Ray? Hi, this is Aroya." A smile stretched across his face. "Yes, yes... I'm fine. How are you?... Yes, I understand. I called to say hello, but I also have a question. Are you familiar with Lord Tennyson?... I don't know the name of the poem, but it's about *freedom*... Oh, really? What time?... Yes, we'll be there. I can't wait to see you.... Okay, bye." He handed the phone back to Abbie.

"What's up?" she asked.

"He has the book...and he's bringing it to the shop. I told him we'd meet him there in 45 minutes."

Abbie and Aroya walked to the bookshop. The windows were boarded up, and the door had multiple locks on it. The entryway in front wreaked of urine.

"God. This is really sad," Abbie said, holding her nose.

"Look! There's Ray!" Aroya jumped like a little boy who just spotted his favorite playmate.

Ray hurried over to the bookshop, carrying a big bag of books. "Well, hello!" he said. Then, noticing the dried puddles of urine on his doorstep, his joyful expression turned to disgust. "I'm sorry about the condition of things," he said, "but I rarely make it by here anymore." He searched for his keys, shifting the heavy bag, not wanting to set it down on the filthy ground.

"Here, let me take your bag," Aroya offered.

While Ray fiddled with the locks, Aroya peered into the bag, curious.

Ray opened the door, and they entered the dark, dusty bookshop. Locking the door behind them, Ray switched on the lights. There wasn't much left of the shop, just some empty tables and shelves, and a few dozen books with missing covers scattered about.

"It's hard to see the shop like this. This place represents 27 years of my life–and now it's gone," Ray said.

"What made you decide to shut it down?" Aroya asked.

"It was either that or watch it burn down. That's what they told me–'close it down, or we'll burn it down,'" Ray replied.

Aroya's mind flooded with disturbing memories about the period leading up to the catastrophe. "This is how it all started," he muttered.

"What started?" Ray asked.

"The fall. It's a sign," Aroya replied.

"The fall of civilization? Yes, I agree. But I couldn't just let them burn the books–some of them were priceless. And besides, it could've endangered the whole neighborhood. Better to admit when you've been beaten and just shut down." Now more excited, Ray addressed the issue of the poem. "Come–I'll show you what I've got."

Ray pulled a book from the bag, holding it up. "It's in here. It's called *Of Old Sat Freedom on the Heights.*

I brought some other books with poems about freedom, if you're interested."

"Thanks, Ray. You're so kind. But I think we'll only need the one. Abbie has some paper, so we can write it down."

"Write it down? Oh no! The book is yours! It's my pleasure! The whole bag is for you. Please take it," he said, handing the bag to Aroya.

Aroya looked through the bag. "Wow, these are wonderful. Why don't you want them?" he asked.

"I should have sold them when I closed down. I knew I had no space for them at home. Hey, you know that Sufi book I gave you? That might have something about freedom in it. To paraphrase Khan: *It's the free spirit in man, that reminds him that freedom is his natural state...*or something like that." Ray opened the Tennyson book and asked, "May I recite the poem for you?"

"Yes! Of course!" Aroya and Abbie replied.

Ray walked to the center of the room. He presented himself in a dignified manner, despite his old jeans and crumpled jacket–as though he were preparing for a dramatic reading on a grand stage. His adoring audience, Aroya and Abbie, pulled open two folding chairs and waited eagerly. In Aroya's time, reciting a poem was almost a sacred act. Apparently, it was equally so for Ray.

Ray adjusted his glasses and cleared his throat. He began:

> *"Of old sat Freedom on the heights,*
> *The thunders breaking at her feet:*
> *Above her shook the starry lights:*

She heard the torrents meet.

There in her place she did rejoice,
Self-gather'd in her prophet-mind,
But fragments of her mighty voice
Came rolling on the wind.

Then stept she down thro' town and field
To mingle with the human race,
And part by part to men reveal'd
The fulness of her face–

Grave mother of majestic works,
From her isle-altar gazing down,
Who, God-like, grasps the triple forks,
And, King-like, wears the crown:

Her open eyes desire the truth.
The wisdom of a thousand years
Is in them. May perpetual youth
Keep dry their light from tears;

That her fair form may stand and shine,
Make bright our days and light our dreams,
Turning to scorn with lips divine
The falsehood of extremes!"

Finished, Ray closed the book. He stepped forward, handing the book to Aroya, who was visibly moved. It was obvious that Dr. Biegel's *prelude to a fall* was pressing down–becoming more severe by the day. They considered the deep meaning of this poem now more than ever.

Abbie and Aroya returned to the apartment with the bag of books and a small shopping bag. Abbie removed a box from the shopping bag, setting it on the table. The illustration on the box depicted a whistling teakettle.

The time was approaching, and both were nervous. When they changed the lake, it was like a game; they were not heavily invested in the outcome. But this was different. Now, they would endeavor to change the future for all of humanity. They both quietly wondered to themselves if they should even try such a thing–or as T. S. Eliot said, should they 'dare disturb the universe?' Night had fallen, and the air was still. They sat together on the couch, silently staring at the altar.

Abbie walked over to the fireplace. "Should I light a fire?" she asked.

"No. It will just remind me of the night we made love, and you know…wild horses."

"Right. Wild horses," Abbie replied. "You know the vision we had? The one with Elijah?" she asked.

"Yes. That's all I can think of now."

"I think we were shown everything we need."

"What do you mean?"

"Well…first, we were shown Lake Merced clearing up, and we presume *we* had something to do with that. So maybe we should just use the same method."

"That's why we saw Elijah reciting the poem?"

"I think so, because the Tennyson poem refers to 'freedom' as *'her.'* It personifies freedom as a woman, just like the poem for the lake did," Abbie suggested.

"Yeah. I noticed that. Maybe the entire vision showed us everything...the method, the poem, and even the results. Then why am I so nervous?" he asked.

"Me too," Abbie replied.

"Okay. Light the candle. Let's do this," Aroya said.

Abbie lit the candle and turned down the lights. They sat on the cushions in front of the altar.

"Should we do the jaguar thing? You know, follow him?" Aroya asked.

"No. We didn't do that when we changed the lake– we only did that for guidance," Abbie replied.

"Then, is there an Archangel to pray to?"

Abbie almost giggled. "I don't think so." She retrieved Aroya's stone from his coat pocket, handing it to him. "I think all we need is this."

"Abbie, help me. What should I say?" Aroya asked nervously. "I know about the poem–but how should I say it?"

Abbie retrieved the book by Tennyson, setting it in front of him.

Aroya opened the book, studying the poem. "But not *everything* is in the poem. You know...the list of things that you wished for. Not all of them are in here–only *'freedom.'*"

"Maybe those other things are like the list of ingredients of the meal we're ordering. Maybe we should just trust the chef?" she answered.

"Perhaps...but wild horses, Abbie. I've got so many thoughts crowding my mind," he said.

"We did meditate before we dropped the stone at the lake. Maybe we should meditate again," Abbie suggested. "But no jaguars, just meditation to quiet our minds."

"I don't remember what we did at the lake. Honestly, I thought we were just playing a game."

"First, we sat facing each other like the two flames–burning brighter and rising higher."

"Yes, I remember now," Aroya replied.

Abbie and Aroya situated themselves on the cushions, facing each other.

"Okay, now close your eyes," Abbie said. "In your mind, see our hearts beating as one. Listen to my breath–and let your breath fall into sync with mine. Imagine that you're unblocking a dam. Then see a gentle stream flowing freely through your mind. Just breathe with me and watch the water flow."

They held hands–and finally, their breath fell into sync.

"I see her," Aroya whispered.

"Who do you see?"

"Freedom. I see the whole drama playing out in every line of the poem. It's like a movie. Just the last line is confusing. Oh, now I see Elijah again. He's reciting the poem like he did before. The last line is: 'the fulness of her face.'"

"What's the message?"

Aroya opened his eyes. "I think we just do what we saw in the vision."

"How are the wild horses now?"

"They're steady…ready to take us to our destination."

Abbie handed Aroya the stone. He closed his eyes. In his mind, he heard the Vision Maker's voice say: *Let the moving waters of your desire…bring you to your destination.* He held the stone in his right hand and began: "My desire is to restore *freedom* to the world, for the benefit of all humanity, and all creation, everywhere. Let *freedom mingle with the human race– to reveal the fullness of her face."* He dropped the stone from one hand to the other.

17– BACK TO THE FUTURE

2019

San Francisco

Timeline 1.0

The morning sun shone like a spotlight through the patio door, landing on Abbie's form. Curled up in front of the altar, she slept on the Persian rug, with Aroya's blanket draped over her and his pillow tucked under her head. Opening her eyes, she stretched and yawned.

Sleeping on the couch, without a pillow or blanket– Aroya cast his sleepy eyes in Abbie's direction. "I didn't want to wake you," he said, yawning. "You looked so peaceful."

Abbie propped her head up. "Do you think we did it?" she asked.

"Changed the future?"

"Yeah."

"I guess we won't know until we go check."

Abbie stretched her legs and whined, "Oh, God–do we really need to go?"

"I guess we don't *have* to–but the feathered man said it was necessary to make the changes more solid."

"Oh yeah, I remember now…" Abbie said, still half asleep, "we have a mission." Then she stood up. "Let's try out the new teakettle."

"Okay. But you better not let Millie see it," Aroya joked.

Abbie shuffled into the kitchen. She turned on the burner, then sat down at the kitchen table. "Do you think the teakettle is really proof that we returned to a different timeline?" she asked.

Aroya put down the Tennyson book. "I don't know. Maybe it's just a theory."

"God, I wish I didn't think about that. Now I'm gonna be all freaked out about going. What if, when we get back, something *major* is different! We still don't even know if we'll be the *same people!"*

"Well, if we're different…let's hope there's some improvement. Of course, I'm speaking for myself."

There was a knock at the door, and Abbie let Millie in. She handed Abbie a grocery bag. "I had a feeling you two were still around, so I picked up some bagels," Millie said.

"Oh, perfect!" Abbie squealed. "Thanks, Millie! And lox too! Look, Aroya! Fish!"

The teakettle started whistling.

"What's that?" Millie asked.

Aroya hid behind his book. "Uh-oh."

Abbie took the teakettle off the burner while explaining, "I really needed one with a whistle…because otherwise, I get distracted, and I burn the bottom," she explained.

"Is that what happened to the one I gave you?" Millie asked.

Embarrassed, Abbie shrugged. "Maybe."

"Well, I've got a show to write. Be good you two…and if you can't be good, for God's sake, be careful! I'll see you later…I hope," she said, shutting the door.

Aroya wandered over to the table, investigating the goodies. "I guess we won't have to go out for breakfast now," he said, somewhat relieved.

"Or lunch! Look at all this stuff! Cheese croissants– even a salad!" Abbie exclaimed. She unloaded the bag, setting out two bagels with lox and cream cheese. "It's probably better that we stay in today anyway," she said, "you know, to avoid distractions. What time should we leave?" she asked.

Aroya was thoroughly enjoying a mouthful of cream cheese and lox. Washing it down with tea, he answered, "I guess we should leave in a few hours, so that we land during daylight. Since we don't know what to expect– showing up in the dead of night might not be a good idea."

"Man, who cast me in this crazy movie, anyway?" Abbie said, stressed. "I mean, look at me! Do I look like a *time traveler?!*"

"Are you forgetting already, what you did in 2050?" Aroya asked. "Not only did you *time travel,* but you fought off evil villains–with *guns and goo!*"

"Oh. Was that me?" she replied.

"Abbie. You were *amazing!*"

"Thanks," she sighed. "I guess I've got a mission then."

"*We've* got a mission. I've already lived in that hellish future, and trust me–you don't want to see the world go that way." He put down his bagel. "Abbie, come here."

He took Abbie by the hand, leading her to the patio. Peering over the balcony, they surveyed the street below.

"Now, take a deep breath," Aroya instructed, "and tell me what you smell."

Abbie refused, holding her nose instead.

Aroya cupped his hand behind his ear. "Listen...tell me what you hear." A siren rang out in the distance, a car honked, and a pedestrian screamed obscenities. "Look down into the street, Abbie–and tell me what you see." A few homeless people wandered about, a drug deal was going down, and a hooker was flagging down cars.

Abbie held her stomach, nauseous. "I get it. It's Dr. Biegel's *prelude to a fall.*"

"Exactly," Aroya replied.

"I'm beginning to understand now, why those nurses ignored those body bags rolling past them–," Abbie said, "because once you acknowledge the atrocities, then I guess, the question is...what are you going to do about it?" She looked directly at Aroya. "It's easy to block that stuff out...when you don't want to see it."

"I know what you mean. When I first arrived here, I thought I was in heaven; because as bad things are–*my* time is a thousand times worse...unimaginably worse. When you went back with me, you didn't even see the worst of it...you didn't see my home for the past 20 years–where the pig people live…the forsaken land of zone 9. That's where this is all heading–if we don't complete our mission. If we wanna confirm the changes that we made last night and make sure they become solid–then we need to go back."

"I know," Abbie sighed. "I don't know what's wrong with me. Our mission is a blessing…and here I am whining like a baby."

"The future depends on us. *Our* future depends on us. The whole world depends on this new reality becoming solid. What did Markus call it? The weighted probability?"

"Yeah. And I guess our mission is to give it more weight," Abbie said.

"When we drop the stone, I'll be targeting Elijah. I'd like to be at my best when I see him. Do you mind if I use the shower first today?"

"Of course, go ahead. How should we dress for the trip?"

"I don't know. In my old 2050, our clothes didn't matter much–just as long as they were warm."

"I'll figure something out. Go on. Take your shower," Abbie said.

Abbie had no idea how to dress for this new 2050. These days, Aroya was most comfortable in casual running pants and tee shirts. In addition to the suit he'd arrived in, he only had one other decent set of clothes, an outfit he wore just once to Markus' place for dinner. She laid his clothes on the couch, then tried to coordinate something for herself. Not knowing what they might face, she chose running shoes and warm jackets for the both of them…just in case.

While carrying Aroya's jacket to the living room, she bumped into him, emerging from the bathroom, all fresh and steamy–barely covered by a skimpy towel. Abbie stopped dead in her tracks, taking a good look at his still moist and mostly naked body.

"What's wrong?" Aroya asked.

"Wild horses," Abbie replied.

Aroya smiled. "It won't be long." He leaned in to kiss her. She playfully pushed the jacket in his face, retreating to her bedroom.

Aroya dressed, waiting in the living room while Abbie took her turn in the shower. He studied the picture of Archangel Michael on the altar, turning it over to read the prayer. Having no idea what they might face in the new future, he thought it might be useful to memorize the Archangel Michael prayer…just in case.

After showering, Abbie dressed in her outfit and joined Aroya in the living room.

"Are you ready?" Aroya asked.

"I think we should pray first. Do you mind?"

"No, I don't mind. I was thinking the same thing."

Abbie slid open a panel near the baseboard, pulling out a large Bible. It was a special edition, complete with colorful full-page depictions of Bible stories. She brought the Bible over to the couch to show Aroya.

"Oh! What a beautiful book! May I touch it?" Aroya asked, amazed.

"Of course. This is my Bible."

"Your Bible? I thought you weren't religious?"

"I'm not. At least, not in the traditional sense."

"Then what do you do with it? Do you read it?"

"Honestly, I find it difficult to understand, but it's useful. For instance, there's a special passage often used for protection." Abbie turned to Ephesians 6:10. "I think we should both read this together, right before we drop the stone."

"I've been memorizing the Archangel Michael prayer, just in case we need it," Aroya said.

"I was planning to say it before we left, but if you carry *that* in your head–we'll be super-protected. First, we'll pray…and then I'll hold on to you while you drop the stone. Okay?"

"Okay," Aroya replied. "But bring your own stone, just in case we get separated."

"Get separated? Impossible! I'll be sticking to you like glue!" she exclaimed.

"Abbie…you really need to learn how to do this on your own," Aroya said. "Let me see your hands."

Abbie held out her hands.

"Now hold up your *right* hand, as if you were holding the stone–and place your *left* hand underneath."

Abbie moved her hands into position.

"I'll hold the stone and drop it into my hand," Aroya said, "but you'll be holding my hands as I do it. Understand?"

"Yes. I think so," Abbie replied.

"Time travel is much simpler than changing things," he said. "First, I'll allow myself to feel a deep longing for my friend Elijah. I'll see his face in my mind. Then, when I drop the stone, I'll see myself with him, at that very moment. That's all there is to it."

"That sounds simple," Abbie replied.

"When we're ready to do this, you'll place your hands in position, holding mine–and you'll repeat after me. Okay?"

"Okay," Abbie replied. "I'm a little nervous, but I think I'll feel stronger after we pray."

"Then let's pray," Aroya said. "Just tell me what to do."

Abbie took a deep breath, straightening her spine. "Begin by closing your eyes," she said. "Ignore all distractions, taking each word I say into your heart."

Aroya closed his eyes.

"I'll begin with myself...then I'll repeat my protection prayer and move my hands around you," she continued. "During these prayers, when you hear me say the word 'Amen', just repeat 'Amen.'"

"Okay, I understand."

Abbie rubbed her hands together above her head to get the energies going. She closed her eyes while moving her hands slowly through the electrified air, then down her sides while reciting the prayer:

> *"Of and by the power of the Lord, Jesus Christ–a living shell of white light is built up all around me, protecting me from harm. I am encased in a shell of living white light and positive energy, protecting me."*

"Amen," she finished.

"Amen," Aroya echoed.

She opened her eyes and turned to Aroya, repeating the protection prayer. Then she moved her hands from the top of his head, down each of his sides. Aroya's legs trembled from the electric charge coursing through his body. Finished, she rested her hands on his knees. The trembling ceased. Now she faced the altar and began addressing God, asking for forgiveness in the name of Jesus–and petitioning for assistance from

Archangel Michael. She took the picture of Archangel Michael from the altar–and turning it over; she began reciting the prayer:

> *"Archangel Michael, defend us in battle.*
> *Come to our aid with your celestial legions.*
> *Bring us protection and guidance, by the power of*
> *the Most-High.*
> *Fill us with your strength, as we fight against the*
> *agents of evil.*
> *Come to our protection and be a refuge–against*
> *the snares of the devil, and all his wicked powers.*
> *Be our defense against all evil intentions, thoughts,*
> *and actions against us.*
> *May the divine fire of your sword, destroy every*
> *evil.*
> *Amen."*

"Amen," Aroya said.

"Now, we'll read the passage from the Bible together," she said. Positioning the Bible so Aroya could also see it, she turned to *Ephesians 6:10-17.* "Okay–here we go."

Together, they recited the passage:

> *"Finally, my brethren, be strong in the Lord and in*
> *the power of his might. Put on the whole armour of*
> *God, that ye may be able to stand against the wiles*
> *of the devil. For we wrestle not against flesh and*
> *blood, but against the principalities, against*
> *powers, against the rulers of the darkness of this*
> *world, against spiritual wickedness in high places.*
> *Wherefore take unto you the whole armour of God,*

that ye may be able to withstand in the evil day,
and having done all, to stand. Stand therefore,
having your loins girt about with truth, and having
on the breastplate of righteousness; And your feet
shod with the preparation of the gospel of peace;
Above all, taking the shield of faith, wherewith ye
shall be able to quench all the fiery darts of the
wicked. And take the helmet of salvation, and the
sword of the Spirit, which is the word of God."

"Amen," she said.

"Amen," Aroya repeated.

Abbie turned to Aroya. "Now it's your turn."

Aroya held the stone in his right hand–positioning his left hand beneath it.

Abbie moved next to him, holding her hands against his–waiting for his direction.

"Are you ready?" he asked.

"I'm ready," she replied.

Aroya instructed her: "See Elijah in your mind–just how you saw him in your vision. Now, repeat my words and feel them ring like a bell inside your chest: *I long for Elijah.*"

"I long for Elijah," Abbie echoed.

"I am *with* Elijah."

"I am *with* Elijah," she repeated.

Aroya dropped the stone.

The floor shifted under their feet, rising and falling like a boat on the water. The carpet rippled, and the curtain billowed. Then suddenly...all was quiet and still.

18– ELIJAH 2.0

2050

San Francisco

Timeline 2.0

Abbie and Aroya landed in 2050–a tangled knot of arms and legs. Looking up at Elijah, seated at his desk–Aroya expected a reaction. There was none–Elijah simply stared back, blankly.

Facing Elijah, waiting for a joyful greeting from his dearest friend–it was quite apparent Elijah did not recognize him.

"Are you from the Council?" Elijah asked.

"No," Aroya replied.

"What do you want then?"

"You don't recognize me?"

Elijah squinted his eyes, shifting his attention back and forth between Abbie and Aroya. "No. Should I?"

Abbie surveyed the room. One entire wall was made of glass, with an amazing view of San Francisco Bay. She peered out over the water. "Wow. Things have definitely changed," she said.

"What do you mean?" Elijah said, still bewildered.

Aroya joined Abbie at the window, peering out over the bay. On the other side of the room was a glass door leading to a patio with a balcony. "Do you mind if I take a look?" he asked, pointing to the door.

"Be my guest," Elijah replied, irritated.

Abbie and Aroya stood in awe, looking over the bright, shining city–populated by pleasant, well-dressed people going about their day.

"We did it!" Abbie exclaimed with excitement.

Elijah was now losing his patience. "Did *what?!* Who *are* you people?!" he demanded.

"We're from the past–I mean *she* is…" Aroya replied. "I'm from *your* time–before it changed." Then, excited, Aroya crossed the room again, looking out over the bay. "Abbie! Come here!" he called out.

Abbie joined Aroya at the window.

"Sky pods," Aroya said, pointing to a small colony of sky pods in the distance. "Maybe some things *haven't* changed," he said, disappointed.

Elijah walked over to the window. "Why are you in my office?!" he demanded again.

"You're the only one I *know* here," Aroya replied.

Elijah rubbed his forehead, perplexed.

"Elijah…" Aroya said, "look at my face. You *know* me!"

Elijah searched his memory. "No, I don't think so." He turned to Abbie, staring. "But *she* looks familiar," he said, pointing his finger.

"Who do I look like?" Abbie asked, surprised.

Elijah scratched his head. "I'm confused. What do you people *want?* For *God's sake,* just tell me what you *want!"*

Aroya had never entertained the idea that Elijah might not recognize him. "My name is Aroya Wallace. And my very best friend in this whole world–is Elijah Stewart," he said.

Elijah raised his eyebrows. "Oh?" Nervously, he smoothed his beard, squinting his eyes again, trying to make sense of the situation. He sat down, searching his memory for the name 'Aroya Wallace.' Then he turned to Abbie. "I heard him call you 'Abbie.' What is your full name?" he asked.

"My name is Abbie Lite," she replied.

Elijah most definitely recognized Abbie's name. His eyes widened, and his chest heaved in rapid succession.

"Are you all right?" Abbie asked, alarmed.

"No. I don't think so," Elijah replied, still hyperventilating.

"Get him some water!" Abbie said to Aroya, pointing to the water dispenser.

Elijah drank the water–looking at Abbie, then looking away, then looking back again.

"Relax, my friend. Things will soon be clear," Aroya said, trying to comfort his old friend.

"How old are you?" Elijah asked Abbie, staring at her like she was some sort of apparition.

"I'm 33," Abbie replied, a little taken aback.

Elijah shook his head in disbelief. "Do you have a relative who calls herself Abigail?"

Now it was Abbie's turn to feel perplexed. "No. Why do you ask?"

Elijah found it unnerving to be in Abbie's presence. Finally, he faced her, with eyes declaring his panic. "You're my *counselor*...my *spiritual counselor*," he blurted out.

"I am?" Abbie asked, confused.

"If Abbie is your spiritual counselor, then who am I?" Aroya asked.

"I don't know. I told you, *I don't know you!*" Elijah replied.

Now it was Aroya's turn to feel perplexed.

All three of them sat down, staring blankly at the wall.

Elijah broke the silence. "I once knew a family named 'Wallace,' when I was a kid. They lived a few streets over."

Aroya perked up. "Were their names Catherine and Brady, and did they have a son?"

He wrinkled his forehead, straining to recall. "I think they had a boy. I never knew him. He was much younger."

Aroya put two and two together. "What happened to the Wallace family?" he asked, in an attempt to confirm his suspicions.

"I don't know. They moved away when I was about 11 years old."

"What did you mean when you said, I'm your *spiritual counselor?*" Abbie asked.

"I have a spiritual counselor. Her name is Abigail Lite. You look just like her, except...."

"Except what?" Abbie asked.

Elijah didn't answer.

"Except, she's older," Aroya said, "about 31 years older. Am I right?"

"*Yes!*" Elijah shouted.

"*This* Abbie," Aroya said, pointing to Abbie, "is the *same* Abbie. She's just 31 years younger...because she's from the year 2019."

Elijah examined Abbie's face again, considering the possibility. "This is really weird," he said.

"Yes. It is," Abbie agreed.

Aroya took a deep breath. "Listen..." he said, "this is going to sound crazy, but you just have to trust me. You don't remember me because, in *your* version of 2050, I moved away with my family when I was six years old. But in another version–me and my mom didn't move away...we stayed in our house in Glen Park. I lived there until I was 17 years old...until the catastrophe in 2030–when both our families were lost."

Elijah became agitated. "Why are you saying these things? What a terrible story!"

"Yes, the catastrophe was terrible...and I don't know what I would've done if it wasn't for you." Aroya struggled not to get choked up. "You took me under your wing–you protected me. We were like brothers."

Elijah's mood suddenly shifted, and his eyes widened. "The *catastrophe!*" he exclaimed, connecting the dots. "I believe you. I've had dreams about it my entire life. That's why I was assigned a spiritual counselor...it was to help me with my dreams." He finally released an enormous sigh. "How did you get here? And why did you come?"

"We used a time travel device. We came to see if this timeline had changed," Aroya replied.

"If all this is true...then apparently, it has changed *a lot*–thank God," Elijah said.

Aroya's attention was now drawn to Elijah's bookshelves. "There it is. *Tennyson!*" he said, tossing a glance at Elijah. He selected a few lines:

"Of old sat Freedom on the heights,
The thunders breaking at her feet:
Above her shook the starry lights:
She heard the torrents meet."

Elijah struggled to find words. "I remember. I remember everything," he said, tears rolling down his cheeks.

Aroya put his arm around Elijah, comforting him. "Elijah, my brother…we've been through dark times together. And we were always there for each other."

Elijah took a deep breath, wiping his eyes. "As weird as all this is–it explains a lot of things. But I always thought they were just dreams…or nightmares." Elijah closed his eyes, pressing his fist against his forehead. "Now that I remember you in that context…your name is coming back. But in my dreams, I always saw you as a kid. I guess I've always thought of you that way–as that 17-year-old boy who I found in the dirt, with bloody hands from digging in the rubble…searching for his mother."

Aroya took a deep breath. "You saved my life, Elijah," he held up the Tennyson book, "you and the poetry."

"Oh, the poetry. I've been obsessed with it all my life. I had dreams about reciting it around a fire–then I'd search high and low to find the poems. It became almost like a religion to me!" He relaxed, leaning back in his chair–then he chuckled. "My family thought I was a little soft in the head."

"No, not soft in the head–but maybe a little soft in the heart," Abbie said. "And actually…it was your love of poetry that saved us all. It was the Tennyson poem that brought us here. We saw you in a vision, reciting it–then we used it to change the world."

"I don't understand. How could my life here be influenced by something that never really happened to me?" Elijah asked.

"I don't understand it myself. It's like the two different times are somehow connected," Aroya explained.

"After all these years…my dreams just suddenly stopped. I have no idea why. It's only been a couple weeks, and honestly, I miss them." He chuckled again. "Oh boy. Wait 'till the *other* Abbie hears about this! She's gonna love it!"

Aroya glanced around the room. "If this is where you work, then where do you live?"

"I have a condominium…over by Lake Merced."

Abbie and Aroya smiled at each other, recalling their adventure at Lake Merced. Little did they know at the time, that their silly game would become the key to changing the future for all humanity. Quite a game indeed.

"Will you be staying? Can I offer you my guest room?" Elijah asked.

Aroya turned to Abbie for approval. "What do you think? Can we stay?"

"The Vision Maker said we shouldn't stay," Abbie said, uneasy.

"But I thought he meant we shouldn't stay permanently. Just one night should be okay?" Aroya argued.

Abbie observed Elijah and Aroya looking at each other. They were like two little boys, asking if they could pretty pleeeease have a sleepover. "Okay. Just one night," she conceded.

Elijah's face lit up. "Great! Then, let's go!"

They took a pod-lift down to the street, where Elijah's vehicle waited at the curb. It was like a fancy aerodynamic automobile, but it had no wheels.

Approaching the vehicle, Abbie peeked underneath. "Where are the wheels?" she asked.

Both Aroya and Elijah laughed.

"It's a hovercar. All vehicles 'hover' in 2050. Some even fly," Aroya explained.

Impressed, Abbie entered the vehicle with Aroya. Elijah entered through the other door, taking a seat next to Abbie.

"Do you have a driver?" Abbie inquired.

"You really are from 2019, aren't you? There's no driver...not here, in the city. City cars are all autonomous." Then he pointed to an upholstered bar located on the back of the front seat. "Lift your arms so we can all buckle in."

They lifted their arms, and a cushy bar automatically slid across their laps.

"Wow–look at you, Elijah," Aroya said, just as impressed as Abbie. "The new 2050 sure treats you a lot better than the *old* one ever did!"

Elijah laughed. "Yeah, I remember…from my dreams. But it's different here. Most people travel this way now–not just the elite. We're generally pretty safe and comfortable. A far cry from that hellish other place!"

A holographic chauffeur suddenly materialized in the driver's seat. Elijah called out: "ES-10-27-2008-8100-2X."

The driver responded, "Verified. Elijah Stewart, plus two unregistered guests. Mr. Stewart, what is our destination?"

"Lake Merced Towers–Number Three, West!" Elijah replied.

"Scenic or commute?" the driver asked.

"Scenic. No stops," Elijah replied.

"Yes, sir," the driver said.

The vehicle rose up a few inches from the ground, then began moving over a wide concave magnetic rail. They drove through the city–passing smartly dressed people on the sidewalks, in the shops, and in the parks; none of them homeless, and none of them begging. The streets were immaculate–even the older structures were in pristine condition. More modern structures could be seen, scattered about the outskirts–mostly sky pods standing on high pedestals, looking down upon the city's tallest buildings.

Abbie pointed to the sky pods. "Wow. Look at those!"

"Those are Administrator Burk's new 'Sky Communities,'" Elijah explained.

"Burk?! He's still here?!" Aroya asked, startled.

"Still here? What do you mean?" Elijah replied, confused.

Aroya toned down his reaction. "Oh, nothing. I just remember the name from *my* time."

Abbie also remembered the name from her first accidental trip to Aroya's 2050. She cringed to think that men like him were still players in this new future.

Abbie continued staring at the sky pods. "Who lives up there?" she asked.

"Mostly government officials. They're all connected to the Sky Council 'higher-ups,'" Elijah said.

"Oh, yeah…the 'higher-ups,'" Abbie said, recalling Dr. Eiffel's words. Just the thought of him made her squirm.

Aroya was also feeling uneasy. He had a sinking feeling that maybe things hadn't changed as much as he'd first thought.

When they arrived at Elijah's condominium, the hovercar lowered itself to the ground. After stepping out of the vehicle–it continued down the road, automatically parking itself in a transport tower.

Inside the lobby of Elijah's building, they entered a glass pod-lift and rose to the top floor.

Elijah used a wrist pad to call his wife. "Hi, honey. I'm on my way up, and I'm bringing two guests. I just wanted to give you a heads up."

"You're married?" Aroya asked, surprised.

"Yes, I am," Elijah replied, "and with two beautiful children…a boy and a girl. Unfortunately, you won't get to meet them. They're attending the Junior Council session this week."

"Junior Council, huh? That sounds pretty official," Aroya commented.

"It's just another one of the new programs here," Elijah replied.

"Of course," Aroya said, definitely uneasy now.

Elijah was confused by Aroya's reaction every time he mentioned the Administrator's name and his programs–but he thought it best to ignore it for now. His lovely wife, Eloise, greeted them at the door–a rather short and curvy woman with a bubbly personality.

"Hi. I'm Elijah's wife, Eloise. It's nice to meet you." She turned to Elijah. "Honey, will your friends be staying for dinner?"

"Yes, dear. My friends will be staying for dinner– and they'll also be taking the guest room tonight."

"Oh, how wonderful. And such good timing too," she turned to Abbie and Aroya, "because I'll be leaving for a few days–and with the children gone, poor Elijah will be here all alone. I'm sure he's delighted to have some company." She turned toward the hallway. "I'm so sorry, but I'm running late. It was nice meeting you."

Elijah brought Abbie and Aroya into the communal room–an ultra-modern and somewhat sterile living environment designed for social activities.

"Please have a seat and make yourselves at home. Would you like something to drink before dinner?" Elijah asked.

"Just water would be fine," Aroya said.

Elijah turned to Abbie. "And for you, my dear?"

"Just water for me, too. Thanks."

Elijah faced the middle of the room. "I'll pull up the menu," he said. Then he called out, "Martha! Dinner menu!" A stylish holographic maid materialized in the center of the room, floating a few inches above a glowing white globe. She waved her hand in the air, and a holographic screen appeared beside her, depicting selections from the menu.

"Good evening. I am Martha," the maid said, in a slightly robotic voice. "May I enquire about your dietary preferences tonight?" she asked.

"Well, that looks good. What is it?" Aroya asked.

"This is the Administrator's preferred balanced meal, with new taste enhancers. This meal will earn you 500 BurkLife points," the maid said.

Abbie and Aroya looked at each other, confused.

Elijah returned with two glasses of water. "Do you see anything you like?" he asked.

"What are BurkLife points?" Aroya asked.

"Oh, that's just the nutrition program. It's an incentive for us to eat healthy," Elijah replied.

"You know, I'm not terribly hungry," Aroya said. "Maybe just something small?"

"Martha! Salads!" Elijah commanded. The holographic screen changed.

"Farmed-fish salad with greens," the maid responded.

"That sounds good," Aroya replied.

"Wow. It's just like having your own restaurant in your living room," Abbie said, turning to the maid. "I'll have the same thing. Thank you."

"Are you sure? We've just upgraded to 26 selections. So there's lots to choose from!" Elijah said.

"Thanks…but fish will be fine," Abbie replied.

"Martha! Two selections of farmed-fish salad and one selection of today's special," Elijah announced.

"Yes, sir. Two farmed-fish salads and one Burk special for 500 BurkLife points. Would you like anything else?" the maid asked.

"No. That's all. Set the serving time for 10 minutes," Elijah ordered.

The maid responded, "Yes, sir." The hologram dissolved.

"Elijah? Are you happy here?" Aroya asked, concerned.

"I guess so," Elijah replied," surprised by the question. "Well, except for the nightmares. But now that I understand what they were all about, maybe I'll be happier."

"Can I ask you something about Administrator Burk?" Aroya inquired.

"Yeah, I noticed you got a little prickly whenever I mentioned his name."

"The sky pods are named after him...and even the *food* is named after him. Why is that?" Aroya asked.

Elijah cast his eyes down. "It's all new. I'm trying to get used to it–mostly to make things easier for Eloise," he said. Then he straightened his back. "I knew if we let them build those sky pods, things were going to change. We don't even know who this Burk guy is. He and the Council just appeared out of nowhere and started implementing all these new programs, all in a matter of months. Honestly, when you guys showed up in my office, I thought you were from the Council."

A chill ran up Aroya's spine. "Oh no. That's not good," he said, shaking his head.

"It all rolled out after the election," Elijah explained.

"What election?" Abbie asked.

"The Presidential election," Elijah replied. "Nobody paid much attention, but a new guy somehow got elected–and then things started to really change. Nobody had even heard of this guy before! It's like he and Burk just fell out of the sky!"

"But didn't the people vote for him?" Abbie asked.

"Who knows? Hardly anyone still votes. We don't pay much attention to that stuff anymore. When they announced his name, everyone just went, 'who?'. His name is *Wolfe*–and let me tell you, he's a real *wolf* alright. I've never felt so hunted in all my life!" Elijah exclaimed.

"Klaus Wolfe?!" Aroya asked.

"Yeah. That's right."

Abbie and Aroya looked at each other in horror.

"Oh, God! What have we done?!" Abbie whispered to Aroya.

"Before Klaus Wolfe was elected, what was it like here? Was life good?" Aroya asked.

"I suppose. Nobody complained much–because there really wasn't much to complain about. We all just did our own thing, lived our lives. Come to think of it–life was pretty easy–pretty carefree. I guess we took things for granted and stopped paying attention." Elijah said, peeking into the dining room, checking on the dinner.

Abbie leaned closer to Aroya, whispering in his ear, "Dr. Biegel's *prelude to a fall*–all over again...just a cleaner and better-organized version!"

The holographic maid materialized in the center of the room. "Your dinner is ready and waiting for you in the dining room. Do you have any further requests?" it asked.

"No, Martha. No more requests."

The hologram dissolved.

Elijah motioned toward the dining room. "Shall we eat?"

None of them found the food very appetizing. Bland and discolored–it had the texture of wet cardboard. They all pretended to eat–shoving portions around on their plates.

Finally, Elijah put his fork down. "I'm sorry. I just can't get myself to eat this crap. I'm trying hard to get with the program, but I can't pretend. I mean, look at this shit! We can't even choose our own food anymore! We now have *26 different selections* of basically the same crap!" He pushed his plate away.

"Why do you put up with it?" Abbie asked.

"If we don't go along with the program, they dock us points! I've always been a stubborn man, and the truth is…that's why my wife and kids are at those stupid training conferences. They were ordered to go to make up for the points we've been docked–mostly because of me." Elijah averted his eyes, ashamed.

"Is it still possible to get a pizza in this town?" Aroya asked, pushing his plate away.

"They discourage it." Then, with a reckless look in his eye, Elijah whispered, "But I know a place. C'mon. Let's go!"

Elijah's vehicle stopped in front of his office. When they got out, he said, "Follow me."

Abbie and Aroya followed him into the lobby. Once inside, Elijah whispered, "Wait a minute."

Looking toward the street, they watched Elijah's vehicle drive away. Elijah put a finger to his mouth. "Shhh…" he said. Then he motioned for Abbie and Aroya to follow him back out to the street. When they were a block away, he finally relaxed.

"The transports track us," he said. "This is the only way I can get real food these days."

They approached a vacant stretch of land near the water's edge. Tucked discreetly into an old brick wall, a forgotten pizza parlor still operated, off grid. They sat outside, at an old weathered picnic table, sharing an extra-large cheese pizza.

"I don't know how this place still exists, but I sure am glad it does!" Elijah said, patting his belly.

"Is it the only one left?" Aroya asked.

"Just about. For some reason, this tiny corner of the city is off the radar." He washed his pizza down with a beer. "You know…when I think about that Tennyson poem about *freedom*–I feel like we're losing it…and it's tearing me up inside."

"If it's tearing you up inside…then you can't go on like this," Abbie said.

"That's what the *other* Abbie says too. I don't feel like I'm being true to myself," Elijah replied.

"You know…since we got here," Aroya commented, "I thought this life didn't fit you. I wondered if you were hiding something–but the Elijah I knew would never hide anything. He always spoke his mind, and nobody told him what to do–not even the Squad. And man, did he have a reputation! I don't mean to make you feel bad or anything, but I can't imagine the old Elijah not being true to himself."

"What about your wife? How does she feel about all the changes?" Abbie asked.

"We don't talk much anymore. She works so hard to get those stupid points. She's kind of lost interest in everything else. The kids are the same way, but at least privately, they admit they hate it," Elijah confessed.

They finished their pizza and returned their plates to the restaurant. While Elijah was chatting up the owner, Abbie watched the news on a holographic screen, floating above a small white globe.

On the news, the anchor said: *"The director of our new national BurkLife program, Dr. Alfred Eiffel, is here with us today...."*

Abbie gasped. *"Dr. Eiffel?!* What kind of alternative hell have we created?!" she exclaimed.

"He's the psychopath from the hospital, right?" Aroya asked.

Elijah overheard them. "What's wrong?"

"Elijah...this is not the world we intended for you. I'm so sorry," Abbie replied.

"Well, it's not perfect–but it's better than the one Aroya came from," Elijah said.

"But don't you see?" Abbie said. "You're on the path to being right back there again. And it's happening at record speed!"

"I know...and nobody seems to notice," Elijah replied.

"They're all asleep," Abbie said. "They've been fed this garbage at such a speed–they've barely had time to digest it! I'm really worried about you."

"We should be worried about *everyone*," Aroya added. "Because now this is *our* future too."

Elijah glanced up at the holographic screen. "C'mon. Let's get out of here," he said.

They walked back to the office–eyes to the ground, quiet–all of them contemplating the situation.

"I'm not sure if we failed," Aroya said. "Maybe we arrived just in time. You say this all started only a few months ago?" Aroya asked.

"Yeah, but it seems like forever," he replied.

They arrived at the office. "Do you guys mind hanging out here for a while? I kind of prefer it to the condo," Elijah admitted.

"You don't like your condo?" Abbie asked.

"It's not really ours," Elijah replied. "We had our own place…a cute little house down by the beach. I'd just started teaching my son to surf–then they designated our area 'off-limits to habitation.' They moved us to the new place, and we didn't have much choice about it. It looked real fancy at first, with all the new technology and everything. My wife and kids went crazy nuts over it for a while. But then the point system began, and we were monitored 24/7." He whispered, "Even in the fucking bathroom!" He sighed, exasperated. "We've been miserable ever since."

Elijah swung open the patio door. "Ah, fresh air! I love the smell of the water." He opened a closet. There was a refrigerator hidden inside. "I've got a secret stash of highly unhealthy soda and beer. What'll you have?"

"You got anything fruity?" Abbie asked.

"You betcha!" Elijah said. He tossed Abbie a can of soda, but it landed on the floor. "Sorry, m'dear. You'd better wait a bit before popping that can. Cherry fizz probably wouldn't complement the décor!" he said, chuckling.

Elijah's new attitude made Aroya smile. "Listen to you! You're starting to sound like the old Elijah I used to know!"

"Yeah? I might be *feeling* like him, too. I think you guys are having an effect on me!" He laughed.

While Aroya perused Elijah's books, Abbie lounged on the carpet–looking up at the stars through the open patio door.

"What kind of work do you do here?" Aroya asked.

"I buy and sell rare books–for collectors, mostly. I also do some publishing for the few independent writers still left out there. There's not a huge market for new books these days."

Aroya pulled a book from the shelf and began thumbing through the pages. He smiled amorously at Abbie. "Hey, Abbie–look what I found. Alfred Noyes. The Hedge Rose Opens–"

Blushing, Abbie put a finger to her lips. "Shhh…"

"Do I detect something naughty between those pages?" Elijah said. He studied the ceiling, trying to recall the poem. He began:

> *"How passionately it opens after rain,*
> *And O, how like a prayer*
> *To those great shining skies! Do they disdain*
> *A bride so small and fair?*
> *See the imploring petals, how they part*
> *And utterly lay bare–"*

Embarrassed, Abbie covered her face. "Oh, stop!" she said.

Elijah laughed. "Uh-oh," then turning to Aroya, "did somebody perhaps, trivialize this beautiful poem by using it as a tool of seduction?"

Aroya closed the book, looking at Abbie. "There was nothing *trivial* about it," he said. "I meant every word of it."

The memory of how Aroya touched her while reciting that poem was still fresh in her mind. She took a deep breath and simply said, "Wild horses, Aroya."

Aroya returned the book to the shelf, echoing, "Wild horses, Abbie."

He plopped down on the carpet next to her, opening another book–this one by Keats.

Elijah studied the two of them, highly amused. "You know...just being in the presence of you two somehow makes me feel more alive." He chuckled. "I'd love for the *other* Abbie to meet you!"

"*Me*...meet the *other me?* Do you really think that's a good idea?" Abbie asked.

"Why not?" Elijah said. "I don't know how this time travel thing works, but maybe there're other people here you might also know."

Aroya lowered his book. "I wonder if Dr. Biegel is here. I'd like to thank him. But then again, I guess he wouldn't know for what."

Abbie sat up, exclaiming, "Wait a minute! Something's wrong!"

"What's wrong?" Aroya asked.

"You guys both saw Dr. Eiffel on the TV thing, right?" she asked.

Aroya and Elijah both nodded.

"How old did he look to you?" she asked.

"I dunno...maybe mid-40s?" Elijah replied.

Aroya agreed.

"But he was in his mid-40s, in *my* time–and that was 31 years ago! Think about it!" she exclaimed.

"I guess he should be in his mid-70s now. He didn't look that old." Aroya said.

"Exactly! So what's going on?! Why does he still look exactly the same after 31 years?!" she asked.

Elijah shrugged. "Well...a lot of people use anti-aging technology these days. And he *is* a doctor, so...."

Aroya addressed Abbie. "Did you tell anybody at the hospital about our time travel?"

"No. Nobody even knew about *you*–except Gina."

"Hmm. There's Markus and Millie... Did either of them know what we were planning to do?" Aroya asked.

"Not exactly. But Carlos did, of course," Abbie said.

"But Carlos wouldn't tell anyone. Biegel knew something, but then again, he died," Aroya said.

"My God. Listening to you two is better than reading a good mystery," Elijah said. "And I have a confession to make."

Aroya put down his book. "What's that?"

"My life is boring...very boring," Elijah confessed.

"Compared to what? Your *other* life in *my* time? Is that such a bad thing?" Aroya asked.

"Yes. It's a *very* bad thing," Elijah replied. "Those dreams of you and me, in the old time...they're considered by most to be a kind of sickness. And I've worked for years to get rid of them. But the truth is, I never really wanted to get rid of them. Secretly, I cherish them–like a beloved friend. No matter how rough and ragged they were, they were part of me."

"I cherish those memories too, Elijah…well, most of them…or at least, some of them," Aroya said. "But bad dreams are probably a lot easier than the real thing."

"I'm sure you're right, but there were many nights when I woke up screaming at the top of my lungs," Elijah said. "So, I guess it felt pretty damn real to me at the time! But then again, we do tend to romanticize our memories. Don't we?"

"We worked very hard to romanticize them," Aroya said, "all those nights, around the fire. It was the only thing we had to make it all just a little more bearable."

"Yeah, we really did work at it," Elijah agreed. "I remember my very last night at the warehouse…before the dreams stopped. There was a tall man from Norway who absolutely begged me to bring him to our dream circle. The man only wanted a few lines of poetry, but he really had nothing to trade–except a stone. You were the only one who obliged him."

"That stone," Aroya said, pulling the stone from his pocket, "happens to be what brought us here…and it saved my life, at least twice!"

Abbie held up her stone. "I've got one too!"

"Well, by God–then how do I get one?!" Elijah asked.

Abbie laughed. "I guess you'll have to find your own Vision Maker," she said.

"Yeah. Your own feathered man," Aroya added.

"Oh, there you go again," Elijah playfully protested. "You two always talk in puzzles…and I absolutely love it! Now, how do I go about finding this man?"

"I don't know. Does Brazil still exist?" Abbie asked.

"Brazil? Hmm…" Elijah wondered what Brazil had to do with anything.

"I don't think it's that simple," Aroya said. "I think you need to be recruited or something. It's not exactly a pleasure ride, that's for sure. It's more like a mission."

Abbie was still staring up at the sky. "Look at those bright stars. They're all in a string, and they look like they're moving."

Elijah and Aroya both peered out the door–then they all walked out together to take a better look.

Elijah turned to Abbie, shaking his head. "I'm afraid those aren't stars, my lovely. It's just the new Burk surveillance system."

"Eyes-in-the-sky," Aroya said with a sigh.

Elijah smiled at Abbie. "The only bright star I see tonight is you, my dear." Then he turned to Aroya with a devilish grin. "Do you mind?" he asked Aroya.

Aroya knew what he was up to. "Be my guest," Aroya replied. He handed Elijah the Keats book, but Elijah pushed it away.

"I don't need it," he said. "I know this one by heart." He stepped to the far end of the patio and addressed Abbie: "Abbie, so sweet and bright–this poem is for you:

> *Bright star, would I were stedfast as thou art—*
> *Not in lone splendour hung aloft the night*
> *And watching, with eternal lids apart,*
> *Like nature's patient, sleepless Eremite,*
> *The moving waters at their priestlike task*
> *Of pure ablution round earth's human shores,*
> *Or gazing on the new soft-fallen mask*
> *Of snow upon the mountains and the moors—"*

Aroya politely pushed Elijah aside–continuing:

"No—yet still stedfast, still unchangeable,
Pillow'd upon my fair love's ripening breast,
To feel for ever its soft fall and swell,
Awake for ever in a sweet unrest,
Still, still to hear her tender-taken breath,
And so live ever—or else swoon to death."

"Wild horses, Aroya," Abbie responded, between sighs. She went inside to conceal her desire.

Elijah was impressed by this romantic exchange between his friends. "What does it mean when you say, 'wild horses?'" he asked.

"It means *control your thoughts*–but mostly it means *not now, Aroya*," he replied.

Elijah laughed. "You're a lucky man."

"I never used to think so–" Aroya said, "but ever since Abbie, I tell myself that every day."

An electronic beeping sound rang out in Elijah's office– and a red light hung in mid-air, flashing atop a glowing white globe. Abbie stepped back, startled by the flashing light.

"My God, it's nearly midnight!" Elijah exclaimed, entering the office. "Do you mind waiting on the patio, just for a moment?" he asked Abbie.

Abbie and Aroya sat on the patio while Elijah closed the glass door. They were out of sight, but they could still hear everything quite clearly.

"Accept call!" Elijah called out.

A holographic image floated above the globe, projecting a nearly life-size replica of Administrator

Burk. Shocked, Elijah's mouth fell open. "Hello, Administrator. What can I do for you?"

Burk's hologram turned a circle in mid-air, scanning the room. "Transport reports two unregistered passengers in your vehicle this evening. Our system was unable to make a match. We'd like their names and IDs."

Elijah concealed his nervousness, taking a deep, slow breath. "Yes, two people *did* come to see me this evening. They said they were travelers. I'm a rare book dealer, and one of them was interested in my books."

Suddenly, a holographic monitor materialized above Elijah's head, displaying his vital signs: heart rate, respiration, and blood pressure.

"Did they make a purchase?" Burk asked.

"No," Elijah replied.

"When did they leave?" Burk pressed.

"They stepped out–just before I picked up your call," Elijah replied.

"What were their names?" Burk asked.

Elijah focused on his breathing, well aware that any lie would be detected and displayed on the monitor. "The man's name was Wallace," he said. "And I believe the woman was his girlfriend."

"Mr. Stewart, you *do* realize that your business does not conform to our new regulations, don't you?" Burk advised.

"What do you mean?" Elijah asked.

"As of today, all physical material in print is to be turned over to the Council," Burk continued.

"I don't understand. Turned over? For how long?" Elijah asked.

"Permanently. If there's a problem, you can petition the Council and plead your case," Burk replied. "The data will be reviewed, and if deemed appropriate, it will be stored for those with privilege."

"But my business depends on real books–they're collector's items and investment instruments–like paintings. If I have no physical books, I have no business," Elijah explained.

"Maybe it's best if you find another line of work, Mr. Stewart. I'll make sure that you're reassigned," Burk said.

"But I don't want to be reassigned! This is my life! I love my work!" Elijah exclaimed.

"Don't worry; we'll make sure you love your next assignment as well. And remember, your assistance is required regarding the unregistered passengers. If you should have any further contact with them, we expect a report from you. Do you understand?" Burk asked.

"Yes, Sir," Elijah replied.

The hologram dissolved.

Abbie and Aroya heard everything. The patio door opened, and Elijah stood before them, defeated.

"Would it be possible to transport a few special books back to your time, Abbie?" he asked.

Abbie turned to Aroya.

"If we keep them close to our bodies, they'll probably travel with us," Aroya replied.

"Then please look through my library before you leave and select a few of your favorites," Elijah said.

"Okay," Aroya replied, sadly.

Elijah sat in a chair, hanging his head. Suddenly, there was another loud beep in the office.

"For God's sake. What now?" Elijah muttered. He entered the office and called out, "Accept call!"

A hologram formed in the middle of the room. It was Elijah's wife, Eloise–and she was crying.

"Hi, honey. What's wrong?" Elijah asked, concerned.

"They're relocating us first thing in the morning. We'll be given a new home somewhere else–I don't even know where," she sobbed.

"What?! But why?!" Elijah exclaimed.

"The Council disapproves of your activities. They think you're hiding information. They've determined you're a bad influence on me and the children," Eloise replied.

"The children?! What are you talking about?!"

"It has something to do with unregistered passengers. I think they're referring to the two people you brought to the condo. I just arrived and was unpacking when I got a call from the Administrator himself! This must be really serious, Elijah–for the Administrator to call personally." She let out a heavy sigh. "Anyway, he said we have no avenue of recourse, so I guess I'm just calling to say goodbye."

"Goodbye? No! They can't do that! Where are the children?!" Elijah pleaded.

"They're taking the children to a training community. They won't tell me where. They say if I pass my evaluation, the children will be placed in my vicinity–so that I can at least visit them. Anyway, there's nothing we can do about it because they seem to have total control now. I don't know what they plan on doing with you, but please be careful. I think you're in big trouble."

"Eloise, I'm sorry. Don't worry. We'll find a way to fix this," Elijah pleaded.

The hologram faded away.

Elijah buried his face in his hands–bawling like a baby. It all happened so fast, he never even saw it coming. Nobody did.

The morning sun rose, casting rays through gray ribbons of fog, still clinging to the Golden Gate Bridge. Slivers of yellow sunlight danced across the patio, through the glass door, and into Elijah's office.

Elijah was asleep in his chair. Abbie and Aroya were crashed out on the carpet.

The sunlight swept over Aroya's face, pushing his eyes open. Not wanting to disturb the others, he quietly stepped out onto the patio. Surveying the street below, he thought to himself, *what a mess we've made for Elijah.* As good as their intentions were, Aroya felt deep regret. Again, he recalled the question posited by T. S. Eliot: *Do I dare Disturb the universe?* It was a worthy question.

Abbie tiptoed out to the patio to sit with Aroya. She whispered, "We really screwed things up. What are we gonna do?"

"It does seem that way…but you know, it really wasn't *us.* The walls were already closing in on Elijah, before we even arrived."

"Yeah, I guess so. But did we somehow make it happen? And isn't it weird that our most hated enemies followed us here? Even Dr. Eiffel, and this isn't even his time."

"Yeah, it's weird," Aroya agreed.

Elijah stepped onto the balcony. "It's a new day!" he proclaimed to the rising sun. Then he turned to Abbie and Aroya, noticing their concern. "Well, that's the one thing we can always count on, isn't it? The sun rising!"

"It was a rough night," Aroya said.

"Are you going to be all right?" Abbie asked.

"I don't know," Elijah replied. "I guess time will tell." He leaned over the balcony railing, looking down into the street.

Aroya thought about Elijah's words. *"Time*...will tell," he repeated.

"You read my mind," Abbie whispered.

"Always," Aroya replied.

Elijah noticed Abbie and Aroya conferring. "Okay, what are you kids up to now?" he asked.

"Me and Abbie were just thinking...that maybe you could come back with us. That is, if you want to," Aroya said.

Elijah turned to Abbie. "Then tell me...what is it like in your time?"

"Don't you remember 2019?" Aroya asked.

"Oh yeah, but I was just a kid," Elijah replied.

"Well, it's worse in some ways...but better in others," Abbie said.

"It certainly isn't as clean and organized as this, but it's still a lot better than *my* time," Aroya added.

"Thanks for your offer," Elijah said. "Let me think about it over breakfast. Are you guys ready for more pizza? It's the only place around where we won't be surveilled."

Abbie and Aroya nodded–and they left for the little hole-in-the-wall pizza joint near the water's edge.

Sitting at the old weathered picnic table, they ate piles of spaghetti with garlic bread.

"I didn't even know they served spaghetti here," Elijah remarked.

A large waterbird landed near their table, and Elijah tossed a spaghetti noodle to the bird. They looked on in amusement while the bird comically maneuvered the noodle down its throat. They all laughed out loud.

"Ah, that feels good," Elijah said.

"What feels good?" Abbie asked.

"Laughing with friends," Elijah replied.

"We love your laugh, Elijah," Abbie said.

"I haven't laughed like this since…well, I don't even remember when," Elijah admitted.

"Don't you laugh with your family?" Abbie asked.

"Not really…not out loud. People here are all very pleasant–they smile, and sometimes they giggle or chuckle, but they rarely laugh out loud," Elijah explained.

"That's weird. Back in my time, you laughed quite a lot! Despite the entire world crumbling down around our feet," Aroya said.

"I know, I remember my dreams. That's why I didn't want to let them go." Then he turned to Abbie. "Would you like to meet yourself today?" he asked.

"Today? I thought we'd go back today," she said.

"But her office is only a few blocks away," Elijah said, pleading. "We can just stop by for a moment. Really quick!"

Abbie checked with Aroya.

Aroya nodded, "Sure, why not?"

Elijah smiled like a happy little boy. Just the thought of the two Abbies meeting each other amused him to no end.

"Do you think there was something about the poem we used that set things off course?" Abbie asked Elijah. "What were the past 31 years like–before things started changing?"

"Let's see… About 20 years ago, there was a big shift," Elijah replied. "Things were terrible before then. But around 2030, there were lots of arrests–and after that, freedom was restored. People danced in the streets for a full year! Gradually, people forgot all about that– and everything became very bland and unremarkable. When I was young, it seems we all used to *feel* more. But now, we've stopped feeling so much–and stopped noticing things. Everything was so dependable and predictable for so long–we couldn't even imagine anything ever changing. I think we stopped imagining altogether. The only excitement left was found between the pages of old books–stories leftover from times when the world was not so predictable. I guess that's why the books became so valuable."

"I'm glad to hear things were good for a while," Abbie said. "Maybe we bought you some time."

Aroya broke off a piece of garlic bread and passed the loaf around. Biting into it, he cringed. "No shortage of salt here, I see," he said, gulping his coffee, trying to wash it down.

Abbie tasted her bread–then she too, began gulping her coffee.

Elijah set his bread aside. "I think I'll pass on the bread," he said, observing Abbie and Aroya's discomfort.

Aroya noticed an old man sitting near the water, fishing. He walked over to the old man, peeking into his bucket. There were only crickets at the bottom. "Are you using crickets for bait? What are you fishing for?" Aroya asked.

"Anything that'll eat 'em, I guess," the old man replied. He smiled, then cleared a spot for Aroya. "You're welcome to join me. There's lots of hungry fish in there. I expect to pull one out any minute!" He pushed his hat up, staring into the sky. "They should be comin' 'round this way soon, but they can't see this little corner–for some reason," he chuckled.

Aroya knew what he was referring to–the 'eyes-in-the-sky.' "Do you enjoy fishing?" Aroya asked.

"Oh, yeah. When the world's gone stupid, there's nothin' left to do but fish," he replied.

"I hear that things are getting worse, but I don't follow the news much," Aroya said.

"Well, ya know what they say…'weak minds follow–and sharp minds watch.' I'm a watcher," he said, chuckling.

Aroya laughed too. He really liked this old man.

"I was watching you and your friends," the old man said. "Not being nosy or anything, just curious 'cause hardly anyone knows about this place. Looks like you didn't like your bread much," he said, chuckling again.

"It was too salty."

"Yeah, salt's kind of like life…it needs to be shaken with moderation. Just a little, but not too much. Balance is always best."

"Is that the secret to a happy life? Balance?"

"Oh yeah, of course." He pointed at a seagull in the sky. "Look at that gull, see how he balances 'tween his right and left wing? If he's perfectly balanced, he goes nowhere at all–he just floats in place, as long as the wind keeps him up. He needs to tilt, one way or the other, to go anywhere. But if his tilt is too extreme for too long–well, then he falls. Everything in moderation–even balance."

"I guess he knows how to move with the wind," Aroya said.

The old man nodded. "Yeah, the wind or the water, if you're a surfer."

"Yeah, surfers really know how to balance and tilt," Aroya agreed.

"A surfer's flexible too, and agile. If he's too rigid, then he can't move with the water. Flexibility and balance keep him from fallin'."

"Do you think that's why the whole world's gone stupid? Is the world out of balance?" Aroya asked.

"Oh yeah, they're outta balance, all right. But that's not the worst of it."

"What's the worst of it?"

"They lost their moral compass–that's the worst of it."

"You mean, they're not moral?"

"Oh, they're moral, alright. Maybe too moral now. Outta balance that way, ya know. But it was even worse before." The old man studied Aroya's face. "Ya mind me askin', how old you are?"

"Not at all. I'm 37."

The old man did some mental calculations. "So maybe you remember what it was like…before everything turned 'round. Things were really crazy then–no moral compass at all. It's like this adventure we call life has hills, and valleys, and tall mountains that we gotta get 'round–and that's what keeps life interesting. But without a moral compass, we can get lost. We need that compass to get back on course if we veer off too far. Yep, things were really crazy back then. Now they're just really stupid!" He chuckled again.

"Hey, it's time to go!" Elijah hollered.

Aroya smiled at the old man. "Thank you for a wonderful conversation. Have a nice day!" he said, heading off in the direction of his friends.

"You have a nice day too!" the old man yelled back.

Aroya caught up with the others, and they started walking.

"Where are we going? To old Abbie's place?" Aroya asked.

Abbie laughed. "I'm not sure she'd appreciate you calling her 'old' Abbie."

"You're right. Maybe I should call her Abigail senior. More respectful."

"Yes, much more respectful," Abbie replied.

"Hey, did the old man catch anything?" Elijah asked.

"Nope," Aroya replied. "But it was nice talking with him. I think I learned something about balance. Maybe that's where we went wrong. There needs to be a balance between extremes, or else everything falls. Maybe that's why Dr. Biegel called it *the prelude to a fall.*"

"A balance between extremes?" Elijah said. "We haven't had extremes here for nearly 20 years. In fact, there's been no movement at all. Oh, wait–everything's been *extremely* still."

Abbie laughed. "Extreme stillness? Some people call that death!"

"Maybe the death of a society," Elijah said. "People here are so afraid to rock the boat."

"But if the boat's not rocking–then you're not moving," Aroya observed.

"That's exactly what's wrong–nothing moves. Everything's been so still, for so long–it's become stagnant," Elijah said. "Nobody likes the new programs–but people are just too polite to complain."

"It's getting like that in my time too–only, it looks different," Abbie said. "People are either indifferent or scared. We can smell the rot, but nobody does anything about it."

"It's worse than indifference here–it's rigidity," Elijah replied. "They fear change so much–they beg for restrictive regulations just to keep things more predictable. There's an obsession with order, and we all strain under the weight of it."

"It sounds like it's out of balance," Aroya noted. "That's what happened in my time too. There was a demand for total order–then suddenly, everything flipped into chaos."

Elijah quoted Tennyson: "*Turning to scorn with lips divine The falsehood of extremes*! "I guess extremes were also a problem in Tennyson's time."

"Maybe all times suffer from extremes," Abbie replied.

"Then what can be done about extremes?" Aroya asked. "Things tip too far one way–and they collapse…then they tip too far the other way–and they collapse again…but if they're extremely still–they fall…or rot." He paused to consider the conundrum. "Abbie, I'm not sure if there's a poem for this situation," he concluded.

19– ABIGAIL LITE 2.0

2050

San Francisco

Timeline 2.0

In a charming alleyway of old brick buildings, adorned with colorful flower stands and trendy outdoor cafés– they approached an office with a polished plaque reading: *Abigail Lite, Spiritual Counselor.* It was nearing the lunch hour, and business people came and went, all chatting merrily.

Elijah pushed a button on the door, and a miniature hologram of Abigail senior appeared above a small white globe.

"Good afternoon!" the Abigail hologram said. "Oh, and just look at you all! Come in, come in!"

The door swung open, and a delightful silver-haired woman stood in the foyer, grinning like a child on Christmas morning.

"Sorry to just drop in like this, but since it's lunchtime, I figured you might be free," Elijah said. "Let me introduce you to—"

"This is surely young Aroya," Abigail senior interrupted. "And of course, this is his sweet Abbie," she continued, admiring young Abbie–who, of course, reflected her own youthful image. "I've been expecting you!" she said.

"You were expecting us? Oh, but *of course* you were," Elijah said, winking at Aroya.

They entered the cozy office. Abigail senior served tea from an English teapot decorated with dainty pink roses. Situated atop a Persian rug, five overstuffed chairs congregated in a semicircle, flanked by a half-dozen floor cushions. Bookcases stood from floor to ceiling–and against the far wall was an antique altar carved in mahogany.

Smiling, Aroya approached the altar. "Look at this. After 31 years, everything's pretty much the same," he said.

There was a vase holding a single rose, an old picture of Archangel Michael, and an ornately framed photo of Abbie and Aroya (versions 2.0) from when they were in their mid-50s.

"Abbie, it's us!" Aroya exclaimed, shocked.

Abigail senior motioned for young Abbie to go take a look. Young Abbie stood at Aroya's side, both of them speechless at witnessing themselves in the future.

"They look happy," young Abbie whispered.

Abigail senior joined them. "Yes. We were very happy."

"Were?" Aroya asked.

"My Aroya, the senior, the love of my life–expired about eight years ago…on his 60th birthday," Abigail senior said. "We didn't know the technology was still inside him…until it was too late."

"Oh, I'm so sorry," young Abbie responded.

Aroya knew what this meant, and it made him uneasy. "That must mean it's still inside me too," he said.

Abigail senior studied Aroya's face. "Possibly, but if that's the case, you can remove it before your 60th birthday and still enjoy your golden years…with your own sweet Abbie."

"Do you have any idea where it was?" Aroya asked.

"I'm sorry, but I don't," Abigail senior replied.

"Then how do you know it was the technology?" young Abbie asked.

"Because right before he went, his skin suddenly turned ice cold and silvery…just like when he had first arrived. It was as though he had a time-bomb hidden inside him that went off right on cue," Abigail senior said. "When his skin began to change, on the day before his birthday…we knew it was his expiration date, but there was no way to stop it."

"That's horrible," Elijah said. "And you never said a thing about it."

"Why recount such a sad story. And besides, if I had mentioned it, how would I honestly explain who he was?" Abigail senior replied. "The world only remembers him now as an antiquated writer of sweet old-fashioned poems: Mr. Wallace A. Roya."

"Of course!" Elijah exclaimed. "And all these years, I thought Wallace A. Roya was an old man that lived by a river."

"He wasn't an old man when he wrote those poems...actually, he was still rather young," Abigail senior replied, laughing. "And the river was the Missouri River in Omaha, his childhood home."

Aroya sat down, visibly moved. "I met my mother again in 2019, and I told her to go with my father to Omaha."

"Yes, I know all about it," Abigail senior said. "He told me of that magical day when he was just six years old–and an Angel came to visit! The Angel warned his mother there would be a great catastrophe, and he advised her to go with her husband to Omaha. There never was a catastrophe, and he always missed San Francisco–his very first home."

"But if the catastrophe never happened, then how did he get *processed*?" Aroya asked.

"His father convinced him to join the military when he was just 17," Abigail senior explained. "He was a gifted psychic. They used his gifts for military purposes. It was before the arrests, and the whole world was falling into a very dark place."

"Elijah told us about the arrests. But he said things improved after that," Aroya remarked.

"Yes, they improved for most. But *my* Aroya worked in special operations until he was 37 years old–it was 2050 for him at the time. That's when they *processed* him. Things may look pleasant on the surface in our 2050, but according to my Aroya, a portion of our military was–and *is*–involved in a very dark agenda."

"How did he revert back?" Aroya inquired.

"I have a friend who is a doctor. He helped him. It was difficult to undo. It took many treatments, and it nearly killed him," Abigail senior replied.

"I'm sorry, but I'm still not following," Elijah said. "What's this about being *processed*?" he asked.

"Both our Aroyas were infused with technology against their will," Abigail senior explained. "We never imagined that science was even capable of such a thing. But the military has all types of advanced technology they keep hidden from us."

Young Abbie rubbed her head. "I still don't understand something. If my Aroya was originally 37 years old in 2050, then how is it that he would also be much older now–when it's still 2050?" she asked.

"If Aroya senior were alive today," Aroya replied, "he would have been 31 years older. And if I stay with you in *your* 2019, then eventually I will also be 31 years older in the year 2050."

"Exactly," Abigail senior replied. "My Aroya disappeared from his timeline in 2050, when he was 37 years old–and from 2019 onward, we aged together."

"So, there was never a catastrophe for him?" young Abbie asked.

"No," Abigail senior replied. "Because of the arrests, we never had to go through that."

"There was never even a catastrophe, and still, I suffered the same fate," Aroya noted sadly.

"*My* Aroya was just another *aspect* of you…another *version* of yourself, but he existed on a distinctly different timeline. If he were still alive, he would be with us today, just like young Abbie is here with me. In most ways, we're the same, but we're also different in some."

Young Abbie squinted her eyes. "I still don't get it. If my Aroya stays with me, after we return to 2019–then what happens to the Aroya, who already lived through the catastrophe of 2030–when 2030 rolls around again?" she asked.

"Well, if you're successful…I suppose that he won't have to live through it again. There will always be a younger Aroya around as he ages, but I'm not sure how the younger Aroya will be affected later on in life. I have a friend who knows more about these things, and according to him, whenever we time travel, there is some sort of splinter."

"If Abbie and I are successful, the six-year-old Aroya I met in 2019, won't *ever* be processed–like Aroya senior was," Aroya added.

"That's right," Abigail senior said. "But even though that happened, he eventually met his Abigail and went on to live a relatively long life–a wonderful life," Abigail senior said.

"And he became an internationally recognized poet!" Elijah added.

"He was really a poet?" Aroya asked.

"Of course. And just like our dear friend Elijah, poetry was always on his mind–especially every night, in his dreams," Abigail senior said.

"Do you know *why* they love poetry so much?" young Abbie asked.

"I never understood," Abigail senior replied, "until I met Elijah." Tears formed in her eyes. "Elijah, you came to me for help…but you have no idea how much you helped me to understand my own husband. I know you never said his name during our talks, but when you described him in your dreams, I somehow knew it was some version of him. And the poems he chose in your dreams were the same poems he loved in real life."

"Was he the one who taught you so much about time travel?" Elijah asked.

"Yes, him and someone else," Abigail senior replied. "My husband escaped danger by using a special stone to travel away from his doomed future in 2050," Abigail senior replied.

"Do you have a stone, too?" young Abbie asked.

"No. I never time traveled with him, and he never time traveled again," Abigail senior replied. "Things were still pretty crazy here in 2019 when he arrived–and he was mugged straight away. At the time, all he had on him was the stone–so they took it."

"But if you never time traveled, then how did you know that *my* dreams were connected to a completely different timeline?" Elijah asked.

"Honestly, I didn't quite understand completely," Abigail senior replied, "but I meditated on it. I followed my spiritual teacher, and he showed me the rest in visions."

"That's just what Abbie would do," Aroya remarked.

Young Abbie sat down, looking at Abigail senior. "I know you're supposed to be a 'version' of me, and actually, you look a lot like my mother–but to hear you describe your journey in meditation…now I really *do* believe that you must be me. And actually, it feels very strange."

"I know what you mean," Abigail senior said. "I can only see you as a kind of daughter…anything more than that, and my mind just ties itself into knots! But in a way, it's kind of like talking to ourselves in a mirror."

"You mean, a *looking glass*...and I'm feeling more like Alice by the minute!" young Abbie said.

"Yes, it's a peculiar feeling. Even though we never met, we actually know each other quite well," Abigail senior said.

Aroya remembered that line. "The feathered man said that! He told us, *you will see a person you never met–but you will know this person very well.*"

"That might apply to me as well," Elijah said. "We never actually met, but in another time, we knew each other well. The common link between the two times seems to be poetry."

"I have a friend who might say you were in 'sync' with an almost identical 'parallel world,'" Abigail senior said. "Maybe it's the poetry that creates the 'sync'."

"Well...I'm not sure I'd call them *identical* worlds," Aroya said. "Things were a lot different in my world, even if some of the people were the same."

"Isn't that interesting," Abigail senior said, "even though some things are different, the actors are mostly the same. According to the theory, there are infinite worlds filled with infinite versions of ourselves."

"I guess that's why Administrator Burk and Klaus Wolfe are also here," young Abbie said, making a sour face. "Wow...infinite versions of evil. That's an unpleasant thought!" Then she recalled Dr. Eiffel. "But why is Dr. Eiffel here? He isn't from Aroya's time, not at his current age, anyway. It doesn't make any *sense!*"

"Does any of this really make sense?" Abigail senior replied.

"Maybe it makes more sense to me because I'm the one who started it all," Aroya said.

"Aroya, we were chosen…remember?" young Abbie replied. "Neither one of us planned any of this."

"Yeah. It was the feathered man who made all the arrangements. I wonder how he got those random people to give us those stones?" Aroya said.

"Ah…the crystal stones. I saw them in my vision. They're slightly different from the one my husband described," Abigail senior said.

"Aroya was taught how to use his stone. But mine didn't come with any instructions," young Abbie said.

"My husband told me he was taught to envision the happiest memory from his childhood when he used the stone. He envisioned a time when he was six years old in San Francisco, before his family moved to Omaha. What memory did *you* use to get here, Aroya?" Abigail senior asked.

"I used Elijah," Aroya replied.

"You *used* me?" Elijah asked.

"I *focused* on you to steer us here," Aroya clarified.

"That's okay. Feel free to use me anytime," Elijah joked. "As long as you get us out of this mess in the end." Elijah turned to Abigail senior and asked, "How did we get into this mess, anyway?"

"I'm not sure, but some say it was the technology," Abigail senior replied. "It developed much too fast, and humanity never had time to mature with it. Originally, it was meant as a tool, but instead, it became the chains of our enslavement. But then again, that's like saying stabbings are caused by knives. Both are only tools. Whether or not they're used as weapons depends on the hand that controls them."

"I can already see it beginning in my time," young Abbie said. "The technology seems almost too powerful to hold back...like it has a life of its own."

"Is the problem balance?" Aroya asked. "Are things out of balance?"

"Oh, the fisherman again," Elijah joked.

"Balance is just the beginning, and it's on balance that everything depends–but there's more to it than that," Abigail senior said. "My own spiritual teacher compares life to music. There is balance in the rhythm of music, but perfect balance does not always create enjoyable music. Maybe it just puts you to sleep, instead." She formulated a better explanation. "Overall, there needs to be a dynamic aspect to it–a change in tempo or a change in amplitude...because the dynamic aspect is what makes us feel alive! But at the same time, there still needs to be a certain balance–otherwise, it's just chaos!"

"Like the bird or the surfer–they tip back and forth– otherwise they fall," Aroya said.

"Exactly!" Abigail senior replied. "So there's a balance in the rhythm, and it's achieved by the beat...but there's more to music than just the beat. There's a variety of instruments and voices and lyrics– all adding to the total experience." She turned to Aroya. "If you are anything like *my* Aroya, then you value beauty over almost everything else. Am I correct?"

"Yes. I'm just like that," Aroya answered.

"Then think about your beloved *beauty:* a woman's face, a painting, a landscape, or a song," Abigail senior continued. "The beauty that you so adore is not found simply in balance, although that is part of it. It is ultimately achieved by harmony–the harmony of the composition. It is an arrangement of elements, both subtle and extreme–all playing a part. Where there is harmony, there is beauty."

"It's like poetry," Elijah said. "The words, the rhyme, the meter…they must all be in harmony."

"That's right," Abigail senior replied. "So you see, our problem is not simply a lack of balance. The sickness in everything is probably more because of a lack of harmony."

"But isn't balance important, so we avoid extremes?" young Abbie asked.

Abigail senior took a moment to compose her answer. "When one begins piano lessons," she said, "one doesn't begin with a lecture about composition. Instead, one begins with the metronome, only a needle, bouncing from one side to the other, keeping the rhythm. If the needle sticks in the center, the movement stops completely, and then there's no rhythm at all. It's the movement, from one side to the other, from one extreme to the other, that creates the bones on which the whole composition is formed. *Extremes* are essential, and if there's rhythmic movement between them, then we have a sort of balance. Balance must be understood first, to understand harmony. But the ultimate goal, overall, is harmony."

Aroya still struggled to understand the root of the problem so that he might choose the perfect poem. After all, one mistake was enough! He really wanted to do a better job in his next attempt to change the world.

"So, we start with balance…and then we move to harmony?" Aroya asked.

"It's more complicated than that," Abigail senior replied, "because, within a state of harmony, there's still additional balance required…whenever opposing extremes are part of a composition. Consider a beautiful painting: there may be opposing colors, but if they are arranged in a balanced way, the painting becomes harmonious and pleasing. Understanding both balance and harmony is important for understanding all aspects of life. In *your* time, Aroya–there was great misery and disgust, due to a complete lack of harmony. And in *our* time, a lack of balance also creates disharmony–leading again to misery and disgust. Too much of a bad thing and too much of a good thing–are both just too much."

"But we've been told it's a good thing–to always keep things balanced and pleasant?" Elijah said.

"Look at our life here, Elijah. Up until recently, was it not perfectly pleasant?" Abigail senior posited.

"Well, it *was* pleasant…until Burk and the Council came along. *Torturously* pleasant and *exhaustively* boring," Elijah replied.

"Yes, because we made such an effort to avoid the unpleasant," Abigail senior said. "All aspects of darkness and light contribute to beauty and happiness. Here is the difference between balance and harmony: the 'balance' of a weighing scale can exist in stasis, but harmony is never static. It is always dynamic, always playing, always moving. Balance is only a rule applied to aspects of life to *achieve* the goal of harmony–which in turn, creates *beauty.*"

"But when we used poetry to change the future," young Abbie said, "our intention was for *freedom.* How did wishing for freedom get things so out of balance?"

"It's not as simple as just choosing one thing over another, or just achieving balance alone," Abigail senior replied. "You must consider the full multitude of aspects, and the dance between them when composing your wish for the future."

"The freedom poem was a bad choice?" Aroya asked.

"Choosing freedom was the natural thing to do. Where people lack water, they sing songs about water. Where people lack freedom, they write poems about freedom. There is nothing without freedom, but life still requires more than that," Abigail senior replied.

"Then it requires harmony...and you can't have harmony if you just choose one thing over another," Aroya said.

"That's right," Abigail senior said. "The whole of life is more like a symphony than a duet. The interplay of opposites is important, or things become static–but it's not just a matter of this or that–freedom or slavery. That way of thinking is a trap. You must begin seeing life as music. We are like the members of an orchestra, all performing a symphony together. There is a composition, and everyone agrees to follow it. If there is no agreement, then there is no harmony, and the music will suffer. The focus should not be on the choice of one thing or another–instead, the focus should be on achieving harmony with all things together. It's an enormous task, and that's why we must call on the Creator for assistance."

"Can't we do something about it ourselves?" Elijah asked.

"Yes, of course," Abigail senior replied. "We must fight to restore harmony, and we must choose brave defenders to fight alongside us. And because it's much more than any *one* man can do by himself, we must call on the Creator and his helpers."

"You mean the Archangels?" young Abbie asked.

"Yes, exactly!" Abigail senior replied.

Young Abbie smiled at Aroya, silently sharing their private memory about Archangel Michael.

Even if there are bad actors in the orchestra, the musicians must keep on playing. If they stop playing, to whine and complain, the music stops! God, the Creator, wants us all to keep playing, and to sing and dance! It is our engagement with the music of life that draws the heavenly forces to us!"

"So, don't stop the music, no matter what!" Aroya exclaimed. "When things bottom out, and you hit a wall, just get back up and start dancing and singing again!" he said.

They all laughed.

Then, Aroya recalled the desperation of his time–and how he learned to cope. "In *my* time, we kept the music going by reciting poetry...no matter what. It kept us alive inside. Your comparison of life to music is beautiful. You learned this from your teacher? Who is your teacher?" Aroya asked.

Abigail senior retrieved a book from her bookshelf.

Aroya read the title: *"The Music of Life."* Then he turned to young Abbie, excited. "Look! It's our Sufi poet–Hazrat Inayat Khan!"

"Of course it is," young Abbie replied with a smile.

"Yes. It was a Sufi teacher who protected my husband," Abigail senior said, "when he was being pursued. He hid my husband away in a desert cave for months. During that time, he taught him many things– and in turn, my husband taught those things to me. That Sufi teacher is the one who gave him the stone–and taught him how to use it for time travel. It saved his life!"

"I came across my stone differently," Aroya said, "but it also saved my life." He remembered his own narrow escape. "I'm familiar with this Sufi teacher, and I like his comparison of life to music–but how will I find the perfect poem to address all those things required for harmony?"

"For this, you will need more than a poem," Abigail senior replied. "For this…you will need a prayer."

"The difference between a prayer and a poem," Aroya said, "confused me once, and the results were–"

"Extraordinary!" young Abbie interrupted.

They all laughed.

"I remember when people used to pray, when I was a child," Elijah said, "but they don't seem to do it much anymore. Why is it–that people don't pray anymore?" he asked.

"Maybe they forgot how," Aroya said. "My mother forgot, and I forgot too. I guess that's why I didn't know the difference between a poem and a prayer."

"The difference between poetry and prayer is that poems address the experience of being human," Abigail senior explained. "Even when the poet describes his experience with God, his poem is still an expression about the human experience. Prayers, on the other hand, although poetic in a sense–instead, address God directly. Prayers ask God for forgiveness, they give thanks, and they petition for assistance."

"Abbie has been teaching me how to pray," Aroya said. "I think I'm beginning to understand. But one time, something happened when I recited a prayer. Something very unexpected." He glanced at young

Abbie, recalling the night on the rooftop. "Where I'm from, they call me a mutant…because I have abilities that others don't have." He bowed his head. "I'm not sure it's safe for mutants to pray."

"What happened when you recited the prayer?" Abigail senior asked.

Aroya breathed a heavy sigh. "I burnt the feet off two men–"

"And you saved my life!" young Abbie exclaimed.

"Wow! How did that happen?" Elijah asked.

Aroya walked to the altar and pointed to Archangel Michael.

"I prayed to him…and when I was praying, I heard Abbie screaming. Suddenly, I turned all fiery and electric!" Aroya said.

"Is it safe then," Elijah asked Abigail senior, "for Aroya to pray?"

Aroya turned to Elijah. "Do you remember the *goo* in your dreams?" he asked. "We used to play with it? It didn't make you crazy like everyone else. Why was that?" Aroya asked facetiously.

"I *do* remember the goo," Elijah replied. "But I don't know why it didn't affect me like that."

"It's because we're *both mutants*!" Aroya said.

"Oh, really?" Elijah said, surprised. "Does that mean it's dangerous for *me* to pray too?" he asked.

"But it only happened that one time!" young Abbie interrupted. "And only because I needed help! I was calling for help!"

"I suspect that's true," Abigail senior said. "Archangels don't just show up if they're not truly needed."

"I'm still confused about it all. I may be a mutant, but I'm not an Archangel," Aroya said.

"No, you're not an Archangel, but he lent you his powers to fight the evil men. Correct?" Abigail senior asked.

Aroya shrugged. "Yeah, I guess. But I didn't turn into an Archangel or anything–I mean, I didn't get *wings* like him."

Abbie stifled a giggle.

"You want wings?" Abigail senior asked.

"Well, ya know...if I'm going to do the Archangel thing, it might be useful," Aroya said.

"Yeah. Wings would be cool!" Elijah said, totally serious.

Young Abbie laughed. "I'm sorry, but this is kind of funny–in a cute way."

"I'm sure if wings were needed, you would have gotten them," Abigail senior said. "Besides, I've always assumed that the wings were really more energetic than physical."

Suddenly Elijah became somber–and turned to Abigail senior. "They took Eloise...and the children," he said.

"What?! But why?!" Abigail senior asked.

"It was because of us...me and Abbie," Aroya replied. "They found out about us being here, and now they're punishing Elijah because he won't turn us in."

"The Council took them," Elijah replied. "They're okay, but they won't tell me where they are. They inferred it's a permanent arrangement–but I'll figure something out. They're also threatening to take my books and close my business. They want to *reassign* me," he said, shaking his head.

"I'm so sorry, Elijah," Abigail senior said, shocked. "Is there anything I can do?"

"Yes," Elijah replied. "You can teach me how to pray, and I'm not scared of turning all fiery and electric. In fact, I look forward to it!"

"Of course," Abigail senior said. "But first, let's think about how we should go about it, considering this is a highly unusual situation."

"I think Abbie's a mutant too–she just doesn't know it," Aroya remarked.

"Why do you say that?" young Abbie demanded, surprised.

"Because you generate electricity from your body when you pray and meditate," Aroya answered.

"If young Abbie's a mutant–then you know what that means…" Elijah said, turning to Abigail senior.

"Yes. I also do that when I pray and meditate," Abigail senior replied.

"So, all four of us are mutants! Wow! Talk about a *highly unusual situation!*" Elijah joked.

They laughed.

"I have a friend who's fascinated with time travel. I told him I was expecting a visit from you today." Abigail senior said.

"But how did you even know they were coming?" Elijah asked.

Abigail senior smiled, indicating there was much more to the story. "I saw it last night during meditation. I was so sure of it that I canceled all of my clients today. And then I called my friend. I've been following your story during my meditations–for many months now. I can't see everything–there are still gaps and holes–but I do know what you've been up to–and what your intentions are."

"You called your friend because you knew they'd be *time-traveling* here today?!" Elijah exclaimed.

"Yes. And my friend is wondering if you might allow him just a few minutes of your time. He has so many questions," Abigail senior said.

"Sure. Okay," young Abbie and Aroya replied.

"But honestly, we don't really know very much. I've only had minimal instruction–the rest is just guesswork," Aroya said.

"Yeah. If we really knew what we were doing, maybe we wouldn't have made such a mess," young Abbie added.

"You didn't make this mess–you simply discovered it," Abigail senior said.

An electronic tone rang at the door. Abigail senior excused herself, attending to the new visitor.

"I knew this was going to be interesting!" Elijah said with a big smile.

Abigail senior returned with her friend.

It was Markus! He was now 73-years-old, and his hair and beard were pure white. With his round belly and rosy cheeks, he looked perfectly jolly. He carried an old-fashioned doctor's bag.

Young Abbie and Aroya were surprised to see him.

"Markus! I'm so happy to see you!" young Abbie said, moving closer for a hug. Then she stopped, realizing he didn't recognize her.

"Well, I guess you spared me the introduction," Abigail senior said.

"I'm sorry," young Abbie said, awkwardly. "I forgot..."

"Do we know each other?" Markus asked, amused.

Again, Aroya repeated what the Vision Maker said: *"You will see a person you never met–but you will know this person very well."*

"Know me very well, do you?" Markus replied, smiling.

"Yes, Markus. You're a very dear friend," young Abbie said.

"Oh, my goodness! Then come here, girl–and give me a big hug!" Markus said.

Young Abbie hugged Markus, delighted–inviting him to sit with her. "We hear you have questions for us…about time travel?" she said.

"Yes, indeed. It's been a lifelong fascination of mine," Markus replied. He leaned forward, whispering. "I'm sure they've been doing it for years, but for some reason, they've been keeping it a secret!"

"I hope you won't be disappointed because actually, we don't know very much," young Abbie said.

Markus turned his attention to Aroya. "And you must be–" He did a double-take, raising his bushy eyebrows. Turning to Abigail senior, he said, "Well…this must be a little strange for you, Abigail…having *Mr. Wallace A. Roya* back from the past!"

"Actually, it's been quite delightful," Abigail senior replied.

Markus extended his hand to Aroya, and they shook. He hesitated before letting go. "Oh, *my*… I think I'm having one of those *déjà vu* moments."

"Maybe you're just in *sync* with a parallel world?" Abigail senior suggested.

"Yes, actually–that could be it! Interesting sensation," Markus noted.

Elijah extended his hand to Markus, but Markus pushed it away, laughing. "Oh, stop it, Elijah! I know you!" he said, joking. Then, taking a closer look, he teased, "Or…do I?"

"Or *do* you?" Elijah returned the joke.

They all laughed.

"Well, I'm glad to see we still all have our sense of humor–even in this highly unusual situation," Markus said.

"Here we go again, with the *highly unusual situation,*" Elijah joked. "Tell me, Markus–are you a mutant too?" Elijah teased.

"A mutant?" Markus replied, confused. "Elijah, what in God's name are you on about?!"

"Apparently, Elijah and Aroya are considered mutants back in the old 2050 timeline," Abigail senior explained. "And Aroya suspects that young Abbie and I must *also* be mutants because our bodies buzz with energy during meditation."

"Mutants? Hardly. Well, I mean the two Abbies anyway…I'm not sure about you boys." Markus laughed. "There are South American tribes who still vibrate–and accomplished practitioners in the East. The vibrating life energy that they generate is quite normal. All humans used to do it–most of us simply forgot how. The two Abbies are fortunate enough to have remembered…something that most of us have long forgotten."

"Well, I guess that's a relief!" young Abbie said.

"A relief, huh? Does that mean you don't wanna be part of our club anymore?" Aroya joked.

"Not until the membership comes with wings," young Abbie teased.

"That's not fair. You know I'd get them for you if I could," Aroya said, playing along.

"I think Abbie just admitted that she wants wings! Now, isn't that kind of 'funny and cute?'" Elijah teased, laughing.

"Hold on! What's all this about wings?" Markus asked.

"It seems that Aroya had a very powerful experience involving Archangel Michael. And for a short period, he was granted some of his powers–but unfortunately, not his wings," Abigail senior explained.

"Oh, I see. So, you want wings, do you?" Markus leaned over and whispered to Abigail senior.

She walked over to the bookcase, returning with something small in her hand.

Markus revealed a little bell and rang it. *DING!* "There you go! You've got your wings!" He chuckled.

"What's with the bell? I don't get it," Elijah asked, confused.

"It's from an old movie. Sorry, I'm sure it predates you. Something about an Angel getting his wings every time you hear a bell," Markus replied, smiling.

"Whatever you say, old man," Elijah joked.

"So Markus… What did you wanna know about time travel?" young Abbie asked.

"My first question is…how do you do it?" Markus asked.

Young Abbie smiled at Aroya. They'd heard those words before, from the *other* Markus. Right on cue, they both pulled out their crystal stones.

"What's this?" Markus asked.

"This is how we time travel," young Abbie said. She handed her stone to Markus.

Markus examined it, holding it up to the light. "What? No fancy Tesla machine or DeLorean DMC-12?"

Abbie and Aroya laughed.

"Now *I'm* the one getting a déjà vu feeling," young Abbie said.

Markus didn't understand.

"When we showed the *other* Markus the stone–in *my* time–he replied in exactly the same way. Word-for-word!" young Abbie said.

"How interesting!" Markus replied. "There must be some kind of bleed over between the timelines–or the parallel worlds. Maybe it has something to do with morphic resonance."

"Morphic what?" Elijah asked.

"Morphic resonance," Markus replied. "It's a theory by Rupert Sheldrake…and it could explain quite a lot of things. It operates on the idea that events in one place can recreate those same events in another place. That is–if they're connected by the same 'morphic field.'" Markus handed the stone back to young Abbie. "So tell me…how does it work?"

"Aroya better explain–because honestly, it's still a mystery to me," young Abbie said.

"You hold the stone straight out, about shoulder high," Aroya said. "And you put your other hand underneath. Then you desire to be with someone–while focusing on the stone. Finally, you drop the stone while visualizing that you're with that person. You catch it in your other hand, and there you are–in another time."

"But what happens when you drop the stone?" Markus asked, unsatisfied with Aroya's explanation. "Do you travel through a tunnel, or fly through the air– or does everything just go black, and you wake up there?"

"When the stone falls, things ripple, and the floor moves–like there's a wave underneath it. It always knocks us down. And when it stops, we've arrived," Aroya explained.

Markus pondered Aroya's explanation. "You say it is as if there were *waves*? Hmm... I think I might know what's happening. But why use the stone? Does it have special properties? Where did you get it?"

"We both received stones in our own times: me in 2019 and Aroya in 2050–both from different people," young Abbie said. "But I never received any instructions...only Aroya did. We've used it to time travel and to change things. Actually, we don't really know what we're doing at all–we just follow the instructions," young Abbie said.

"Who gives you the instructions?" Markus asked. "I mean...if that's okay to ask?"

"A man with a painted face, wearing feathers on his head. He's called the Vision Maker," young Abbie said.

"A painted face and feathers. He sounds like a shaman," Markus replied.

"Yes. Something like that," young Abbie said.

"Have you ever tried it without the rock...I mean, by just holding your hand out while desiring something?" Markus asked.

"No. I was never taught that," Aroya said.

"Maybe you should try it sometime...on something small and inconsequential, just as an experiment,"

Markus suggested. "My suspicions are that it might just be a matter of quantum physics working along with your mind," Markus said. "It's the *wave* phenomenon that points to this."

"Yeah, you said that before…in 2019," Aroya replied, smiling.

Markus chuckled. "Well, I guess it's nice to know that I'm consistent…even throughout parallel universes!"

"Oh, Markus, you're nothing if not consistent!" Abigail senior joked.

Markus stood up, preparing to leave. "I suppose you're right. I'm an old man, set in my ways."

"Markus, before you leave," Abigail senior said, "our young Aroya has a problem. I'm wondering if you might offer him some advice. I told him about how *my* Aroya expired."

"Oh, the implant!" Markus exclaimed. "Yes, I could see how that would concern him. When I removed the technology from the *other* Aroya, I didn't know about the implant…not until it was too late," he said, sadly. "Hold on…I have something here." Markus dug around in his bag and pulled out a meter. "Here it is. I use it to locate metal fragments in wounds at the hospital, but it should work for implants, as well." He approached Aroya, holding the device. "Now, Aroya, just stand here, perfectly straight–with your arms raised, so I can scan you."

Aroya stood, raising his arms while Markus scanned his body–up and down and all around. While scanning the back of his head, the device came alive with escalating numbers and a high-pitched whistling sound.

"Aha! I found something!" Markus said.

Young Abbie moved closer to watch the meter while the numbers continued to climb.

"Aroya, he found it!" young Abbie exclaimed, excited. Then she remembered Dr. Biegel in the old hospital. "Oh, that's why Dr. Biegel wanted that surgical tray. He was preparing to cut it out!"

"But Klaus and Burk showed up!" Aroya exclaimed, recalling how they'd burst through the doors.

"I'll be glad to remove it for you if you'll drop by my office tomorrow," Markus said.

"I'm not sure we can stay. But if it's set to go off when Aroya turns 60, then don't we still have time?" young Abbie asked.

Aroya ran his fingers through his hair, trying to detect the implant in his head.

"I'm afraid you won't find it that way—it's rather small and embedded quite deep," Markus said. "Wherever you end up next...you'll need to find yourself a trustworthy doctor to cut that thing out. Oh, wait a minute! Odds are wherever you go—*I'll* be there!" He laughed. "Well, that is...in timelines involving 2019 and 2050, anyway."

"Except not in *my* time," Aroya said. "I don't remember you being there at all. Unless you were in the Sky Council."

"The Sky Council? Oh, my! I certainly don't resonate with that! But the doctor's name you spoke of—Dr. Biegel—that name is familiar to me. Would that, by chance, be Dr. *Samuel* Biegel?"

Young Abbie and Aroya perked up.

"Yes, I think that was his first name," Aroya said.

"Well, well, well… *Dr. Samuel A. Biegel* happened to be my department head. He was an acclaimed researcher, widely published in his field."

"You said he *was*? young Abbie asked. "Does that mean he's–"

"I'm afraid so," Markus replied. "He recently passed away quite suddenly on his 60th birthday, just like Aroya senior did. Odd coincidence. His heart just stopped beating in his sleep. It's quite a mystery, really."

Young Abbie recalled the grisly way that Dr. Biegel died in the old 2050–with a bullet in his chest, falling into a puddle of goo. "At least it was a peaceful death," young Abbie added.

"Yes…at least there's that," Abigail senior agreed, handing Markus his coat and bag.

"Well, I'm afraid I must be going," Markus said. "But I had such a lovely time with you all–and honestly, I haven't laughed like that in a very long time!" Putting on his coat, he said, "Thank you, all–and good night."

Abigail walked Markus to the door.

"Apparently, the *morphic field* resonates loudly with Markus," young Abbie joked. "It's kind of comforting to know that we're not much different, even in parallel universes."

"When we first arrived, I wasn't so sure about Elijah," Aroya said. "It sure is nice to have the *old* Elijah back!"

"Thanks, Aroya. I guess I just needed a little push," Elijah joked.

Abigail senior returned. "Well, now. Are we ready to get to work?"

"What do you mean?" Elijah asked.

"I think she's asking if we're ready to change the future again," young Abbie replied.

"Balance the future? Or is it harmonize the future?" Aroya asked. He was still unsure about the whole thing.

"It's more like inviting God, the Creator–and his Angels to assist us in harmonizing the future," Abigail senior said. "But yes, it is a matter of balance and harmony."

"Is this where you teach me to pray?" Elijah asked.

"Well, I usually begin with prayer and then move on to meditation. But this time, I think we need to *begin* with meditation," Abigail senior replied.

"What's different this time?" Elijah asked.

"This time, we need to look for guidance in our meditation–about how we pray," Abigail senior said. "It's important to be clear about what we're praying for, especially when we ask for divine intervention. Words matter. We need to be careful about what we intend to manifest, because sometimes it comes with unexpected baggage." Abigail senior spoke as though she'd learned this lesson the hard way.

"That makes sense," young Abbie said.

Elijah chuckled at her.

"What's so funny?" young Abbie asked.

"Watching you, agree with yourself in the future. I just find it amusing," Elijah said. "Sorry."

"Okay. Let's all remove our shoes and socks," Abigail senior instructed, "and loosen our clothing." Removing her shoes, Abigail senior retrieved a small ceramic pot filled with sand, and four slender tapers. She set the pot on the altar, then passed out the candles while young Abbie arranged the floor cushions in front of the altar. Lighting her own candle, she used it to light the others. "We will now join our flames, and together they will rise higher," she said. "Come to the altar and push your candles close together in the sand so that our flames conjoin into one."

They each pushed their candle into the sand, and Abigail senior fastened the burning tapers–so that all four flames danced together. Then, taking her place on a cushion, she said, "Abbie, would you please bless us with a protection prayer before we begin?"

Young Abbie stood facing her friends. She recited her protection prayer, the one she had learned from the old Catholic priest. Then she moved her energized hands around her body, and then around her friends' bodies. Her hands buzzed with a vibration so intense that her fingertips trembled. She sat on a cushion, closing her eyes.

Aroya and Elijah noticed both women had their eyes closed, and they followed suit.

Abigail senior spoke in a gentle, monotone manner. "We will purify our hearts now by combining the energies of Earth and Heaven–while sending out love to the world. Follow my instructions: In your mind, see the floor beneath you as green earthen soil. You hear birds singing in the trees, and smell the scent of flowers drifting through the air. In the distance, the sound of water causes you to wonder if there might be a stream nearby. Now, focus on the ground beneath you, and see the Earth's rainbow colors circulating around your feet. When I say, 'breathe-in'–see the rainbow colors rise up through your body–and at the same time, see the pure light of Heaven rush down through the top of your head. The colored light from Earth and the white light from Heaven–meet in your heart as you inhale them both, simultaneously. When I say, 'breathe-out,' see your heart as a multifaceted crystal…exploding with light and love, out to the world as you exhale your breath. Okay, we will begin now." Abigail instructed: *"Breathe-in…breathe-out,"* for three cycles. Then she said, "See yourself standing beneath a tree. Listen to the wind gently blowing through the leaves. We are waiting now for someone to come and lead us on our walk. We will stand quietly in this peaceful place, watching and listening. Now…you are all on your own."

In her vision, young Abbie saw her friends there, under the tree with her. To her surprise, there were also three very tall men dressed in ancient robes, standing by a stone wall–each with a very long beard. They beckoned–and a heavy wooden door swung open. The three tall men stepped over the threshold–once again, beckoning. Abbie and her friends followed them, stepping over the threshold–passing through the door. One after the other, they entered a beautiful rose garden. Rose perfume filled the air, and the sound of water bubbling from a fountain, along with bird songs, created an enchanting kind of music. Beyond the fountain, they saw four smooth marble statues. They each approached a statue: Abigail senior and young Abbie stood facing female statues, while Aroya and Elijah stood before male statues. They gazed upon the statues, witnessing the marble faces come alive with flesh-like color and texture. Young Abbie's statue had the sweet face of a loving mother, soft and tender, with eyes, wise and gentle. Abbie's heart swelled with a sense of love and beauty, and finally, she recognized the statue as Mary, mother of Jesus–the same image she had previously seen with the Vision Maker. Once again, Mary's face became like a mirror, and Abbie found herself looking into her own eyes. The experience was overwhelming, and tears moistened her cheeks. As she became aware of her tears–the statue dissolved into the garden wall.

Now, the sound of soft drumming drifted through the garden. Young Abbie turned to see her friends, all with wet cheeks–peering into a thick hedge of foliage. Together, they moved through the foliage until they came to a small clearing. Sitting on an old log in the clearing was Carlos, drumming–and the Vision Maker, singing a tribal song. The Vision Maker stood, smiling. He addressed Abbie and her friends, but this time he spoke in very clear English.

He said: *Your journeys have taught you well. When you recite a poem, you are addressing other men. When you say a prayer–you are addressing God, the Creator, and the Angels of his Heavenly court. The Creator creates the music. He understands the ingredients of harmony better than any man. You have only to ask, and the influences will appear–the ingredients will present themselves. Your role is to use what he gives you to make it happen. It is up to you to keep the music going. When you are ready to address God and his Angels, you need only to touch your heart–for God, the Creator, resides in the heart of every man. When you pray, you must forget about the past and the future–the only real time is 'now'–therefore, always formulate your prayers in the present tense because God can only be fully realized in the moment. That moment can be found in the space between your breaths–it is the space where the crystal stone falls. As you hold the stone, you focus on your desire. Then you see yourself arriving at your destination, and you drop the stone. You have done it without even realizing it. You inhale, holding the image in your mind, then you drop the stone and exhale. The secret is the space between your breaths– the infinite space of the moment. The human story is driven by the past and the future–and in those ideas, there is always a spell. The people must be released from the spell, so they can regain their freedom from the chains of dark influences. They must reconnect to their Creator in the stillness of each moment.*

You cannot do their work for them, but you can petition to bring about the influences necessary to awaken them. When you are petitioning, you must train your mind–you must tame the wild horses–and you must open your heart to God, the Creator. Abbie and Aroya have been chosen for a mission. Their mission is to connect the agents and influences that will bring together harmonious music makers. Because it is their mission, this prayer must arise from their own hearts. It need only be a simple petition–spoken in the moment, with the awareness that God, who is both the conductor and the composer, will know best how to bring about the outcome. Abbie and Aroya will state their intention– and finally, they will drop the stone. Elijah's part has always been, and is still to be, a great supporter and friend to Aroya. Abigail senior is given the work of clearing your hearts so that you may hear God's instruction more precisely. She has received a special song to accomplish this. Before you leave, she will offer you protection–but it will be up to Aroya and Elijah to petition the Archangel Michael. From this point onward, they need only touch their hearts to receive divine powers from the Archangels. Abbie, you will go forward now, protected by the energies of both Earth and Heaven–and the forces of God's Angels.

The Vision Maker sat down, finished, puffing on his pipe.

Now Carlos stepped forward, addressing Abbie: *Abbie, thank you for assisting my brother at the time of his transition.*

As if on cue, Tulio walked into the clearing. He smiled and offered his hand to young Abbie. Tears formed in her eyes while she took his hand in hers. It felt warm

Tulio said: *Yes. I am alive. Here is the truth: life is everlasting. Thank you for fighting for me. Never stop fighting–never stop the music.*

With those words, the vision dissolved, and suddenly, they all became aware of the flickering candles on Abigail's altar. They opened their eyes, stretching their limbs, gradually returning to physical awareness. They stared at each other in silence, each wondering what the other had experienced.

Finally, Aroya spoke. "Yes, we all want to know. Were we really all together there, in that garden with those statues–and with the feathered man in the jungle?"

"I was there," Abigail senior answered.

"I was there too," young Abbie replied.

"I was there…but I don't understand," Elijah said, clearly emotional.

"Elijah…are you sure you want to do this?" Abigail senior asked.

"Yes," he said, "I just need a moment to digest it." Taking a deep breath, he continued, "Okay, all digested. I'm ready."

"Then let's take each other's hands," Abigail senior said. "I will open our session by addressing God, the Creator with the *Lord's Prayer.*"

Finishing her prayer, Abigail senior continued, "Now, it's time for young Abbie and Aroya to compose and recite their own special prayer."

Young Abbie turned to Aroya. "Shall I begin, and you finish?" she asked.

"Yes. Thank you, Abbie," Aroya said.

"When you're finished saying your part, just say 'amen,'" young Abbie whispered.

Aroya nodded.

Abbie began the prayer: "We address this prayer to God, our Creator, and the Angels of his court. We honor the music of life, and we continue to play our part. Dear God, Creator, the Source of all: we recognize it is only *you* who know the required ingredients to achieve harmony on this Earth. We ask for your guidance and the ability to discern those ingredients in our own lives. We are honored to be of service, and we take up this mission to restore harmony to all the people of the world. Help us to connect the essential agents and influences, to bring together the music makers–for the benefit of all humanity. We pray this from our hearts, and we trust in you to show us how to manifest the very best outcome."

Abbie turned to Aroya, cueing him to begin his part of the prayer.

Aroya began: "Dear God, send your Angels to work with us, to release people from the dark spell that has captured their minds. Show the people how to reconnect with their Creator and his Angels. Help them to remember how to pray and fill their hearts with light. Awaken the people and encourage them to keep on fighting for truth. We trust in you to provide the tools, and we wait for your instruction. Where there was once darkness, let there now be light. If it be your will, then let it be done. Amen." Then Aroya remembered something else. "Oh, and thank you, for my dear friend Elijah, and for Abigail senior, and thank you for all the good people who help us, and thank you for Archangel Michael, who fills me with fiery electricity and helps me to defeat evil. And most of all—thank you, God, for Abbie, my partner on this mission."

Aroya turned to Abbie, taking the crystal stone from his pocket. "Let's do this together," he said. "Remember how I taught you?"

Abbie moved close to Aroya, placing her right hand over his—and her left hand beneath his.

Aroya continued, "It is our desire to petition God and the Angels for harmony in the years 2019 to 2050—and beyond. It is our desire to call for Divine intervention to introduce just the right influences, at just the right moments, to manifest harmonious cooperation among all the people of the world. We hold that vision in our minds, and we trust God, the Creator, will provide all that is necessary to achieve this harmonious outcome."

Aroya closed his eyes—and dropped the stone.

The entire room quaked, and the ground rolled under their feet. The curtains billowed, and the carpet rippled.

Elijah held his stomach, then finally lost his breakfast in a nearby trashcan.

Then...everything was still.

"What was that? An earthquake?" Elijah asked.

"Markus calls it *the wave,*" young Abbie replied.

Abigail senior collected the dirty trashcan, removing it to the bathroom.

"Sorry," Elijah said.

When Abigail senior returned, she glanced around the room. "I expect that was a sign that something happened," she said. "Now, let's get on with our work." She turned to Elijah. "Are you all right?" she asked.

"I just need some time to get my sea legs," Elijah joked.

Abigail senior instructed the others to stand. She began with young Abbie, taking her hands and turning her palms up. Abigail senior rubbed her hands briskly against young Abbie's palms, creating friction–then she stopped for a moment, scanning the space for energy. Satisfied, she began moving her energized hands around young Abbie's head and body, clearing her energy field. Then she moved down the line, repeating the same process with the others.

When she finished with Elijah, she moved back to young Abbie and told her, "Close your eyes and listen to your heart." She placed her left hand on young Abbie's right shoulder, then her right hand on Abbie's heart. Closing her eyes, she moved her head near Abbie's chest as if she were listening for something. Then, she began singing directly to Abbie's heart–a song that was at first gentle, like a baby's lullaby– gradually building in amplitude and emotion. Abigail senior was now in direct communion with young Abbie's heart, singing forth the shadows hidden deep inside. The language of her song was unknown, but still, the emotion moved young Abbie. She wept silently, and Abigail senior embraced her. Affectionately, she brushed young Abbie's hair from her face–kissing her forehead. Now Abigail senior moved on to Aroya, repeating the same process with her song. Aroya was also moved to tears. When she finally moved on to Elijah, she found he was already weeping–his heart had opened spontaneously, even before Abigail had begun singing.

When the session concluded, Abigail senior went to her altar and retrieved a bowl of herbal water. She dipped her fingers in the bowl and patted the liquid onto their heads, then on to their forehead, face, neck, hands, and feet. Young Abbie recognized the minty smell from her visit to the Vision Maker, and she wondered how Abigail senior knew about these things in the year 2050.

Finally, Abigail senior spoke. "Before we conclude, I'd like to say one last thing. While you're on your mission, remember this Sufi saying: The heart is the seat of the King, and the mind is the King's wise advisor. For harmony to exist in the kingdom, the King must consult his wise advisor–but the advisor must never dethrone the King. In other words, rule with your heart and always consult with your disciplined mind– but never let your mind shut down your heart."

"What a beautiful image," Aroya said. "The King, seated on his throne in our heart–and the wise advisor, working at his desk in our mind."

"Now, if you're ready–we'll begin the prayers to send you off," Abigail senior said.

"Ready," they all replied.

Abigail senior recited the *Armour of God* Bible verse from *Ephesians 6:10-17*. Then she asked Aroya and Elijah to step up to the altar.

"This last part is just for you," she said. "I found this prayer and this picture, nestled deep inside an old book. It was peculiar because it was actually a Sufi book." Abigail senior reached for the picture of Archangel Michael. "It's rather weathered...but I believe it's still legible." She handed the picture to Aroya.

Aroya smiled. "I think that was my book...and this was young Abbie's picture, from her altar."

"Of course," young Abbie said. "But I'm confused. That was a completely different timeline."

"Maybe some things will always remain a mystery," Abigail senior replied.

Aroya flipped over the picture. "Here," he said, handing it to Elijah. "I already know it by heart."

"Show off," Elijah joked.

"I'll introduce the prayer," Abigail senior said, "then I'll motion for you to begin. Go slowly, Aroya. Remember, this is Elijah's first time, and we need you to recite it in unison."

"We will recite this prayer as if it were the rarest and most sought after of all poems," Aroya said.

"I'm ready!" Elijah said, excited.

Young Abbie settled down on a cushion.

Abigail senior faced Aroya and Elijah. She began: "O God, the Creator, the Source of ALL. We call on your most powerful Archangel–the glorious Archangel Michael." Then she motioned for Aroya and Elijah to begin.

They took a moment to compose themselves, then Aroya faced Elijah and nodded. Elijah held the prayer high–indicating he was ready. As if standing in the spotlight, before an entranced audience, the men began in unison:

> *"Archangel Michael, defend us in battle.*
> *Come to our aid with your celestial legions.*
> *Bring us protection and guidance, by the power of*
> *the Most-High.*
> *Fill us with your strength, as we fight against the*
> *agents of evil.*
> *Come to our protection and be a refuge–against*
> *the snares of the devil, and all his wicked powers.*
> *Be our defense against all evil intentions, thoughts,*
> *and actions against us.*
> *May the divine fire of your sword, destroy every*
> *evil.*
> *Amen."*

A palpable wave of vibration rushed through the room. Both men's faces were glowing, radiant from within. They examined their hands, amazed by the tiny sparks and arching currents–dancing across their fingertips. Elijah touched Aroya, and they both jumped.

Suddenly, the room's atmosphere turned hazy–and then, as if coming through the wall, four tall beings appeared. Their features were smooth and indistinct, like glowing statues sculpted of pristine white marble. They seemed to glow from within, and although nearly translucent, they were definitely not holograms. Not only were their qualities different, but their effect was incomparable. Young Abbie fell into a wide-awake trance. A marble floor, composed of the same glowing material, appeared beneath her feet, with a step landing right in front of her. Young Abbie stood up, not knowing why–but the four beings seemed to be waiting for her. She stepped onto the marble floor and slowly moved across it–facing the tall, glowing beings. In her mind, young Abbie could hear them speaking to her. *You find this life difficult. Your own emotions are what you find so overwhelming. At times, the pain seems unbearable, and you wish to block it. What you don't realize is that emotion is what gives life its value. And your emotional response here helps others elsewhere. It is the whole point of this life.*

Now, one of the tall glowing beings stepped forward, handing something to young Abbie. It looked like a large scroll, and she wondered what was written on it–but in her trance-like state, it didn't occur to her to open it.

In her mind, she asked the beings, *who are you?*

We are your true family. You were with us before you came to this life, and you will be with us again, afterward. Your light was the strongest among us–and only you had the power to come into the physical. We are grateful to you for your sacrifice.

Young Abbie stood frozen in place, filled with emotion, unable to speak. She observed the marble floor fading away–then, looking up, she discovered the beings were gone. Their sudden departure filled her with intense panic and grief. In her mind, she flashed back to the first day of kindergarten when her mother left her with strangers for the very first time. The panic of being abandoned pained her heart. She thought she understood now why we come into this life with spiritual amnesia, unable to recall our true origins. She knew that if we could fully remember our true home and our true family, we might live out our days here, suffering unbearable longing.

The atmosphere in the room normalized, but the air was still electric and tingly.

Aroya and Elijah approached young Abbie.

"Abbie, are you all right?" Aroya asked.

Abbie nodded.

"What happened? What did you see?" he asked.

Young Abbie turned to Abigail senior for support. "Did you see them?" she asked.

"Yes. But not as *you* did. I knew what you were experiencing because it also happened to me–many years ago," Abigail senior replied.

"But what happened?" Aroya asked.

"Give her some time. She'll tell you, eventually– when she's ready," Abigail senior said. She guided the bewildered young Abbie over to the table and poured her a cup of tea. "Drink the tea, my dear. It will bring you back."

Worried about Abbie, Aroya and Elijah sat with her at the table.

"The entire day has passed," Abigail senior said, "and soon it will be dark. Is there anything else you want to do before you return?"

Aroya peered out the window. "You're right. The sun is already on this side of the city."

Still spaced-out, young Abbie stood up. "I think…we should return before dark," she said. Still a little unsteady, she held onto the chair.

"Do you think *this* timeline changed?" Elijah asked Abigail senior.

"We'll just have to wait and see," she replied.

"Can you walk?" Aroya asked Abbie.

"I think so," she said.

Elijah turned to Aroya. "I need to get back to my office to connect with Eloise. I don't want to involve Abigail by connecting here."

"I guess we'll be going then," Aroya said.

Young Abbie was a bit wobbly but determined to soldier on. "Let's go," she said.

Abigail senior escorted them to the door. "Try to find a green patch of earth and place her bare feet on it. She'll need some grounding to come back."

Aroya understood. "Thank you, Abigail. The King will always rule in our hearts."

Young Abbie reached out to Abigail senior with a hug.

20— THE LAST FIGHT

2050

San Francisco

Timeline 2.0

Aroya guided Abbie across the busy streets. "Where should we take her?" he asked Elijah.

"Over by the pizza parlor. That whole strip is nothing but dirt and grass," Elijah replied.

Abbie thought it remarkable that her feet were somehow moving beneath her without any physical sensation–as if she were floating.

Arriving at the pizza parlor, they sat Abbie down at the picnic table, removing her shoes. Abbie dug her toes deep into the grass, hoping to find some cool, moist earth.

The old man was still sitting near the water, fishing. "Do you mind if I go talk with the fisherman for a moment?" Aroya asked.

"Go ahead. I'll stay with Abbie," Elijah replied.

Aroya approached the old man. Peeking into his bucket, he discovered a big fish. "Wow! What kind of fish is that?!" Aroya asked.

"A striped bass," the old man replied. "The boats used to take people way out to catch these. I'm not sure what it's doin' so close in–but I sure know what it'll be doin' tonight! It'll be sittin' pretty on my dinner plate, that's for sure!"

"It's a beautiful fish. Congratulations!" Aroya said.

The old man gestured toward the picnic table. "Is the girl alright?" he asked.

"She had an unusual experience today. She just needs some grounding," Aroya said.

"I might be able to help–if you like," the old man offered.

"What do you mean?" Aroya asked.

The old man dug into his pocket, pulling out a slim metal case. He opened it, showing Aroya a set of acupuncture needles.

"What's that?" Aroya asked.

"You never seen acupuncture needles before?" the old man asked.

"No. What are they for?" Aroya inquired.

The old man laughed. "It balances the chi...the life energy."

Aroya brought the old man over to meet Abbie.

"Hello, young lady. I'm told you had an unusual experience today," the old man said. "I hear it left you kind of outta balance."

"I do feel a little out of balance," Abbie said.

"May I feel your pulse?" the old man asked.

Abbie gave him her hand, and the old man placed three fingers across her wrist. He concentrated for a moment, then released her hand. "If you like, I can fix that for you," he said, opening the box of needles.

"Oh, acupuncture. Where will you put the needles?" Abbie asked.

"A few just inside your wrist–and one up near your shoulder. Is that okay?" the old man asked.

Abbie agreed, and the old man inserted the needles.

Fascinated, Aroya and Elijah looked on.

"While we're waiting...would you like to tell me what happened?" the old man said.

"I think I met four tall Angels today. But I don't know for sure–because they didn't have any wings," Abbie said.

"They didn't have any wings," Elijah whispered to Aroya.

The old man chuckled. "Well, not all Angels have wings, ya know." He smiled, recalling the movie. "That's why you've gotta ring the little bell...so they can get 'em!"

Abbie giggled.

"It sounds like you're feeling better already," he said. "Let's check your pulse again." The old man checked Abbie's pulse. Satisfied, he located the needles and removed them. "There ya go. All back in balance now."

"Thank you!" Aroya said. Then he turned to Abbie and asked, "Do you feel well enough to walk to the office now?"

"Yes. I feel much better," Abbie replied.

Aroya glanced up at the sky. "The sun is setting," he noted. Then addressing the old man, he said, "You sure know a lot about balance."

"Oh, yeah–I've been balancin' energy for nearly 50 years!" the old man said. He gestured to Aroya, taking Abbie's hand again. Pointing to three spots on her wrist, he said, "Look here. If you don't have needles– just press like this." He used his fingernails for pressure. "Ya know…just in case they come back!" he whispered with a smile. "Okay. I'll be off now, to cook my fish. Y'all take care!" Chuckling again, he scooted down the street.

Before heading back to 2019, they thought they'd spend a few last moments with Elijah, enjoying some bootlegged sodas. Approaching the office door, they spotted new drag marks across the carpet.

"What the hell is this?!" Elijah exclaimed. He waved his hand over the door sensor, unlocking the door.

They stepped into the office, and their hearts sank. The entire office had been cleaned out: every book was gone–and sodas were smashed all over the desk.

Elijah was in shock. He turned a circle, surveying the room. "They took them all! They were irreplaceable!" he exclaimed. Then, looking like he might explode, he hurried out to the patio for some fresh air.

Abbie and Aroya followed him.

Leaning over the balcony, they stared down at the bustling city below. It was getting dark.

"Well, there goes my business," Elijah said.

"You know that our offer still stands," Aroya reminded him. "We'd love to take you with us."

"Yeah, Elijah," Abbie added. "2019 isn't that great, but at least we know how to change it now."

"You figured that out?" Elijah asked.

"Well...we kind of know," Abbie admitted.

"I'm gonna try to contact Eloise," Elijah said. "I wanna see if anything's changed."

Abbie and Aroya sat on the patio, giving Elijah some privacy for his call. They moved their chairs away from the glass door. Now familiar with the holographic communication system, they worried about being seen.

Pushing smashed cans off his sticky desk, Elijah prepared himself. "Call Eloise. Track her last number," he called out. A green light blinked in mid air. Finally, an image materialized. Eloise appeared frightened.

"Eloise! What's wrong?!" Elijah asked.

"Elijah! They know where you are! Get out! NOW!" she pleaded.

Her image dissolved as the communication globe disconnected–then suddenly it beeped, and a red light flashed. Elijah called out: "Accept!–*NO! WAIT! CHECK ID!"* It was too late. The image of a man in uniform began forming. Before it was fully formed, Elijah yelled: *"DISCONNECT! DISCONNECT!"* Instantly, the hologram dissolved.

Elijah rushed out to the patio. *"We need to leave–RIGHT NOW! They know you're here!"*

"But what about you? Come with us, Elijah!" Abbie begged.

"I can't!" he replied. "I could never be happy in another time, knowing I left my family behind."

Just then, a hovercraft lowered itself down to the balcony. They ran inside, and Aroya searched his pocket for the crystal stone. A loud noise came from the hallway. Alarmed, they pushed bookcases against the door.

"Elijah, you're trapped. You need to come with us. It's the only way out!" Aroya pleaded.

Suddenly, everything was quiet. There was no more hovercraft and no more noise in the hallway.

"Did they leave?" Abbie asked.

"I doubt it," Elijah replied.

Aroya got down on his knees, peering under the door. Satisfied that all was clear, he walked out to the patio, listening for the hovercraft. He heard nothing–only the sound of a squawking gull.

Elijah joined Aroya on the patio. He looked over the balcony–and then up at the sky. All was quiet.

Abbie approached the patio, but Elijah motioned for her to stay inside.

Leaning over the railing–Aroya looked up and down. "What do you think?" he asked Elijah.

"I think they're toying with us," Elijah said.

Walking back into the office, they closed the door behind them.

"What should we do?" Abbie asked.

"Wait," Elijah replied.

Aroya kept his eye on the door, periodically pressing his ear against it.

"Shhh…" Elijah said, pointing to the holographic globe. "I'm sure they're listening," he whispered. Removing his jacket, he threw it over the globe.

A few minutes passed, and still, there was no sound.

"Maybe they changed their plans," Abbie whispered.

"No. They're waiting for us to come out...like a cat waits for a mouse," Elijah replied.

"Should we move more furniture in front of the door?" Abbie asked. "What about the chairs?"

"I don't see the use...but maybe it'll buy us more time," Elijah replied.

They pushed all the furniture against the door.

Aroya ran to the window, looking out over the bay. "There's no way out," he said. He held up the stone for Elijah to see.

Elijah paused, reconsidering Aroya's offer.

BOOM! AN EXPLOSION blew open the door! Elijah and Abbie flew across the room. Chairs and bookcases were tossed in every direction.

Aroya rushed to Abbie, holding the stone. "Hold on to me!" he cried. "I'm dropping—"

A large boot kicked Aroya—he crashed against the desk, his stone rolling onto the carpet.

Abbie and Elijah got to their feet.

Elijah ran to Aroya, then stopped—spotting a weapon aimed at his head. He froze. "Aroya, don't move!" he warned.

Abbie shouted, *"Touch your heart! Call the Archangel!"*

Elijah reached for his heart—a guardsman smashed him in the head. Elijah fell to the floor, unconscious.

Now, Burk walked through the door—followed by Klaus and Dr. Eiffel. Abbie gasped in shock!

Dr. Eiffel pointed at Abbie. "Check her pockets!" he shouted.

Klaus took the stone from Abbie's pocket. Then, spotting Aroya's stone on the floor, Burk scooped it up.

Dr. Eiffel smirked at Abbie. "Well...it looks like you're both stuck here now. Just like I was *stuck in that jail cell* after your heroic interview!" He jeered at Abbie. "You've always been a little troublemaker, nurse Lite!"

Still face-down on the carpet, with a boot on his back and a weapon pointed at his head, Aroya reached for his heart.

"Don't move, or I'll dustify you!" the guard warned.

"What are you doing here?!" Abbie shouted at Dr. Eiffel. *"This isn't even your time!"*

Klaus approached Abbie. "What about us, girlfriend? Aren't you wondering why *we're* here?" he said, flashing his black teeth.

"No. Not really," Abbie replied, trying to act tough. "It's your time...isn't it?"

"Is it? Are you *sure* about that?" Burk asked. Joining forces with Klaus–both pressed their faces closer, flashing their black eyes at Abbie.

"Look at *my* eyes." Klaus hissed. Abbie cringed, turning away. Klaus continued, "We're *goo-bots* now, girlie. Time-traveling *goo-bots!*" he growled. "That silly Dr. Biegel...he was such an old-fashioned man. Do you know he used to write little notes? Something about a dark stone with unusual properties. But we found those notes in his pocket," he said, grinning, "and *then* we found the man with the *stones*! The rest wasn't that hard to figure out. And so...*here we are!!"* he exclaimed, cackling.

Burk laughed at Klaus. Then he focused his attention back on Abbie. "We combed through dozens of universes looking for you!" Pointing to Dr. Eiffel, he continued, "And *this* fool–he swore he could find you!

But in the end–it was a common *hovercar* that tracked you down!" He glared at Dr. Eiffel. *"Useless!!"* he shouted, pointing his finger.

Dr. Eiffel panicked, backing out of the office–but a guard hurled him back inside. He smashed against the wall, landing next to Abbie.

"I'm suddenly in the mood for a little entertainment," Burk said, adjusting his weapon. "Now…let's have a little fun!"

The guards backed away.

Trapped against the wall with Abbie–Dr. Eiffel trembled. *"Wait, wait!"* he pleaded, trying to devise an argument to spare his life.

Burk gestured for Abbie to get out of the way. "I think your boss is about to piss himself," he said, smiling.

Abbie distanced herself.

Burk trained his weapon on Eiffel, slowly pressing the trigger. Nothing happened immediately, but soon Dr. Eiffel began squirming–clearly uncomfortable. Beads of sweat rolled down his face. He threw off his jacket, unbuttoning his shirt.

"What's wrong, doctor? Is it too hot in here for you?" Burk said, jeering. "Oh, but…we're just getting started!" Again, he adjusted his weapon.

"No! No!" Dr. Eiffel pleaded. *"Please! I'll do anything!"* he begged.

Klaus thoroughly enjoyed the entertainment, but he wanted more. "I'm surprised he hasn't pissed himself yet," he said with a grin.

"Yes, me too," Burk said. "Maybe it's time to–"

"No! Please! What do you want me to do? I'll do anything!" Dr. Eiffel groveled.

"Then why don't you piss yourself?" Klaus demanded. "You know that's what we want!"

"Yes–go ahead. Piss yourself!" Burk ordered. Noting Eiffel's lack of response, he adjusted his weapon again.

"No! Please!" Eiffel cried. He swallowed hard, then closing his eyes, he urinated. A large wet spot formed on his crotch–and urine leaked out his pant leg, forming a puddle on the floor.

Burk and Klaus burst out laughing. The guards also laughed.

As much as Abbie despised Dr. Eiffel, witnessing his humiliation disgusted her.

Taking advantage of the distraction, Aroya moved his hand to his chest, trying to touch his heart.

"Don't move!" Burk hollered, pointing to Aroya. "Okay–that's enough entertainment! Let's get on with it!" he snapped. Pointing his weapon at Dr. Eiffel–he dustified him on the spot.

Shocked, Abbie witnessed Dr. Eiffel's body disintegrate before her eyes, falling in a mound of powdery dust.

Elijah regained consciousness, making eye contact with Aroya on the floor.

Klaus zeroed in on Aroya. "It was *you*, Recruit Wallace! It was *you* who was supposed to be the *goo-bot!*" he growled. "Look at what you've *done!*" he hissed, pointing to his black eyes. Then he grinned, turning to Abbie. Moving to her side, he fiddled with her hair, purring like an animal. "You know…" he said, "even goo-bots like a little fun, now and then." He leaned in closer. "Do you know what's fascinating about that? When a goo-bot fills a woman with *goo,* guess what she becomes?"

Burk watched on, howling like a hyena–while Klaus tore at Abbie's clothes.

Finally, Abbie screamed, *"Aroya! Aroya!"*

Her scream activated Aroya's powers, just like on the rooftop. Aroya's body instantly transformed, throwing the guard off his back. The room exploded with electricity as 10-foot-tall Aroya towered over the men.

The guards aimed at Aroya–then suddenly, they shrieked–their weapons melting in their hands.

The sound of a hovercraft shook the room–and through the window, Abbie spotted men aiming weapons at Aroya. *"Aroya, behind you!"* she shouted.

Elijah got to his feet, grabbing his heart, commanding, *"Archangel Michael, come to my aid!"* Elijah's body instantly expanded with such force that the window in front of him exploded outward–spraying fiery daggers of glass into the hovercraft, causing it to crash.

Just like Aroya, Elijah was now 10-feet-tall–all fiery and electric!

Klaus still had Abbie in his grip. Aroya fixed his gaze, projecting fire from his eyes–instantly cremating Klaus into a pile of black ash. Now, Aroya turned to Burk.

Suddenly, Elijah bellowed, *"No! This one is mine!"* Elijah glared at Burk, his chest expanding. Finally, he projected fiery beams from his eyes. Burk cried out, falling onto the carpet, rolling in agony. His charred form remained for a moment before disintegrating into a little pile of ash.

Elijah turned towards the guards–now trapped against the broken window. Surveying what remained of their commanders, the guards chose to jump. Their screams echoed above the bay–until they hit the ground with a dull thud.

Just as quick as they'd expanded, Elijah and Aroya shrunk back to normal size. Collapsing on the carpet, exhausted, they could barely move.

Abbie held Aroya in her arms. She'd been through this before on the rooftop–and she knew it was only a matter of time before he recovered.

Elijah pulled himself off the floor–stumbling and staggering over to Aroya and Abbie. "Will he be all right?" he asked, still out of breath.

"Yes. He just needs rest," Abbie said. "And so do you."

"No, not me. I've got business to take care of," Elijah huffed. Then he fell back on the carpet, collapsing next to Aroya. "I just need to catch my breath," he gasped. He rolled onto his side, crawling along the carpet. Pushing his hands through the ash, he found the crystal stones. "It's time for you to go now," he said, handing the stones to Abbie. "I can lie low...but you need to get out of here."

Aroya opened his eyes, reaching for Elijah. "Come with us," he pleaded.

"I can't," Elijah replied. "I can't leave Eloise and the children. I promised."

Aroya expected his response. With Abbie's help, he sat up. "You were always a man of your word," Aroya said. Then he turned to Abbie, asking, "Do we really need two stones?"

Abbie knew what he was thinking. "No, we don't," she said, handing one stone to Elijah.

"You saw how we used them," Aroya said. "If you ever need anything, just hold the stone in your right hand, and think of me. Then imagine that you're with me–and drop the stone, from one hand to the other."

Elijah examined the stone. "I sure will miss you two. You made life worth living again."

"I guess we're just a couple of boat-rockers," Abbie joked. "We'll miss you too, Elijah," she said. "Come here and give us a big hug."

Elijah hugged his dear friends one last time. Then he stood back. Aroya dropped the stone...and they disappeared.

21– THE CONVERGENCE

2019

San Francisco

Timeline 3.0

When the shaking stopped, Aroya and Abbie found themselves on Millie's bedroom floor.

Millie was in bed, watching a movie, snacking on potato chips. She observed Abbie and Aroya tangled up on the floor. "Why am I not surprised?" she responded.

"Sorry, Millie," Abbie said.

Millie noticed Aroya's weakened state. She crawled out of bed to take a better look. "What's wrong with him?" she asked.

"He saved my life again," Abbie replied.

"I saved her from the goo-bots," Aroya added.

Millie rolled her eyes. "You can explain later. C'mon, let's get him to your place."

Abbie lifted him on one side, and Millie on the other–dragging Aroya back to the apartment. Upon entering, Millie naturally pulled Aroya toward the couch, but Abbie stopped her.

"Uh-uh. Tonight he's sleeping in *my* bed," she said.

"Well, it's about time!" Millie huffed.

They tucked him into bed, leaving him to rest–then moved to the kitchen table for a brief chat.

"It sure is good to be back home," Abbie said, "even if it is…just the same old 2019."

"My God, Abbie…one of these days, you're gonna drop in while I'm on the toilet!" Millie said, shaking her head. "It's late, and you look tired. G'night, Abbs'," she said, heading toward the door.

"G'night, Mil'."

In the morning, Abbie shuffled into the kitchen, putting the kettle on for tea. Aroya was already sitting at the kitchen table, with his nose in a book.

"I'm surprised you're up so early," Abbie said. "I guess you're feeling better?"

"Yes, much better," Aroya replied.

Digging through the refrigerator, Abbie poked her head out. "I'm not sure if anything's still edible in here. Do you feel strong enough to go down to the café for breakfast?"

"Sure. It feels like it's been a while."

Abbie turned off the burner. "I'm just gonna hop in the shower," she said.

When Abbie finished her shower, she heard running water in the kitchen. Peeking in, she caught Aroya shaving, using a shiny pot lid as a mirror.

"We've really got to work out this bathroom routine," she said.

Aroya put down his razor, smiling. "Maybe we can work it out together?" He pulled her close.

"Well…somebody's feeling recharged this morning."

"Yes, all charged up. And tonight, my love, there will be so many wild horses–"

"It'll be a friggin' stampede," Abbie said, smiling.

They kissed.

Sitting at the café, they admired each other's stylish outfits. "Apparently, in this timeline–we're pretty snazzy dressers!" Abbie said. "I was shocked to find this stuff in my closet, but I have to admit–the entire wardrobe suits me to a T."

"It's almost as if you picked it out yourself," Aroya joked. "And now…I've got my own closet! I wonder how that happened?"

"Yeah, it's weird that we can't remember."

They sipped their tea, finishing their bagels. "Hey– look across the street! It looks like Ray reopened the shop!" Aroya exclaimed, peering out the window.

"Yeah–it looks great! Like it was never even–" Abbie took a closer look. "I don't see any homeless people," she said, popping the last bit of bagel in her mouth. "C'mon, let's go check it out!"

They walked up and down the street, surveying every hidden nook. There was not one bag of poop in the alleyway, no used syringes on the sidewalks, and no homeless people camped out on the curbs, anywhere.

Stopping at Ray's bookshop, the little bell jingled as they entered. "Sounds like another Angel just got his wings!" Abbie teased.

"Hey, Aroya! Long time no see!" Ray said, delighted. "I've been holding a book for you!"

Aroya approached the counter. "When did you reopen? It looks great in here! Just like nothing ever happened!"

Ray brought out the book. "What do you mean?" he asked.

Abbie said 'hello' to Ray, joining Aroya at the counter–then glancing at the book, she said, "Ah, of course–*The Music of Life.*" She smiled at Aroya.

"Oh, you've already read it?" Ray said, surprised.

"No, I haven't. But a friend showed it to me. I'd love to read it!" Aroya said.

Ray handed the book to Aroya. "It's yours," he said.

"Wow–it looks brand new! Thank you! I'll be gentle with it and return it when I'm finished," Aroya said.

Ray gave Aroya a puzzled look. "What did you mean by…'just like nothing ever happened?'"

Aroya turned to Abbie–she raised her eyebrows. There was definitely something off with Ray. "Oh, nothing," Aroya replied. "We just thought that… something might have happened over here. But it looks like we were mistaken."

"Thank goodness!" Abbie added, playing along.

Confused, Ray studied their faces.

Abbie couldn't resist testing him a little. "You know, Ray…there used to be a homeless guy who slept in your doorway. Whatever happened to him?" Abbie asked.

"A homeless guy?" Ray asked, concerned. "Are you sure?"

"Aren't there any homeless people around here?" Abbie asked.

"Of course not." Ray tilted his head, squinting at Abbie. "Were you two out late last night?" he asked. "You're acting kind of strange today."

Aroya put his arm around Abbie, guiding her toward the door. "Yeah! I guess we *were* out a little late last night. Maybe we should go take a nap."

As they were leaving, Ray hollered out to them, "Wait a minute! I have something else for you!" He came out from behind the counter, carrying a journal in his hand. "It occurred to me that a man who loves poetry so much, might wanna try his hand at it. I've had these journals in my store for a long time. I'm afraid I haven't sold one in more than a year." He handed the journal to Aroya.

"Thanks, Ray. It's beautiful! I can't believe nobody bought this!" Aroya said, impressed with the hand-tooled leather.

"I guess people just don't write anymore," Ray replied.

Aroya recalled hiding out in the warehouse, teaching the boys to write. He shook his head, thinking about how people take things for granted. "If they only knew what a privilege it was," Aroya lamented.

Ray had no idea what he meant.

"Thanks again, Ray," Aroya said. "I guess we'll see you later."

"Be sure to get some rest!" Ray called out.

They strolled down the street, taking in every detail. The area was now completely devoid of garbage and homeless people. When they arrived back at the apartment, Abbie opened her laptop and scrolled through the Internet.

"I could use some more tea. You want some?" Aroya offered.

"Sure." Abbie continued scrolling.

"Hey, Abbie…didn't we just buy a brand-new teakettle?" Aroya asked.

"Yeah. Why?"

"Because this one's got a big chip on the bird's beak."

"Huh? I didn't notice it this morning. Maybe it's that Mandela thingy again. Well, as long as it whistles, I'm okay with it," she said.

Aroya sat down at the table, waiting for the water to boil. "I guess we'll see if it whistles," he said. Propping his chin up, he thought about it more. "If our clothes are different…and the teakettle is different…then are *we* different?" he asked. "And whatever happened to the *old* teakettle, anyway?" He thought harder. "And if *we're* different…then what happened to the other *Abbie* and *Aroya*, who used to live here?"

"Stop it!" Abbie said. "If I think about it too much more, my brain will explode!"

"It's too late for me," Aroya said, rubbing his head.

Abbie continued scrolling the Internet. "Well, that's weird. I can't find anything significantly different in the news. When I search the term 'homeless people,' it doesn't even come up. And when I search for 'crime in San Francisco', it says we have the lowest crime rate in 60 years! Maybe it's this new search engine."

"Maybe we should celebrate! Look at all the positive changes: Ray's bookshop wasn't closed–and now, there are no more homeless people."

"It's more like they never existed," Abbie said.

"Hey, let's go see Markus today. That oughta be interesting."

"Okay. I'll text him and see what's up."

22– COMING OUT

2050

San Francisco

Timeline 3.0

Abbie and Aroya entered Markus' office, taking note of the new plaque on his door. Not only had the door-plaque been upgraded, but Markus' education had been upgraded as well–he now had an M.D. after his name. Somehow this made sense to Abbie since the Markus of 2050 was also an M.D. In addition, there were other improvements. Markus' old office was kind of funky, especially for a medical professional–but now it had the atmosphere of a lush spa.

Markus' receptionist, Liz, was now dressed to the nines, and she supervised three additional office assistants. "Abigail! How are you?" she said. Then, turning to her staff, she announced, "Okay, crew. It's lunchtime!" The staff dropped their work and grabbed their jackets as Markus sauntered into the waiting room with his own upgraded look.

"Oh, here they are! The lady Abigail and her gallant prince, Aroya!" Markus said, in a jovial mood. "Should we dine at Enrico's today? I only have an hour, so actually, we'd better."

Abbie had never heard of Enrico's. She examined her attire. "Do you think we're dressed for it?" she asked.

"Oh, you know Enrico," Markus chuckled, "he wouldn't mind if you dined in your PJs, just as long as you order from the *deluxe* menu."

"Then I guess Enrico's it is!" Abbie said. "Lead the way!"

Behind Markus' back, Abbie shot a bewildered look at Aroya. She had no idea who Enrico was or where they were going.

Following Markus, they ended up downstairs, at the old lunch café–which, of course, was now *Enrico's Pizza Extravaganza.* Upon entering, Abbie was relieved to see that it wasn't the stuffy high-class restaurant she had imagined. Instead, it was a colorful Bohemian café, with live music and an international pizza menu.

Enrico spotted them entering the restaurant. "Oh, there he is again! He just can't get enough of me!" Enrico joked, addressing Markus. He waved to Abbie and Aroya. "Abigail–Aroya, it's nice to see you!"

"Our regular table then?" Markus asked.

"Sure, lead the way!" Abbie replied, again concealing her confusion.

On a small stage near the back of the restaurant, a guitarist and percussionist played sensual samba to a packed house.

Sitting at a cozy table near the stage, the waiter handed them menus.

"Should we order the usual?" Markus asked.

Abbie and Aroya nodded. "Sure. That sounds good."

Markus handed the menus back. "Thanks, Kevin. We'll have the usual."

"Will it be a Chianti or Cabernet today?" Kevin asked.

"I think California coolers might be a nice change." Markus checked with Abbie and Aroya. "What do you think?"

"Sure. Why not?" they said, just rolling with it, even though neither one of them drank.

Enrico approached the table. Glancing between Abbie and Aroya, he playfully pinched Abbie's shoulder, teasing, "Ya know, I'm still waiting for your RSVPs. You *did* get the invitation, didn't you?"

The drinks came. "No. I don't think we did." She glanced at Aroya, who played along, shaking his head.

"Oh, my God! And the wedding's in two weeks! I hope you're coming! I mean, you have to, right?" Enrico joked.

"Well, of course!" Abbie replied, still playing along.

"Well, of course!" Enrico echoed. He bent down and whispered, "It would be kind of awkward if the *groom's maid* didn't show up." He and Markus laughed while Abbie and Aroya did their best to fake it.

Now Abbie was ultra-confused. Kevin brought the pizza, while Enrico pranced off into the kitchen.

Markus sighed. "He's so nervous," he said. "Always such a perfectionist! Every night he stands in front of the bedroom mirror, practicing his posture and reciting his vows. After five minutes of that nonsense, I just turn out the light–but then an hour later, he's back at it again!"

Abbie raised her eyebrows. "Oh, really?" She turned to Aroya, dropping her jaw.

"I guess he just wants to get it right," Aroya replied, shrugging.

"Is there something wrong?" Markus asked. "You don't seem like yourselves today."

"What do you mean?" Abbie asked.

"Oh, never mind. I guess it's just me. Maybe I'm a little nervous too," Markus said, sipping his drink.

"Markus?" Abbie began with hesitancy.

Markus put down his drink. "Yes, Abigail? Do you wish to tell me something?"

Abbie turned to Aroya, nudging him.

"No…I think you'd better do it," Aroya said.

"Is everything all right?" Markus asked. "Abigail…are you…?" he asked–waiting for her to fill in the blank. "What I mean to say is…will you be eating for two today?"

Abbie and Aroya laughed.

"No…," she said, smiling. "We just wanna talk about our trip."

"Oh, of course!" Markus said, letting out a sigh. "I want to hear all about it! You know, I was trying to reach you for days, but there was no answer. So finally, I dropped by to check up on you–and Millie said you were off somewhere. Where did you go?"

Aroya wondered if this new Markus even knew about their time travel. He did a little testing. "Markus?" Aroya asked. "Are you still interested in time travel?"

Markus surveyed the room–then, leaning closer, he asked, "Are you feeling okay, Aroya? Is your condition returning?"

"I'm fine," Aroya replied. "But I'm wondering…if it *did* return, what should I do?" Aroya asked, still fishing for clues.

"Well, I suppose you'd need to go back then–to find that doctor again. I did everything within my power last time, and between me and Abigail, we nearly killed you!" Markus said.

Relieved, Abbie and Aroya were now sure he remembered.

"Markus, we just got back from the year 2050," Abbie said.

"Another version of it, anyway–" Aroya clarified, "kind of, the new and improved version."

"And we met you there," Abbie said, "when you were 31 years older!"

"You did?" Markus said, surprised. "Well, what was I like? I mean–what was it like? Oh, my!" Leaning closer, he whispered, "Are you sure we should be talking about this in public?"

Abbie glanced around the room, confused. "Why shouldn't we?"

"Well…the reason I came to check on you, was that a strange man came by my office. He was looking for you, and he said you were in big trouble. He was a dreadful man, Abbie. So, I thought you really were in trouble–and that maybe you'd actually left town!" Markus said, speaking just above a whisper.

"Did the man tell you his name?" Aroya asked.

"No, he didn't. He just said he worked with Abbie," Markus replied.

"Was it Doctor Eiffel?" Abbie asked, alarmed. "Was he kind of short, with dark hair and beady blue eyes?"

"Yes! That's him! But why didn't he say he was a doctor? I thought he might be from one of those *ABC agencies* or something," Markus said.

"What day was that?" Abbie asked.

"It was Monday morning. He scared poor Lizzie nearly to death!" Markus replied.

"He was the doctor I told you about–the one who was killing patients!" Abbie whispered. "He must have heard me on Millie's podcast. In fact, I know he did– because we also received a visit! Two thugs snuck up on me in the garden. They nearly pushed me off the roof!!"

Markus's eyes grew wide. "Oh, my! Do you think he's really dangerous?" he asked.

"Well, he *does* have a history–" Aroya began.

"Yes, of *killing* people!" Markus interrupted. "Oh, this is not good!" He glanced around the room, then whispered, "Let's not talk about it here. Meet me back at the office in an hour. I only have a few patients left. I'll let the staff go home early."

"Okay. We'll be there," Abbie said.

Markus beckoned to Kevin. "You can take my plate, but Abigail and Aroya will be staying. And of course, give them anything they want."

Kevin took the plate. "Sure thing," he said.

Aroya noticed a cozy spot near the stage. "Should we listen to the music while we wait?" he suggested.

"Okay," Abbie replied.

Settling into the overstuffed cushions of a red velvet loveseat, they cuddled–enjoying the soft sensual beats of Brazilian samba. They only had a few sips of their California coolers, but still, they were feeling a bit buzzed from the alcohol.

Kevin asked if they'd like anything else, but Abbie only requested two cups of tea. She took out her cell phone and began entering search terms.

"There *does* seem to be a few changes with this new Internet," Abbie said. "I noticed it on my laptop, too. There's no more *Google.*"

"What are you looking for?" Aroya asked.

"Millie's podcast...the one I did with her," she replied. "I wanna see if anyone left comments."

Their tea arrived, and they sat up. Still groggy from the drinks at lunch–they blew on the tea to cool it, in a hurry to get some caffeine down.

Abbie continued scrolling. "Oh, God help me. It's 'anonymous,' but I know it's him!" she said.

"What's it say?" Aroya asked, leaning over to read the comment.

"It's mostly profanities. Oh, wait! Jeez...he's posting threats now! When was this?" she asked, trying to make out the date.

"It was Monday," Aroya said, pointing to the date. "Dr. Eiffel was a busy man on Monday. He must have written this just hours after visiting Markus." He kept on reading (it was a very long comment). "It looks like his blood was really boiling, too. I'm surprised he didn't hunt down Millie!"

"Yeah...but Millie would've said something if he was harassing her." Abbie sighed, putting her phone away. Then she pulled it back out to check the time. "It's been almost an hour. Let's get going," she said.

They entered Markus' office. The staff had all gone home, and Markus was checking out his last patient. Once the patient had gone, he double-locked the door.

"Okay. We're all alone now," Markus said. "I know I seem paranoid, but that guy was really scary–and honestly...there's been a weird *'agency'* vibe in the air lately. I half expect the *'men in black'* to show up any minute!"

"I'm sorry," Abbie said. "We don't mean to cause you any trouble."

"Oh...it's not about me, really. I'm just worried about Enrico finding out," Markus said. "He's already on edge about the wedding, and he doesn't even know about Aroya's past. I thought it best not to tell him."

They sat down in the waiting room.

"So, tell me about this new 2050?" Markus inquired.

"Well, we actually went back–or *forward*...to see if anything had changed. And it *had* changed," Abbie said. "When we first got there, things seemed much better. But then, gradually, we began noticing things. Apparently, everything had been good for a very long time–*so* good that everything became stagnant. Things were rotting, just beneath the surface–and it was all just about to flip!"

"But how did you meet me–I mean, the *other* Markus?" he asked.

"It's complicated," Abbie replied.

"It was through Abigail," Aroya said. "Not *this* Abigail, but the older Abigail."

"And you know what else?" Abbie added. "Before we left… you never used to call me 'Abigail'…unless you were joking or something. You always called me 'Abbie.' We've noticed a few other changes as well. Like, there used to be homeless people all over the city, and now they're gone!"

"Homeless people? You mean, like bums?" Markus asked.

"No. Like third-world homeless people–addicts, and crazy people–and families, too," Abbie said.

"Here in San Francisco? My God–that's unbelievable!" Markus exclaimed.

"Lots of things are different now," she said.

"Am I different?" Markus asked.

Abbie turned to Aroya, smiling–but Aroya picked up a magazine, pretending not to hear.

"Well…" Abbie started, "Enrico was not in your life before we left. And not only that, but before we left, you were dating women," Abbie replied.

Markus raised his eyebrows. "Women? Really? Now, isn't that interesting?"

"Markus, please forgive us…we had no idea," Aroya explained.

"So, you don't remember anything about the wedding?" Markus asked.

Abbie and Aroya both shook their heads.

"Well, I guess I'll have to fill you in then," he said, scratching his head. "What about other changes? Are there any other improvements, other than no more homeless people?"

"Well, our wardrobe, I guess," Abbie said, giggling. "And it's not an improvement, but my teakettle was *not* chipped before we left, and now it's chipped," Abbie said. "It makes me wonder...because if *I'm* not the same 'Abigail' you planned your wedding with...then where did the other 'Abigail' go?! And who am I now?!"

Markus pondered the question. "I think what's happening...is that the timelines are converging," he said. "The 'Abigail' from the old timeline...who apparently, I used to call 'Abbie', must be coalescing with the one here. It's the only explanation I can come up with at the moment."

"Coalescing?" Aroya asked.

"Merging together," Markus replied.

"Ever since we got back, it's been like waking up with amnesia," Aroya said. "We really have no idea what's going on...or even where our clothes came from."

"When the timelines converge, does it happen all at once?" Abbie asked. "Or does it happen in haphazard pieces? Because in the 'new' 2050, there were strange anomalies that seemed very out of time."

"I really don't know how it happens," Markus replied. "But I suspect that time isn't what we think it is. We tend to see it as linear, and I suppose it would be difficult to manage our human experience without some sort of sequential organization. But the reality might be something else entirely. Maybe what's really happening is just one continuous moment, encompassing both the past and the present, all at once–and in infinite universes, in ways that we're not even capable of comprehending. You two are the only time travel pioneers that I've ever met! I've always loved thinking about it, but I never imagined I'd ever really know anybody who actually did it!"

"I know," Abbie said. "And it's not like either one of us planned any of this! We were just kind of tossed in– and it was like, sink or swim!"

"So far, you seem to be treading water quite well," Markus said. "So tell me, what are your plans now?"

"We have a mission," Aroya replied. "A mission to connect people so that the world becomes more harmonious."

"Connecting people to create harmony? Hmmm. Do you think it'll work?" Markus asked.

"I don't know," Abbie replied. "I hope that we're not like those people who spent their last moments rearranging the deck chairs–while the Titanic was sinking."

"Yes, I see what you mean," Markus said. "But so far, you say everything appears to have improved. And maybe it's improved for me too, because apparently–I finally came out of the closet!" he said, laughing.

Abbie laughed too. "Yeah, that was another little surprise."

"We're still kind of assessing the situation," Aroya said. "Last time…we thought we got it right with a poem about freedom. But it turned out we needed more than just freedom, and we needed more than just a poem. We learned a lot from Abigail senior in 2050."

"Oh? What did you learn?" Markus asked.

"We learned that life is like music; it's composed of many tones and opposing aspects. And if they're not all in harmony, then everything just turns to chaos," Aroya replied. "But if it's too steady and rigid, then it's just tyranny–and both tyranny and chaos eventually rot and stink."

"Life does indeed stink sometimes," Markus said, laughing. "May I ask what action you took in order to improve our time here?"

"We said prayers," Aroya replied. "Some of them were new prayers that Abbie and I made about harmony, and some were more traditional...really old prayers."

"Well, that makes sense," Markus said. "Prayers from old traditions, recited so many times, by so many people–they've likely been stored up as memories in the morphic field–giving them more weight and more power. The more weight added to anything in the morphic field, makes it more likely to manifest physically. Anyway, that would be consistent with Sheldrake's theory, and it would also support the 100th monkey idea."

Abbie smiled. "Yeah. You mentioned the morphic field in 2050."

Markus chuckled. "Well, it's nice to know that I'm consistent throughout time!"

"Oh, Markus, you're nothing if not consistent!" Both Abbie and Aroya laughed, recalling when Abigail senior said the same thing.

"I think I detect an inside joke," Markus said, smiling. "But I do believe it's true about old rituals and prayers: they're quite powerful because they've grown, layer upon layer, due to so much repetition. They contain all that stored up power!"

"So far, their power seems to have had a positive effect," Abbie said. "The only loose end right now...is that psychopath, Dr. Eiffel."

"No, Abigail...there's another loose end," Markus said. "Apparently, you have no idea that in two weeks, you will be playing a significant role in my own personal future! I guess we'll need to get together soon, so I can refresh your 'converged' memory–because if this doesn't go off without a hitch, I'm afraid poor Enrico may never recover."

Abbie agreed. "Give us a few days–you can come by and fill us in " Then, remembering something, she said, "Oh, I almost forgot! When we were in 2050, we discovered that the *other* Aroya expired from an implant in his head. The 2050 version of Markus located the implant in *our* Aroya with a meter. It still needs to come out. Can you do it in your office?"

"That depends on how deep it is, and if it's connected to anything vital," Markus replied. "Toying with the unknown, when it comes to Aroya's health, still makes me a little bit nervous," he said. "Is it urgent?"

"The other 'me' lived with it until he was 60 years old," Aroya replied, "so I think we still have some time."

"That's good because I'd like to think it over before rushing into anything," Markus said. Then he smiled, amused by something. "So... I must have been about 73 years old when you met me in 2050? How did I hold up?"

"You were quite the dapper gentleman," Abbie replied. "But you might wanna lay off the desserts as you approach retirement."

"I see! I had a potbelly, did I?" he asked, laughing.

"Yes, you had quite the potbelly. But Markus, you were still as handsome as ever," Abbie replied.

Markus smiled. "Funny how flattery even feels good 31 years in advance!"

"We'd better get going now. We need to find out if Dr. Eiffel has been harassing Millie, as well," Abbie said.

When they returned to the apartment, Abbie sent a text message to Millie. Just as soon as she had finished, there was a knock at the door. Of course, it was Millie. When it came to Abbie, Millie was sometimes just as psychic as Aroya.

"I've gotta show you something," Millie said. She flipped open Abbie's laptop. "Pull up *Camelot* and click the *Town Crier*."

Abbie had no idea what she was talking about–she had never heard of *Camelot* or the *Town Crier*. She entered her password–but it didn't work. She tried again.

"There's something wrong with my password," Abbie said.

"Then just use your phone and search 'San Francisco news,'" Millie suggested.

Abbie found the headline Millie was looking for: ANOTHER ARREST MADE AT PUBLIC HOSPITAL.

She read the story out loud: *"After a complaint was filed by Millie Grace, a popular podcast host, another doctor has been arrested in connection with the 'Dark Angels of Death' cult. After receiving multiple threats,*

Ms. Grace cooperated with local police, resulting in the arrest of Dr. Frederick Eiffel, an attending physician at San Francisco Public Hospital. Dr. Eiffel is being charged with 300 counts of criminal negligence and manslaughter for actions resulting in the deaths of elderly and indigent patients as part of a larger scheme that is suspected to involve a multitude of government agencies and officials. The 'Dark Angels of Death' cult is thought to have been operating for months as part of an international ring, taking advantage of the recent influenza epidemic to cover its deadly deeds. Dr. Eiffel is currently being held in an undisclosed high-security detention facility, without bail."

Abbie dropped her phone on the table. *"He's in jail!"* she shouted.

"Yes!" Millie exclaimed. "While you two were away, that son-of-a-bitch came looking for you, and he threatened me in the most demented ways…describing to me, in detail, what he planned to do to me–if I didn't tell him where you were!"

"Oh my God, are you all right?" Abbie asked, alarmed.

"Yes, honey. I'm fine," she replied. "Me and the cops set a trap, and it worked like a charm! You should've seen that weasel squirm when he was cuffed!"

"Well…," Abbie sighed, "I guess we can all relax now. Maybe justice will finally be served on behalf of those poor patients–and for Tulio Guterres." Suddenly, her eyes widened. *"The box!"* she shouted, running over to the altar.

"I guess I'll catch you guys later!" Millie called out as she shut the door.

WHEN WE WERE WARM

23– TULIO'S BOX

2019

San Francisco

3.0

Abbie and Aroya were so preoccupied with the box that they barely said goodbye to Millie. They sat together on the couch with the box on Abbie's lap.

"Should we open it now?" she asked. "I'm kind of nervous." She looked at the address. "It says it's for *Mr. Guterres*...I assume that's Tulio. I wonder why Carlos gave it to us?"

"It was probably meant for Tulio, but he died before he received it. Remember...from the vision at Abigail senior's place?"

"You saw him too? I wasn't sure if everyone saw the exact same thing."

"Yes, I saw him, and I heard him. And I assume the others did too. The only thing that we all didn't see were your tall Angels."

"Yeah. That was intense."

"Do you think you could call them back? I mean–if you wanted to?" Aroya asked.

"Maybe. But I'm not sure I want to. It was amazing, but when they left, it felt like my heart was being torn from my chest."

"I think I understand. I didn't say anything, but when I left my mother, my heart ached for days. I feel the same way about seeing her again…since things can never be the same."

"She thought you were an Angel," Abbie said, smiling.

"Yeah. But Millie knew who I was."

"Millie knew?"

"My dog. Remember? Her name is Millie. She recognized me."

Abbie held up the package. "Well? Should we open it?"

"Yeah! Let's do it!"

Abbie took a deep breath. Removing the tape, she discarded the paper. Inside, there was a large shoebox with a picture of a boot on it.

"It looks like he gave us Tulio's boots?" Abbie joked.

Aroya peeked under the lid. "I don't think so."

Abbie removed the lid, revealing a colorful feather headdress. She took the headdress from the box, finding a carved wooden pipe underneath.

"Wow! Look at this!" She unrolled the headdress, spreading it out across the coffee table. "It's just like the one the Vision Maker wore."

"I've never seen feathers like these," Aroya said, running his finger along the edge of a tall feather.

"They must be from Brazilian birds," Abbie said.

Aroya lifted the pipe to his nose. "Whoa! That's really strong!"

Abbie walked over to the altar, holding the headdress against the wall. "I think we should put it right here…for added power."

"Do you think we really need added power?" Aroya asked. "Oh, wait…*feathers!*" he exclaimed.

Abbie laughed. "Oh no. You're not thinking about wings again, are you?"

"Yes, actually."

"You're so cute." She peered into the box again, locating a white envelope–with the words *Para Tulio* written on it. "It's a letter–but it's in Portuguese. I can't read it." She carried the letter over to her laptop for help with translation–but again, her password wouldn't work. "That's so weird…it worked this morning. If the timelines are converging, you'd think our memories would converge along with them!"

Aroya held the pipe in his mouth. "Just type something you think *she* would have used."

Abbie typed the password, *ArchangelMichael7*, but nothing happened. She typed it again, this time adding two more 7s–and *voila!* "It worked!"

"Maybe you've already 'coalesced' more than you realize," Aroya suggested.

Abbie moved her laptop to the coffee table, sitting next to Aroya on the couch. She set the letter down next to her computer, noticing a new icon on the desktop that said *'Camelot.'*

"I guess *everything's Camelot* now," she said. "No more *Google*."

She began translating the letter:

> *My dear brother,*
> *You went to the hospital before the Vision Maker*
> *arrived. I could not be with you because the*
> *hospital prohibited visitors. I will ask them to give*
> *you these things. They will keep you strong and*
> *protect you.*
> *The Vision Maker saw a woman during his*
> *meditation. He said she will come to you in the*
> *hospital–and she will comfort you. He said that a*
> *special mission will be given to her.*
> *He will not tell me more. He only tells me to wait.*
> *May God bless you and keep you well.*
> *Your loving brother,*
> *Carlos*

"The Vision Maker didn't want to tell Carlos that Tulio would die," Aroya said.

"Yeah. And Carlos had no idea it would happen so fast. Neither did I. God, I was so torn that day. My head was saying, *don't make a scene, Abbie!*–but my heart screamed, *fight for him!*"

"It's just like what Abigail senior said about the heart and the mind ruling together. Your heart is King–so in the end, it ruled over your mind."

"You really thought about that a lot, didn't you?"

"It was one of the most important lessons I learned from Abigail senior. I even made a little poem about it." Aroya opened his journal and recited the poem:

"Let not your heart
Hide like a coward
Instead, let it go forth
Armed with reason,
Standing in defense,
Of the one true thing–
Love"

"Aroya? Is that your very first poem?" Abbie asked, surprised.

"Yes. I guess it is."

"Could you possibly be *coalescing*–with the renown Wallace A. Roya?"

"Maybe."

Aroya placed the pipe back in his mouth, contemplating the possibility.

"If the feathers and the pipe are for strength and protection," Abbie said, "then I guess they really do belong on the altar." She spread the feathered headdress against the wall, atop the altar–then taking the pipe from Aroya's mouth, she placed it underneath. "Should we order dinner tonight to celebrate our success?"

"I suppose just making it back alive qualifies as success."

"Yes, but there *do* seem to be a lot of improvements since we returned: there are no more homeless people on the streets, Ray's shop never shut down, Dr. Eiffel is in jail, and Markus is getting married!"

Aroya laughed. "You're right. I guess there are plenty of reasons to celebrate."

Abbie picked up her phone. "Pizza or fish?" she asked.

"Pizza will always remind me of Elijah now–but Abbie, you know how I love fish."

"Then sushi it is."

"How about a fire tonight," Aroya suggested, "and some nice music?"

Abbie smiled, imagining what Aroya had in mind.

Reading her mind, he said, "You'd better believe it." He leaned closer, stroking her cheek. "Those wild horses are restless, Abbie."

24– EACH OTHER'S GAZE

2019

San Francisco

Timeline 3.0

It had been a long and torturous wait for both of them, but now they could finally relax and enjoy each other.

"How 'bout some sexy Brazilian samba?" Abbie asked with a beguiling smile. She scrolled on her laptop, looking for Brazilian music.

Aroya took a velvety blanket from the couch, spreading it over the carpet in front of the fireplace. He gathered the floor cushions, setting them near the hearth, recalling their first night of lovemaking in front of the fire's warm glow. Of course, he was setting the stage–and planning out each seductive move in his mind.

"I think I'll take a quick bath," Abbie said. "Can you listen for the door?"

"Alright," Aroya said, leaning back on a cushion.

Before she left the room, Abbie switched on the music, setting the volume on low.

Soon, there was a knock at the door. The sushi had arrived. It was a full platter, a veritable feast. Aroya spread it out on the hearth. He could barely resist picking at it. He turned the music up, dimming the lights, lying back on the cushions, closing his eyes.

The Brazilian beat moved through his body, and the sensual sound of Portuguese soothed his soul. He imagined he was on a cloud, floating high above the city–drifting away.

A sweet perfume filled his senses, and he opened his eyes. Abbie was fresh out of the bath, kneeling beside him in her silky robe–still warm and dewy, smelling like flowers.

"I've been thinking about your Angel experience at Abigail senior's place," Aroya said. "You never told me exactly what happened."

"That's because I'm not sure what happened," Abbie said, pausing to revive the memory. "I was watching you and Elijah, and suddenly, I felt like I was in a dream. Four tall figures appeared in the room–it was like they just came out of the wall. They were smooth and white–and glowing from within. Their features were indistinct, almost like marble statues."

"Who were they?" Aroya asked.

"I don't know. They only said they were my family– my original family. They handed me something and spoke to me–in my mind."

"What did they hand you?"

"It appeared to be a very large scroll. I held it with both arms."

"Was something written on the scroll?"

"I don't know. It seemed like they were honoring me for something. I was confused by it all because in my eyes, these were powerful beings–and I was just an insignificant little person."

"What did they say to you?"

"They seemed to know my thoughts, and they told me it was I who was the powerful one. They said that only I had the power to come here, and that others were depending on me."

"Depending on you for what?"

"They acknowledged how hard this life was for me…because of my deep emotions. They were right about that. There were so many times that I wished I was one of those cold, unfeeling people who could just go along with the program. Life always seemed easier for those people."

"I understand. In my time, the survivors were usually the ones who were cold and unfeeling. But those who were able to hold on to their feelings–they were the special ones. People would come from far away to meet with us secretly–to be reminded of the beauty of emotional expression. We bore the pain for the others, and we fiercely protected the gifts of the human heart."

"That's kind of what they said to me, that the pain I carried in my heart was an important part of the human experience. They told me to honor that part of me and said my emotional experience here affected others, in another place."

"It must have been a powerful experience. You were really shaken up afterward."

"It was. But the experience itself wasn't traumatic–it was the separation afterward…it was almost unbearable. I remember thinking to myself: this must be why we have spiritual amnesia when we come here, because to remember that separation might be too painful for most."

"The pain of losing your family. Like when I lost my mother in the catastrophe. You're right…it was almost unbearable."

"Yes, I can imagine. They say we're the strong ones for keeping our hearts open, but I never felt very strong or powerful when my heart was breaking. I always felt weak and ashamed. But these beings said it was proof of our strength, to be able to feel so deeply–and to carry that pain."

"But who were they, really?"

"I feel they were Angels, but they never said they were–" she smiled, "and they didn't have wings."

Aroya found that amusing. "They didn't have wings," he said. "Maybe the wings really *are* only metaphorical. But if they said they were your original family…then that makes you an Angel too, Abbie."

"Or maybe I was…before I came here."

"Abbie…I think you *are* an Angel. It would explain a lot of things. Why you vibrate with energy like that, and why you were called for this mission. Let me see..." Aroya closed his eyes for a moment. "I can't see everything…but I can see that you're only beginning to realize who you truly are. I don't think it'll be long now before you start getting all fiery and electric. Uh-oh…we'd better watch out!" he laughed.

Abbie also laughed. "I'm not sure about that!" Then smiling, she said, "The only thing I know for sure is that right now…I am most definitely a woman."

Abbie held a piece of sashimi to Aroya's lips, teasing him with it. She fed him, one piece at a time, pausing every so often–waiting for the anticipation to build, then rewarding him for his patience. When they had finished the sushi, she slowly and methodically unbuttoned Aroya's shirt and unzipped his pants. Of course, Aroya became excited and began kissing her lips–but she pulled away. "Wait," she said. "Tonight, I want you to feel what it was like for me to be caught in your gaze by the fire. Please remove your clothes."

Abbie stood back, observing Aroya's best attempt at disrobing gracefully. He managed his shirt with some grace but was quite clumsy with his pants–and he knew it.

"Where do you want me?" Aroya asked.

"Near the fire, just as I was for you," Abbie replied with a smile.

Aroya remembered that first night as though it were the most sacred moment of his life. He found the proper place, and only now was he realizing how difficult it was to be gazed upon, restraining all urges to physically engage.

Abbie caressed every inch of Aroya's skin with her gaze. He watched her as she watched him–and then she let her silky robe fall to the floor. Now, they both stood in each other's gaze, illuminated by the fire's glow–silently studying the other's rising and falling breath.

"Abbie, I'm not as strong as you," Aroya said. "I need to touch you."

"Wait," she said. "Me, first."

Abbie moved behind Aroya, stroking the back of his neck with her finger. Then, sliding her hand down his back to his buttocks, she knelt, placing delicate little kisses over his skin. She moved to his front, studying his face–watching his lips quiver, anticipating a kiss that was just out of reach. She stroked his lips with her fingertip–as though it were a paintbrush, applying delicate color to his mouth. She caressed his earlobes, then moved closer to enjoy his masculine scent–warm and concentrated in the hollows around his neck and chest. Of course, he was fully erect by now, and his size made it difficult to move around without brushing against him–and every time she did, he gasped, trying with all his might to resist touching her. She returned to his lips–teasing them with her tongue but never fully kissing his mouth. Stroking his chest, she scattered kisses–then she moved her hand down to his thighs. Standing directly in front of him, she spread her legs– grasping him between her thighs and pressing her full breasts against his chest. Now, she used her tongue to open his mouth, finally surrendering a deep, full kiss.

"Abbie, please. Can I touch you?" he begged.

"Soon. First, watch me as I lay–preparing myself."

Abbie laid down on the blanket–moving one cushion under her head, scooting another under her hips. While gazing into his eyes, she traced the contour of her own breasts and belly, then she reached inside her thighs and slowly opened her legs.

Aroya's body quivered. His gaze danced between her body and her eyes, awaiting her invitation. He thought he should take her gently, but right now, he was almost exploding with anticipation–like a racehorse at the starting gate.

"Now, my love," Abbie said, "take me with your hands… and your mouth…then come inside me."

Aroya lowered himself over Abbie's body. He caressed her and tasted her. He let her scent carry him to faraway places of almost unbearable beauty and pleasure, beyond the limits of any romantic poem. Her body quivered–and now he understood the quivering, for she had taught him all about it. He came into her, entering slowly–waiting for her to move with him. In a moment of deep intimacy, their eyes wandered into that hidden space of the soul–where all defenses dissolve, and one's true nature is revealed. Their breath fell into sync, and their hearts swelled. Between quick breaths, they whispered sweet sentiments of love–finally, surrendering into a wondrous climax a place where time stood still. There was no floor, no arms, no legs– only a single point between breaths–where they met, floating weightlessly in union.

As the motion stopped, Aroya settled down onto Abbie's body.

"Stay," she whispered, stroking his back.

"I will," he said.

"Forever," Abbie added.

"Forever," he echoed.

25– LESSONS LEARNED

2019

San Francisco

Timeline 3.0

The following day, Abbie and Aroya strolled around the city, visiting cafés, chatting up locals, and gauging people's feelings about the state of the world. Grabbing a newspaper, they searched for clues about changes that may have occurred since their last trip to 2050. In general, there seemed to be an all-around improvement.

But the improvements had not yet solidified for Abbie's original timeline–the changes were only fully realized on the new 3.0 timeline. Abbie and Aroya's mission, going forward, would be to fully meld the old timeline with the new timeline, guiding the convergence into a positive outcome for both.

The process of convergence and coalescence was sometimes very confusing. The stage was set for an optimistic future–and yet, several new groups fresh on the scene were out there pushing their dark agenda. Few people paid much attention, most laughing at their rhetoric and calling them crazy. Abbie and Aroya recognized the danger in their ideas, but now they also understood the need for balance. They remembered the old fisherman's description of the seagull riding the wind; skillfully shifting from wing to wing, maintaining balance between opposing sides. They understood now that the urge to eliminate contrasting ideas ultimately resulted in stagnation, and just like the weak and lazy bird who rests too long in one place–eventually, it falls. They learned that dark influences must coexist with the light in a dynamic dance, supporting healthy progression and growth. But they also learned–just as it is detrimental to allow the royal advisor to dethrone the King, it is equally detrimental to allow dark ideas and perverted deeds to multiply unimpeded, like a cancerous disease. They understood that blind freedom was not enough on its own, and if there was no *truth*, then there would only be *freedom* to choose between lies…and if there was no *justice*–then lies would always prevail.

Now, they understood why it was necessary for them to experience both extremes of 2050. Their adventures had taught them essential lessons about balance and harmony, preparing them for their mission: to connect others, to keep the music going, and to personally be the checks and balances against both chaos and stagnation–in support of harmony–and ultimately, to prevent the fall of humanity.

In the evening, Abbie and Aroya visited the rooftop garden. They surveyed the city and breathed in the cool, misty air. Tonight, they would rest in each other's arms, not knowing what tomorrow might bring. Things appeared promising, but the new future was still yet to be solidified. They had no idea how they would accomplish their mission…they only knew they *must*.

Abbie clipped a half dozen roses from her rooftop garden, and when they returned to the apartment, she placed them in a large vase on the kitchen table. Preparing her altar, she arranged the floor cushions and lit the candle.

Curled up in his favorite spot on the couch, Aroya was writing in his journal. Although he was now free to share Abbie's warm and fragrant bed, he would always remember her couch as his first place of refuge–upon his arrival in 2019.

"I think, considering all we've been through and all we've survived," Abbie said, "–we should offer a prayer of gratitude. We might also petition the Angels for strength and guidance on our mission going forward."

"Abbie…is it okay to make a prayer that is also a poem?" Aroya asked.

"I don't see why not."

"Then may I go first?"

"Of course."

Aroya walked to the kitchen table, selecting one special rose from the vase. "This one is perfect," he said. "It's only beginning to bloom–just like our new future. It must be aware of its unsurpassed beauty–and yet, every exquisite petal still blushes with innocence."

He approached the altar, kneeling. "I offer my appreciation to God and the Angels for manifesting so much beauty in this world." He placed the rose on the altar and continued, "This is my prayer to God, our Creator. It is a prayer for the future of humanity." He stiffened his spine and readied himself. Then he began:

"May God sit as King in the hearts of humanity.
May he inspire us all to reach toward perfection.
May we discern the wrong from the right,
And may we be guided to always choose light.

May our leaders command our lands with
benevolence.
May our eyes be opened to corruption and
malevolence.
May our minds be freed from manipulative spells,
And may the fallen be saved from the pits where
they fell.

Take the pain from their wounds wash the dirt from
their feet,
For those who were tricked by lies and deceit.
Take the mask from their face, command
corruption to cease.
Welcome a renaissance of beauty, harmony, and
peace.
Amen."

THE END

WHEN WE WERE WARM

AFTERWORD

TIME TRAVEL

There are many theories about time travel, and thinking about them in any serious way is enough to twist the mind into a pretzel. Of course, weaving a story that addresses some of these theories was, at times, extremely challenging–especially for someone with poor math skills, like me.

The time travel aspect of Abbie and Aroya's story was based upon accounts offered by mysterious visitors and courageous whistleblowers. Due to the difficulty of keeping track of timelines and ages–I was compelled to create a TIMELINE CHART of sorts–so that when they traveled from one time to the next, the supporting characters showed up at their appropriate ages. It is one thing to time travel forward or backward–to a time when you did not exist. But it's quite another thing to travel to a time when you do indeed exist–being there at the same moment–when you are either younger or older. If you add to the complication, by creating a time traveler who exists in two timelines–as two different versions of himself–well, it is then that you definitely need some kind of map.

This book is the first of a series–and because I never knew what the characters might do next (until I began writing)–I can only imagine that their subsequent adventures will be equally unpredictable and amazing!

If you would like a FREE COPY of the TIMELINE CHART I used to keep track of my time traveling stars and their supporting cast–please subscribe to my NEWSLETTER with the link on my website: ABRaphaelle.com.

If you enjoyed this book, please leave an honest review for *WHEN WE WERE WARM* on Amazon.com.

For more information about the author and new releases, please go to my website: **ABRaphaelle.com.**

May our future be filled with Love, Harmony, and Beauty.

A. B. Raphaelle

ACKNOWLEDGMENTS

Although this book is a work of fiction, I must thank the many muses, sages, whistleblowers, and time travelers–who influenced my ideas and sparked my imagination. Of course, special thanks must go to the poets–and all lovers of Beauty.

I'd also like to thank David Byrne, whose extraordinary music colored my mind with thought-provoking words and images during the writing of this story.

POETRY CREDITS

Song of Myself, by Walt Whitman
The More Loving One, by W. H. Auden
Mazeppa, by Lord Byron
Of Old Sat Freedom, by Lord Tennyson
The Hedge-Rose Opens, by Alfred Noyes
She Walks in Beauty, by Lord Byron
Do I Dare Disturb the Universe, by T. S. Eliot
Bright Star, by John Keats
Let Your Heart Not Hide, by A. B. Raphaelle
Prayer for Humanity, by A. B. Raphaelle
(Also sprinkled throughout this story,
are various quotes by Hazrat Inayat Khan, Plato, and
The I Ching)

ABOUT THE AUTHOR

A. B. Raphaelle is a teacher and a native of San Francisco. After three generations, it breaks her heart to watch the once beautiful and highly eclectic city of San Francisco– falling to her knees. May our prayers bring the city that we once knew and loved–back to us for a renaissance in beauty, art, and culture.

Made in the USA
Las Vegas, NV
16 September 2021